Kate Fortune's Journal Entry

I can no longer bear to stay silent. My family is crumbling, and Jake needs my support. I believe all the plots to destroy the Fortunes have been unearthed. Now we must unite and stand proud against our enemies. It's not easy being rich and powerful, always in the spotlight. Everyone wants a piece of you. But I know that together we can triumph over any adversity. I know justice will prevail and Jake's innocence will be proven. Then we can get back to what really matters — love and family.

A LETTER FROM THE AUTHOR

Dearest Reader,

I have always been a firm believer in family and family ties. The idea of big family gatherings has always filled me with a warm, nostalgic feeling. And year after year, I still manage to get choked up at those greeting-card commercials. You know, the ones where siblings and children overcome great obstacles to walk into a house and a warm hug just in time for the holidays. They never fail to make me misty.

For the longest time, my own family was tiny—just my two brothers, my parents and me. I can remember envying people with grandparents, aunts, uncles and cousins. That was why it was such a treat to be one of the authors included in the Fortune's Children series. While writing *Forgotten Honeymoon*, I could close my eyes, put myself in Kristina's place and pretend to have scads of family scattered all around the country. Family that, no matter what the differences involved might be, come through for you when the chips are down. And after all, isn't that, along with having five different flavors of ice cream in the refrigerator, what the American Dream is really all about? To always have people to rely on, to watch over and to have watch over you?

I hope you enjoy reading *Forgotten Honeymoon* half as much as I enjoyed writing it. Now go and hug someone close to you.

Love,

Marie Ferrarella

MARIE FERRARELLA

Forgotten Honeymoon

Published by Silhouette Books
America's Publisher of Contemporary Romance

To Jessi and Nikky,
the beginning of my legacy

SILHOUETTE BOOKS

FORGOTTEN HONEYMOON

Copyright © 1997 by Harlequin Books S.A.

ISBN 0-373-50187-0

Special thanks and acknowledgment to Marie Ferrarella
for her contribution to the Fortune's Children series.

This edition published by arrangement with Harlequin Books S.A.
® and TM are trademarks of Harlequin Books S.A., used under
license. Trademarks indicated with ® are registered in the United States
Patent and Trademark Office, the Canadian Trade Marks Office and in
other countries.

Printed in U.S.A.

MARIE FERRARELLA

is the author of sixty-eight books for Silhouette Books, and has written for several other publishing houses. She has garnered four RITA Award nominations and won the RITA Award in 1992 for *Father Goose*. She has also won three awards from *Romantic Times*.

Marie was born in Germany, raised in New York City and currently lives in Southern California with her husband, their two children and a German shepherd named Rocky. She holds a Masters of Arts with a concentration in Shakespearean comedy from Queens College. Her interests include old movies, old songs, and musical theater, and her motto is Always Be Prepared. (She sewed her own wedding dress and made it wash-and-wear "just in case"!)

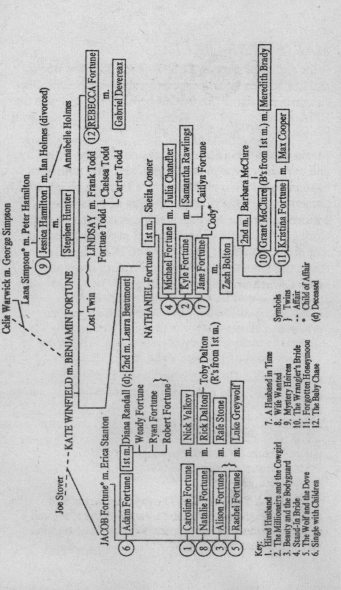

Joe Stover

Celia Warwick m. George Simpson

Lana Simpson* m. Peter Hamilton

⑨ Jessica Hamilton m. Ian Holmes (divorced)
m.
Stephen Hunter

Annabelle Holmes

LINDSAY m. Frank Todd
Fortune Todd ┬ Chelsea Todd
             └ Carter Todd

⑫ REBECCA Fortune
m.
Gabriel Devereax

KATE WINFIELD m. BENJAMIN FORTUNE

Lost Twin

NATHANIEL Fortune | 1st m. | Sheila Conner

④ Michael Fortune m. Julia Chandler

② Kyle Fortune m. Samantha Rawlings
                    └ Caitlyn Fortune

⑦ Jane Fortune ┐ Cody*
m.
Zach Bolton

⑩ Grant McClure (B's from 1st m.) m. Meredith Brady
2nd m.
Barbara McClure

⑪ Kristina Fortune m. Max Cooper

JACOB Fortune m. Erica Stanton

⑥ Adam Fortune | 1st m. | Diana Randall (d); 2nd m. Laura Beaumont

Wendy Fortune

Ryan Fortune ┐
Robert Fortune ┘

Toby Dalton
Rick Dalton ┘ (R's from 1st m.)

① Caroline Fortune m. Nick Valkov

⑧ Natalie Fortune m. Rick Dalton

③ Alison Fortune m. Rafe Stone

⑤ Rachel Fortune m. Luke Greywolf

Symbols
} Twins
-- Affair
* Child of Affair
(d) Deceased

Key:
1. Hired Husband
2. The Millionaire and the Cowgirl
3. Beauty and the Bodyguard
4. Stand-In Bride
5. The Wolf and the Dove
6. Single with Children
7. A Husband in Time
8. Wife Wanted
9. Mystery Heiress
10. The Wrangler's Bride
11. Forgotten Honeymoon
12. The Baby Chase

FORTUNE'S Children

Meet the Fortunes—three generations of a family with a legacy of wealth, influence and power. As they unite to face an unknown enemy, shocking family secrets are revealed...and passionate new romances are ignited.

KRISTINA FORTUNE: She is beautiful and wealthy, but there's more to Kristina than her spoiled rich-girl attitude. However, it isn't until she loses her memory that she proves she is more than just another pretty face....

MAX COOPER: The tough blue-collar loner has had to make his own way in life. He resents that pushy and pampered Kristina is his new business partner. And when amnesia renders her at his mercy, he decides to teach her a lesson.... But could he be the one who ends up learning about love?

JAKE FORTUNE: He stands accused of murder. But will justice set him free, or will he end up imprisoned for life?

KATE FORTUNE: She can no longer stay hidden while her family faces a relentless adversary driven to destroy them. So she reappears to provide the emotional support that binds the Fortunes together in their crisis.

REBECCA FORTUNE: The mystery writer and amateur sleuth is determined to unravel the clues and prove Jake innocent of murder. Will her investigation succeed before it's too late?

LIZ JONES— CELEBRITY GOSSIP

Kate Fortune is alive and well! Many friends and family members grieved the death of this wonderful woman. But apparently the crafty matriarch of the Fortune family has been hiding out. She survived the plane crash—which was an attempted murder, not an accident!—and has remained in hiding, trying to discover who's been out to destroy her family. With Monica Malone dead and Jake on trial for murder, Kate could no longer remain silent. She's back to support the family and resurrect the mighty Fortune empire.

Go, Kate!

One

Kristina Fortune hung up the telephone. A bittersweet smile played on her lips, a reflection of her ambivalent feelings. Grant was getting married. And while she felt happy for her older half brother, she couldn't help feeling sad for herself. She doubted it would ever come to pass for her, that knock-your-shoes-off kind of love that left you tingling and wanting more.

Especially since she wasn't about to let her guard down anymore. Not after David.

Nothing ventured, nothing gained, she thought. And nothing ripped apart.

With a sigh, she wandered over to the window. The view from the fourteenth floor of the Fortune Building was next to nonexistent today. Visibility, according to the radio, was zero. Air traffic was at a standstill. Looking out the window was like looking into the interior of a cloud. A dense fog was embracing the city, swirling its long tentacles around the tall Minneapolis skyline and smothering it like a white feather boa thrown about the shoulders of a call girl.

She remained standing there, staring, though there was nothing to see. Staring and thinking.

There was no doubt about it, she felt restless. Edgy. Grant's phone call had just brought it to the fore. It was as if there was no place within the chrome-and-black-enamel office where she could comfortably alight. So she didn't bother moving at all.

The feeling of restlessness, of dissatisfaction, was due largely to her grandmother's sudden death.

Kristina still couldn't believe it.

Death happened every day. The newspapers and the rest of the media were full of it. But it was always someone else's family, not hers. Death wasn't something that she wanted to think about at twenty-four. It had no place in her life.

Except that it had entered, hoary and unannounced, claiming someone she cared about a great deal.

Grandmother would have been happy for Grant.

Kristina smiled to herself. The sad curve of her mouth mocked her as she looked at her reflection. Funny, she'd just assumed that Kate Fortune would go on forever, like the sun, like the tides. Never once had her grandmother given any hint that she was actually mortal. She'd never been sick, and she'd worked long, endless hours tirelessly. She'd been more an institution than a flesh-and-blood woman.

Except that she could be warm and kind when a granddaughter was needy, Kristina thought sadly. She fingered the silver charm around her neck, the one shaped like a lace valentine. It had been specifically bequeathed to her, taken from her grandmother's charm bracelet. It was the charm her late grandfather had given her grandmother the day Kristina was born. "Another valentine joins the lot," Ben Fortune had told his wife, continuing the tradition of giving her a charm for each birth.

As she touched the charm, Kristina remembered the way Kate had held her and let her cry her heart out over David, the one and only time she'd allowed her heart to be vulnerable. David, who had turned out to be far more interested in the Fortune name and inheritance than he was in her love. David, who had gone on to marry well, ensconcing himself in a political dynasty. Breaking off her engagement, Kristina had spent the night at her grandmother's house. They'd stayed up all night and talked. Kate had been the only one to ever see this softer, vulnerable side of her.

Kate had understood how much it hurt to discover that you had been made a fool of.

She pressed her hand against the glass. Winter was just outside, harsh and unforgiving. Like life, she thought, if you let your guard down and made one mistake. Kristina blew out a long, tired breath. It didn't help ease the tension.

David and politics deserved each other, she decided, her mouth hardening. But her grandmother didn't deserve what had happened to her.

She thought of Kate as she had last seen her, her hand lightly resting on her lawyer's arm as she inclined her head toward him, quietly commanding center stage, just by her presence. Kate Fortune had been a magnificent woman, even when approaching her seventh decade. She hadn't aged the way other people did. There were no telltale wrinkles, none of the mocking badges that the passage of time awarded, like hands that shook, or a mind that became progressively more vague and enfeebled. Kate Fortune had embodied the very essence and vibrancy of life.

That was why having that life snuffed out in a plane crash seemed so highly impossible. The ultimate insult. Kristina could barely make herself believe it.

And yet, if her grandmother had picked a way to die, that was the way she would have chosen, Kristina was certain. She would have elected to go out in one astounding blaze of glory, crashing somewhere in the middle of a mysterious jungle.

Leaving the rest of her family to realize just how much they missed her. How much they needed her. Not to run Fortune Cosmetics, but just to be.

Kristina's throat tightened with the swell of tears that insisted on forming. Tears she hadn't allowed herself to release. Kate Fortune wouldn't have wanted tears. She would have wanted them all to go on, to forge an even greater legacy than the one she had worked so hard over the years to give them. The Fortune success was due as much to Kate's efforts as it was to Ben's. Perhaps even more, for she had continued the expansion even after her husband died.

God, but she missed her.

Kristina sighed again. The weather was getting to her. It was so gloomy, so pervasive and disheartening.

She needed to get away for a few days, she thought. Kristina glanced at the official document on her desk, the one she'd been studying this morning. Maybe, she considered, for more than a few days.

She thought of Grant and Meredith and their pending marriage. And the honeymoon to follow. A gleam entered her eyes.

Why not?

With the enthusiasm that was the hallmark of everything she did, Kristina turned back to her desk and began making notes. The idea that had been born yesterday morning began to take on depth and breadth at a speed that would have astounded anyone who didn't know her.

Those who did knew that Kristina never did anything slowly or in a small way.

At twenty-four, she was already successful and recognized as being insightfully creative, a definite asset to the advertising department she had joined. She was also driven. She took after her grandmother that way. A powerhouse who enjoyed making a difference, leaving her mark upon everything she came in contact with.

Buffered by inheritances, completely devoid of monetary concerns, Kristina could very well have done nothing with her life but attend parties from dusk till dawn.

That wasn't her.

Kristina thumbed through the folder Sterling Foster, their family lawyer, had been thoughtful enough to send on to her. There was a very lackluster-looking brochure included in the packet. Four pages in total, it featured three rather homey, unflattering photographs of a bed-and-breakfast inn, one her grandmother had made a sentimental investment in so long ago. Every word she read within the brochure generated more notes on her pad. And sketches that she kept for future consideration.

The youngest in her large family, Kristina made certain that she would never have the adage "Last but not least" attached to her. She was never going to be last, in any manner, shape or form. She was too conscious of being first. Of being a winner.

If, in winning, it cost her a friendship or two, well, she rationalized, those people couldn't have been such very good friends after all. Not if they didn't understand what making her mark upon things meant to her. Being part of the Fortune family meant having to try harder to make an impression. She didn't want to be just one of the Fortunes, an interchangeable entity. She wanted to be distinguished from the rest. To do things her way and stand out.

Like Grandmother.

This might just be her key, she mused, turning the brochure over to the back page—even though the inn looked tacky. Tacky could always be fixed.

Moving the brochure aside, she looked at the cover letter on her desk, the one Sterling had sent with the deed and the information on the inn.

How like her, Kristina thought. Even in death, Kate had seen to everyone's needs, leaving each of them not only a monetary legacy, but something else, as well. In Kristina's case, it was a half interest in a country inn located in southern California.

Until she was notified by Sterling, Kristina hadn't even known her grandmother had the inn among her holdings. From what she'd gathered, it seemed Kate Fortune had remained a discreet silent partner in it for over twenty years.

Kristina smiled fondly now. It was hard to envision her grandmother being a silent partner in anything. They had that in common, too. Neither of them had ever believed in keeping her opinions to herself.

"The silent aren't heard," her grandmother had once said to her.

At the time, Kristina had thought that the line was just a quaint, self-evident homily, but now she understood the deeper meaning behind her grandmother's words. You had to make yourself heard in order to get your own way. If you didn't, no one would ever know what you had to offer.

And she had a lot to offer, especially to this tacky little place. Kristina tapped a well-manicured pink nail on the photo on the cover of the brochure for emphasis. In fact, she'd guess that the bequest had arrived here just in time. Just in time for the inn.

As a matter of habit, she'd requisitioned the tax information on it from their accountant. It had taken some doing to find the information for her, but it had wound up on her desk this morning, just as she had requested.

The statement wasn't heartening, but that hadn't been completely unexpected. There was a huge margin for improvement. As far as investments went, this hadn't been a shrewd one for Kate.

Kristina decided that Kate must have kept her hand in for some sentimental reason. Maybe she had even met there with Grandfather Ben for a lovers' tryst.

The thought pleased her. Kristina would have wished her grandmother that kind of heart-quickening happiness.

The kind that Grant now had. The kind that had completely eluded her.

Kristina banished the thought before it could make her maudlin again, and made up her mind. Her career was established and flourishing. She was a natural at creating ad campaigns that were simple yet sleek and caught the public's attention. But after two years, it was a case of "Been there, done that."

What she wanted now was a challenge, something new to try her hand at. Something that was hers alone, not an integral part of the Fortune dynasty. She looked at the paper on the desk. The place was begging for help.

And she was just the woman to give it.

With a nod of her head, Kristina swept together the papers on her desk and deposited them in their manila envelope. Her pensive, restless mood had vanished, now that her course had been established.

"Thanks, Grandmother. You always knew how to set things right for me."

Frank Gibson had been part of the advertising department at Fortune Industries for the last fifteen years. He had slowly worked his way up within the framework, losing a little more hair with each advancement. Now, as the senior VP, a title that he felt at times was more decorative than lucrative, he retained only a slight fringe of brown just above his ears. And even that was in danger of going.

Such as now.

He looked at the blond slip of a girl who had been all but foisted on him two years ago and digested what she was saying to him. He might have accepted her into the fold reluctantly, expecting nothing, but he had been more than just a little pleasantly surprised. He'd quickly discovered that Kristina Fortune pulled her own weight and then some. If at times that meant she ran over some toes, allowances could be made, not just because she was the boss's daughter, but because she was damn good.

He didn't like the idea of doing without her for any long extended period of time.

Frank rubbed his large palms along the edge of his desk, a sure sign that the news he was receiving was making him nervous.

"You want *what?*"

She knew she could do this without asking. No one's opinion really mattered, when you came right down to it, except her father's. And he would give her her head, as she was requesting, especially since it involved his mother's bequest.

But, technically, Frank was her boss, and she got along with him a great deal better than she did with her father.

So, to avoid any bad feelings, she went through the proper channels and put her request to him.

"A leave of absence."

They were unveiling a new perfume in a little more than two months. There were still a thousand details to see to. It had been Kristina's baby all the way.

"Now?" Frank asked. "In the middle of an ad campaign?"

Kristina laughed. She couldn't remember a single day going by when Frank hadn't behaved as if everything were a matter of life and death.

"Frank, we are *always* in the middle of an ad campaign." Sitting down on the sofa against the wall, she crossed her legs and saw Frank's eyes drift to her hemline before he quickly looked away. Frank's romantic life began and ended in his mind. "It's nothing you can't handle." She genuinely liked the mousy little man. He was kind to her without being obsequious. She tucked her tongue into her cheek. "Maybe not with my flair, but at least with my notes." She nodded in the general direction of her office. "I left everything organized for you. It's under Redemption." Which was the name she had given to the new scent.

Kristina had made her mind up to handle the inn herself a week ago, when she first received Sterling's letter. But she had taken the extra time to do her homework on bed-and-breakfast inns. She never ventured into anything unarmed.

Frank frowned. After years of trying, he could finally find his way around a keyboard, as long as it was attached to a typewriter. Word-processing and spreadsheet programs were completely beyond him. You might as well ask him to pilot a starship.

"You know I hate computers. That's what I have you for." Finally comfortable with her, he was not above putting a teasing spin on their working relationship.

She laughed as she leaned forward. "You have me for a lot more reasons than that, Frank."

In actuality, at this point, Frank was content to let Kristina head most of their campaigns. The TV spot she'd come up with for Hidden Sin had single-handedly upped sales a full ten percent across the board.

"All right," he agreed. "Rub my nose in it, but don't leave."

"Leave of absence, Frank. Leave of absence." Kristina enunciated the words slowly. "That doesn't mean forever." She knew how quickly Frank could come to rely on something. It was flattering, but right now, it was getting in the way of the new pair of wings she wanted to try.

Kristina rose, giving the appearance of being taller than she actually was. "I'll only be gone for about two months." She thought of the photographs of the inn. "Two and a half, tops."

He knew it was useless to argue with her. She would do what she wanted to do. She was a Fortune and could afford to, unlike the rest of the world. "And what is it that you want to accomplish in those two months?"

"Something new." She couldn't quite put it into words, but something was calling to her, telling her that this was right. That she had to do this. Maybe it was even her grandmother, whispering in her ear. She wasn't certain. She just knew she had to go. "Grandmother left me her share in a bed-and-breakfast inn in California."

"California?" he echoed, horrified at the thought of the place. "They have earthquakes."

She laughed at the expression on his face. Frank was one of those people who were content never to try anything new in their lives. He ascribed the feeling to everyone. "And we have fog and tornadoes."

Frank snorted shortly. Nothing in the world could get him to travel to California, even on business. He would delegate trips if he had to. "A fog can't kill you."

She looked out the window. The gauzy texture of the fog hadn't changed since this morning. "No, but it can depress you to death." She knew she didn't have to explain herself, but because she liked him, she wanted Frank to understand. "I don't know, Frank, I just feel that I want to try my hand at something that doesn't have the Fortune stamp all over it."

"It will when you get through with it," he pointed out, in case the fact had escaped her.

She turned to look at him, her smile wide, satisfied, as if he'd gotten the point. "Exactly, but it'll be my own stamp."

"Your mind's made up?" It was a rhetorical question, uttered for form's sake. He already knew the answer.

"When have you known me to waver?"

Never. She was the most self-assured woman he'd ever encountered, next to her grandmother. Frank sighed. "All right." Cocking his head so that he resembled a sparrow eyeing an early-morning worm, he gave it one last shot. "I suppose there isn't anything I can say to make you change your mind?"

Kristina slowly moved her head from side to side, her amused eyes on his.

Frank spread his hands wide, helplessly. Surrendering, since he'd never had a chance of winning. "Then there's nothing for me to say except yes." He frowned as he sighed, resigned. "When has a man ever said no to you?"

She grinned. "Hasn't happened yet." Even with David, she'd been the one to say no. But that had only been after she discovered that his one and only love was the Fortune money. "And I don't see it happening anytime soon."

He had no reason to disagree with her. "When it does, let me know."

She patted his face affectionately, with the camaraderie that had arisen in the trenches over the past two years. "You'll be the first, I promise."

She'd begun to leave when he called out after her, "Really, what are you going to do there in..." His voice drifted off as he waited for her to tell him the name of the city.

"La Jolla," she supplied.

"La Ho-ya," he repeated incredulously. What kind of a name was that for a place? "You don't belong in a place like that," he insisted, "With all those laid-back, surf-obsessed weirdos running around. You'll go stir-crazy inside a week."

Spoken like a man who had never traveled outside of Minneapolis. "You're getting your information from some bad movies made in the seventies, Frank." She knew that, in his own way, he was concerned about her. That touched her. "I'll be fine," she assured him. After debating with herself, she decided to confide in him, at least partially. "I want to turn this little side holding of Grandmother's into something she would have been proud of."

Not everything needed to be tampered with, Frank thought. He didn't want to see her fail. God only knew what sort of repercussions that would have on her work when she returned. Not to mention on her. "Seems to me that if Kate Fortune would have wanted to change it, she would have done it herself."

Maybe. And maybe there was a reason she hadn't. "Not necessarily. She might have been too busy."

He thought of the mountain of details still waiting to be tended to before the campaign was launched. "And you're not?"

It was time to go. If she let him, Frank could go on like this all afternoon. And she had packing to do. "You can handle it, Frank."

He rose behind his desk, his voice rising with him. "How will I reach you?"

"You won't." She tossed her reply over her shoulder. "I'll call you."

When I feel like it, she thought.

She had left everything in her customary meticulous order. Frank had all her notes on the new ad campaign and though she knew for a fact that she was the new blood that had been pumped into the veins of the stodgy department, she also knew that there wasn't anything here that couldn't keep, or be handled by someone else, until she returned. She'd done all the preliminary work. All that remained now were the uninspiring details that had to be overseen and implemented.

Kristina placed all thoughts about the department and the pending ad campaign on the back burner and turned her attention to the future.

A new future.

Who knew? This could be the start of something big. She had a feeling...

"Hey, Max!" Paul Henning cupped his mouth with one hand as he shouted above the noise of the crane. "It's for you."

He held up the portable telephone and waved it above his head, in case Max couldn't hear what he was saying.

Max Cooper turned toward the trailer. He'd thought he heard his name being called. The rest of the men were too far away for him to hear one of them. Then he saw his partner waving the telephone receiver.

With a sigh, he took off his hard hat and ran his hand through his unruly dark brown hair. He sincerely hoped that this wasn't from someone calling about yet another delay. The construction of the new housing development was already behind schedule. The December mudslides had set them all back at least a month. He had his people and the subcontractors working double shifts to try to catch up. The last thing he wanted was to pay the penalty for bringing the project in late.

Every time the phone rang, he mentally winced, anticipating another disaster in the making. Nature didn't use a telephone, but errant suppliers and subcontractors did, and they could wreak almost the same amount of havoc Mother Nature could.

Replacing his hard hat, he waved at Paul. The latter retreated into the trailer that, at the moment, housed their entire operation. Max followed.

He made his way into the cluttered space, hoping that by the next job they could see about getting something larger. Right now, a new trailer was the least of their priorities.

Paul, a tall, wiry man, was as thin-framed as Max was muscular. He pressed himself against the wall to allow Max access to the telephone.

"We've built closets larger than this," he muttered, still holding the telephone aloft.

Max indicated the receiver. "Who?" he mouthed.

Paul knew who it was, but he thought he'd string Max along for a minute. It appealed to his sense of humor, which hadn't been getting much of a workout lately.

"She said it was personal," he whispered.

He was between "personals" right now, Max thought as he took the receiver from Paul. He and Rita had come to a mutual agreement to go their separate ways. Actually, the word *agreement* was stretching it a little. She'd been screaming something about his "freaking fear of commitment" at the time. Those had been her parting words to him, ending what had otherwise been a rather pleasant, albeit short, interlude.

Warily Max put the receiver to his ear, wondering if Rita had decided to try to make another go of it. He hoped not. He'd kept his relationships short and predominantly sweet—the former fact being responsible for the latter— ever since Alexis.

But then, no one had touched him, or hurt him, like Alexis. And no one ever would.

"Hello?"

"Max? It's June," the voice on the other end of the line said. Normally pleasant, June's voice was anxious and uncertain. "I hate bothering you at work, but I think you'd better come out here. You're going to want to see this."

June Cunningham, sixtyish, even-tempered and efficient, was the receptionist at the Dew Drop Inn, the small bed-and-breakfast inn that Max had found himself the unwilling half owner of. He would have sold his share in it long ago, if it wouldn't have hurt his foster parents' feelings. John and Sylvia Murphy were the only parents he had ever known, taking in a scared, cocky thirteen-year-old and turning him into a man, when everyone else had elected to pass on him. He owed them more than he could ever hope to repay.

So if they wanted him to take over their half of the inn, he couldn't very well toss the gift they offered back at them. He left the management in June's hands and stopped by on Fridays after six to look in on everything. Right now, knee-deep in construction hassles, the inn was the last thing on his mind. When he thought of it at all, it was in terms of it being an albatross about his neck.

He couldn't imagine anything that would prompt the unflappable June to telephone him here, of all places, and request his presence at the inn. She'd *never* asked him to come by. What the hell was wrong?

"This?" he repeated. "Exactly what do you mean by 'this'?"

"Ms. Fortune."

It was a minute before he reacted. "Kate? She's dead. She's been gone for nearly two years." He remembered seeing an article in the paper saying that the woman's plane had gone down in some isolated part of Africa or South America, someplace like that. Her lawyer, Sterling Foster, had sent him a letter saying probate would take a long time, considering the size of Kate's estate, so he should just continue to run it as always. But now it seemed there would be some changes.

"Not Kate," June quickly corrected. "Her heir. Kristina Fortune."

This was all news to him, although he had to admit that he'd been rather lax as far as things at the inn were concerned. It hadn't even occurred to him, when he read about Kate, that whoever inherited her half would be coming by to look the place over.

"She's there?"

"She's here, all right." He heard June stifle a sigh. "And she wants to meet with you. Immediately."

June took everything in stride. He couldn't remember ever seeing her hurry. "Immediately?" It was a strange word for her to use. "Immediately?"

There was no humor in the small, dry laugh. June lowered her voice, as if she were afraid of being overheard. "Her word, not mine. But I really think you should get here, Max. I heard her murmuring something to herself about knocking walls out."

That caught his attention. Just who the hell did this Kristina Fortune think she was? He didn't particularly want the inn, but he didn't want to see it destroyed, either. It was part of his childhood. The best part, if he didn't count John and Sylvia.

Covering the receiver, he turned to Paul. "Would you mind if I left you with all this for a few hours?"

Paul grinned as if he'd just hit the mother lode. "Hell, no, I was just wondering how to get rid of you. I love playing boss man."

Max knew Paul meant it. He took his hand off the mouthpiece. "I'll be there as soon as I can, June." He cut the connection.

"Must be great to have a piece of so many different enterprises," Paul joked. When Max didn't return his grin, he asked, "What's up?"

I don't need this, Max thought. He liked things uncomplicated and this was probably the worse possible time to have problems rear their pointy heads. "Seems that the new partner at the inn has some fancy ideas about what to do with the place."

Paul poured himself another cup of coffee. "New partner?"

Max nodded, hanging up his hard hat. "Kate Fortune owned the inn with my foster parents. She was killed in a plane crash a while back. June just called to say her 'heir' arrived. She thinks I'd better get over there immediately.''

"Doesn't sound like June.''

Max pulled his jacket on. "She was quoting Kristina Fortune.''

"Oh.'' He got the picture. "Better you than me, pal.'' Paul saluted Max and then walked out of the trailer, back to the construction site.

"Yeah.'' Max bit off the word as he strode out. He wasn't looking forward to this.

Two

It had possibilities.

Stepping away from the taxi she had taken from the airport, Kristina had slowly approached the inn. It had no real style to speak of. The photographs she had seen in the brochure had turned out to be flattering and too kind. Still, the inn was rustic and charming, in its own quaint way. But it was definitely run-down. It reminded Kristina of a woman who was past her prime and had decided that comfort was far more important to her than upkeep, but it did have definite possibilities.

With a good, solid effort, and an amenable, competent contractor working with her, who understood what she had in mind, the inn could readily be transformed into a moneymaker.

The forerunner of several more.

Kristina had seized the thought as soon as it occurred to her, and begun to develop it. Her mind had raced, making plans, putting the cart not only before the horse, but before the whole damn stable.

The horse was just going to have to catch up, she had thought with a smile as she walked up the stairs to the porch.

Kristina had done her homework and boned up on the subject. She liked the idea a great deal. Why just one bed-and-breakfast inn? Why not a chain? A chain that catered to the romantic in everyone. If she could make it work here, she could continue acquiring small, quaint inns throughout the country and transform them, until there was a whole string of Honeymoon Hideaways.

Her mood had altered abruptly as she stumbled, catching the handrail at the last moment. Her three-inch heel had gotten caught in a crack in the wooden floor. Kristina had frowned as she freed her heel. Someone should have fixed that.

Fixed was the operative word, as she'd discovered when she went on to examine the rest of the ground floor, finally returning to the front room, where she had begun. The woman who had introduced herself as June had remained with her almost the entire time. She wasn't much of a sounding board, preferring to point out the inn's "charm." It seemed that around here "neglect" was synonymous with "charm."

Having seen more than enough, Kristina turned now in a complete circle to get a panoramic feel for the room. Ideas were breeding in her mind like fertile rabbits.

Her eyes came to rest on the large brick fireplace. It was dormant at the moment, but she could easily envision a warm, roaring fire within it.

"Fireplaces."

"Excuse me?" June looked at her uncertainly.

Kristina turned to look at her. "Fireplaces," she repeated. "The other rooms are going to have to have fireplaces. I'm going to turn this into a place where newlyweds are going to be clamoring to spend the first idyllic days of their life together."

She ignored the dubious look on the other woman's face. She made a quick mental note as she continued to scan the room. The coffee table was going to have to go.

June pointed out the obvious. "But there's no room for any fireplaces."

"There will be, once a few walls are knocked down and the extra bathrooms are put in," Kristina responded, doing a few mental calculations.

Placing her escalating ideas on temporary hold, Kristina

looked at the woman behind the counter. She'd had one of her assistants obtain information from June's personnel file before she flew out. She had a thumbnail bio on everyone who worked at the inn.

June had been here for over twenty years. She looked very comfortable in her position. Too comfortable. From the way she talked, June probably would resist change, and that meant she was going to have to go. It would be better to have young, vibrant people working at the inn, anyway. Young, like the idea of eternal love.

The success that loomed just on the horizon excited Kristina.

"I need a telephone book," she told June suddenly. No time like the present to get started getting estimates. "The classifieds."

June had a really bad feeling about all this. Kristina Fortune had announced her presence with all the subtlety of a hurricane. The very few, very leading questions that the woman had asked made June believe that the inn was in danger of being torn apart, piece by piece, staff member by staff member. She liked her job and the people she worked with, the people she had come to regard as her extended family. She felt very protective of them, and of Max.

She wondered what was keeping him. She'd called him nearly an hour ago.

Kristina noticed that June gave her a long, penetrating look before bending down behind the front desk to retrieve the telephone book.

It only reinforced Kristina's intention to replace her. June Cunningham moved like molasses that had been frozen onto a plate all winter.

No wonder this place was falling apart. Everyone moved in slow motion. The gardener she had passed on her way in looked as if he had fallen asleep propped up against a juniper bush.

And there was supposed to be a maid on the premises to

take care of the sixteen rooms. If there was one, Kristina certainly hadn't seen her since she arrived.

June placed the yellow pages on the counter with a resounding thud. "Planning on calling a taxi?" she asked hopefully.

The sentiment wasn't lost on Kristina. *Don't you wish.*

It wouldn't be the first time she had run into employee displeasure. If she was in the business of trying to make friends with everyone, it would have bothered her. But Kristina had learned a long time ago that most people were jealous of her position in life. Jealous of the money that surrounded her. It had them making up their minds about her before she ever had a chance to say a word. So Kristina ignored the opinions so blatantly written across their faces and did what she had to do. She wasn't out to make friends, only a reputation.

Kristina frowned as she flipped through the pages, looking for the proper section. She wondered where she could get her hands on an L.A. directory. This one was relatively small. There weren't many companies to choose from.

"No, a contractor." She spared June a cool glance. "This place needs work."

"Antonio is our handyman," June told her easily. "He doubles as a waiter."

That would undoubtedly explain the condition of the inn, Kristina thought. "It's going to take more than a handyman to fix up this place. It needs a complete overhaul."

June thought of telling the woman in the crisp teal business suit that Max was a contractor, but decided against it. Max could tell her that in person, when he got here. It could be the icebreaker. And from where she stood, it looked like there was going to be a lot of ice to break, June thought.

Kristina looked around. There was no sign of a telephone on the desk. "Where's your telephone?" Impatience strummed through her as she marked one small ad. Jessup & Son promised that no job was too small or too large. It was as good a place as any to begin.

The answer didn't come quickly enough. Kristina waved a dismissive hand in June's direction. If this was a sign of the service, no wonder there was no one staying here. "No, never mind. I'll just use mine."

Kristina opened one of the compartments in her purse and extracted her cellular telephone. Reading the numbers on the ad again, she punched them into the keypad. She raised her eyes to June's face when she heard the audible sigh of relief. The next moment, the woman was hurrying to the front door.

Phone in hand, Kristina turned to see who had managed to liven the woman up enough for her to actually display some speed.

June hooked an arm through Max's as she pulled him over to the side. "Max, she's calling contractors. Do something."

So this was the other owner of the inn. Kristina flipped the telephone closed. The call could wait. "Home is the hunter," she murmured, quoting one of her favorite lines.

Slowly her eyes took the measure of the other half owner, from head to foot. There was a lot to measure. Tall, Max Cooper looked, in Kristina's estimation, like a rangy cowboy who had taken the wrong turn at the last roundup. He was wearing worn jeans that looked as if they'd been part of his wardrobe since he was in high school. They adhered to his frame with a familiarity reserved for a lover. The royal-blue-and-white work shirt beneath the faded denim jacket made his eyes stand out.

Even from a distance, she saw that they were a very potent blue. The kind of blue she would imagine belonged in the face of a Greek god. If that Greek god was smoldering.

From what she could see, the hair beneath his slouched, stained cowboy hat was brown and long. As unruly and unkempt as the inn appeared to be.

Kristina was beginning to see the connection.

The man's appearance might have impressed someone

from Central Casting, as well as a good handful of her female friends, unattached and otherwise, but it didn't impress her.

Business sense was what impressed her, and he apparently didn't have any.

She was looking him over as if he were a piece of merchandise to be appraised, Max thought. He did his own appraising.

So this was the whirlwind June had called him about. He'd met Kate Fortune only once, years ago. She'd come out for a long Memorial Day weekend to sign some papers with his foster parents. He remembered the way she'd looked, sitting on the terrace, with the sun setting directly behind her, haloing her head. Even as a teenager, he'd known he was in the presence of class.

Right now, what he felt he was in the presence of was a brat. A very lovely brat, with great lines and even greater legs, but a brat nonetheless.

She had no business here.

He knew he read her expression correctly. Kristina Fortune looked as if she wanted all the marbles and didn't care who she had to elbow out of the way to get them. Well, half the marbles were his, and he intended for them to stay that way.

Just the way they were, and positioned where they were, without any walls coming down.

Knowing the value of getting along with the enemy, June, her arm still hooked through Max's, drew him over toward Kristina.

"Max, this is the new half owner." Kristina heard the way the woman emphasized the word *half.* June's smile deepened. "Kristina—"

Not waiting to be introduced, Kristina shifted her cellular phone to her other hand and stepped forward, thrusting her hand into Max's.

"Kristina Fortune, Kate's granddaughter. At least, one of them," she amended, thinking of her half sister and cousins. Kate had treated them all equally, but only she was going to turn her bequest into a shrine for her grandmother.

Maybe I'll hang her portrait over the fireplace, Kristina thought suddenly.

Yes, that would add just the right touch. She knew just the one to use, too. The one that had been painted on Kate's thirtieth birthday. Her grandmother had still had the blush of youth on her cheek. Her beautiful red hair had been swept up, away from her face, and she had had on a mint-green gown...

He'd just said a perfunctory "Glad to meet you" and gotten no response. When he dropped her hand, she suddenly looked at him.

He had the distinct impression that she was only partially here. Which was fine with him. He'd like it even better if none of her were here. June and the others did a fair job of maintaining the old place, and he firmly believed in the adage that if it wasn't broken, it shouldn't be fixed.

He damn well didn't want this intruder "fixing" anything. "You look a million miles away."

Kristina cleared her throat, embarrassed at having been caught. "Sorry, I was just thinking of what I want to hang over the fireplace."

There was a huge, colorful tapestry hanging over the fireplace now. His foster mother had spent long hours weaving it herself. He remembered watching her do it. Her fingers had seemed to sing over the loom. She was one-quarter Cherokee; the tapestry represented a history that had been handed down to Sylvia Murphy by her grandmother's people. He was very partial to it.

Max's eyes narrowed. "What's wrong with what's over it now?"

It was natural for him to challenge her. She'd already made up her mind that he would resist change. The unimaginative always did.

"It doesn't fit the motif," she said simply.

What the hell was she talking about? They hadn't discussed anything yet. They hadn't even gotten past hello. "Motif? What motif?"

"The new one I've come up with. We're turning this into a Honeymoon Hideaway." She watched his expression, to see if he liked the name. He didn't.

Kristina paused and blew out a breath. Since he was the other owner, she supposed she had better explain it to him, even though she hated explaining herself to anyone. She preferred doing, and letting others watch and see for themselves.

Kristina got the distinct impression that Cooper wasn't going to be as amenable to her methods as Frank was. "I guess I'm getting ahead of myself."

Now there was an understatement. Max exchanged a look with June and missed the fact that it annoyed Kristina. It would have been a bonus, as far as he was concerned.

After pushing his hat back on his head, he hooked his thumbs on the loops of his jeans. "I'd say you were getting ahead of just about everyone. What makes you think we need a 'motif'?"

He said the word as if it left a bad taste in his mouth. "Well, you certainly need something."

He didn't care for her condescending tone of voice. "The inn is doing just fine."

"Just fine," she repeated softly. She gave him a long, slow look, as if she were appraising him again, and this time finding him mentally lacking. He could feel his temper rising. It was the fastest reaction he had ever had to anyone. "I take it that you don't bother looking at the inn's books."

No, he didn't, not really, but he didn't care for her inference. "June handles the books." He nodded at the woman, who was once again safely ensconced behind the counter. "I review them."

"Not often enough." Probably every leap year, Kristina guessed.

He'd had just about enough of this. His real business

needed him, not the inn. The inn would do just fine continuing the way it had. Without her fingers all over it. "Just what gives you the right to come waltzing in here—"

She had to stop him now, before he got up a full head of steam and wasted both their time. He might have time to kill, but she didn't.

"I didn't 'waltz,'" she corrected sharply. "I walked— nearly breaking my neck on the loose board in the front, I might add."

He set his mouth hard, his eyes narrowing to slits. "Pity."

She got the distinct feeling that he wasn't apologizing for the presence of the loose board, he was lamenting the fact that she'd avoided the injury.

Ignoring that, she continued, getting to her point. "And I've had a good hour to look around—"

One hour, and she was passing judgment on his foster parents' lives' work. "That makes you an expert."

She raised her chin as she took up the challenge in his voice. "No, I arrived being an expert."

God, talk about brass. Hers was glinting in the sun, and could have served as a beacon to guide ships home in a fog. "On inns."

Kristina ignored the obvious sarcasm. "On profit margins, and how to sell something."

He took his time in responding, instinctively knowing that it annoyed her. "And what, exactly, is it that you sell?"

She could have slapped him for what he was obviously thinking, but it wouldn't have gotten them anywhere. After all, she'd come here to work. Even with an insufferable mental midget like him. "I'm an ad executive. I'm responsible for the Hidden Sin campaign."

He was vaguely aware that she was referring to a perfume. The latest copy of a magazine he subscribed to had arrived in the mail smelling to high heaven, because one of the pages had been impregnated with the scent. "Congratulations. I heard sin came *out* of hiding."

"The perfume," she retorted.

Inexplicably enjoying the fact that he could bait her, Max responded, "Never heard of it."

If he thought he was getting to her, he was mistaken. "I don't doubt it. We haven't found a way to pipe the commercials into people's sleep yet."

He heard her message loud and clear. At another time, it might have amused him. But she, and her manner, irked him beyond words. "You're implying that I'm lazy?"

Kristina crossed her arms before her chest. Her expression congratulated him on finally catching on. "The inn is run-down, the bookings are off," she pointed out, warming up. "You're in the red—"

He cut in curtly. "It's the off-season." From the corner of his eye, he saw June shaking her head in disapproval. What was he supposed to do, humor this crazy woman?

Right there was the beginning of his problem, Kristina thought. "There shouldn't be an off-season in southern California."

He looked at her, completely mystified by her reasoning. "Is this something you just made up?"

She sighed. She was trying to hold on to her temper, but he wasn't making it easy for her. She'd carried on better conversations with her parakeet. "If you're going to challenge everything I say, Cooper, we're not going to get anywhere."

He took a moment to compose himself. "What makes you think I want to get anywhere with you, Ms. Fortune? I like the inn just the way it is."

He might, but what he wanted alone didn't count. She eyed the wide sofa before the fireplace. If it had a style, it might have been Early American. That, too, would have to go.

"Not good enough." She ran her hand along the floral

upholstery and wondered when it had last been cleaned. "I'm half owner."

He read her intentions loud and clear. Very deliberately, he removed her hand from the sofa. "And you can't do anything without my half."

Can't had never been part of her vocabulary. "I can buy you out."

Ironic, wasn't it? He had wanted to sell his ownership in the inn. Ever since his foster parents had given it to him, he'd wanted to sell it and devote himself completely to his business. Now the perfect opportunity was presenting itself, but he wasn't about to take it.

He wasn't about to sell his share to her, because that would mean selling out, selling out and abandoning people he'd known for a long time. He had no doubt that within ten minutes of his signing the deed over to her, Kristina Fortune would send the staff packing and hire some plastic people to take their place.

He'd be damned if he was going to let her fire people he had known and liked for years. There was a place for loyalty in this world, even if fancy ad executives with creamy skins didn't know it.

"No, you can't," he told her. "Not if I don't want to sell."

He wasn't making sense. It was clear he didn't have any interest in the place. If he did, he wouldn't have let it deteriorate to this extent. She hated things that didn't make sense.

"I don't understand. Why would you want to let all this go to waste?"

There was a fantastic view of the ocean from the rear of the inn. People would pay dearly for the opportunity to wake up in the morning to it. Yet the hotel's bookings were way off, even for the so-called off-season.

People like Kristina Fortune only had one view of things—their own. He'd had experience enough with her kind. Alexis had been a great teacher.

His mouth hardened. "What makes you think it's going to waste?"

Oh, God, the man was an idiot. Good-looking, but an idiot. She looked at his face again, taking in the rugged lines, the sensual sweep of his lashes. The bone structure that was faintly reminiscent of the tribes that had once walked this land freely. He was probably accustomed to getting by on his looks and nothing more.

But that wasn't going to cut it here, not with her. Especially not when it got in the way.

"Anyone with half a brain would know—" Kristina began testily.

Having stood on the sidelines long enough, June came around from behind the desk and placed herself between the two of them. She could almost hear the lightning crackling on either side of her. This exchange wasn't going to get anyone anywhere. They both needed to cool off and begin again. She didn't care a whit about Kristina and what she did or didn't want, but she did care about the inn and Max.

"Ms. Fortune, why don't I have Sydney take you up to your room?" June suggested brightly, as if Kristina had just walked in. Her smile was warm and genial. "You must be tired, after your long flight out here from—" She let her voice trail off as she raised her brow inquiringly, waiting for Kristina to supply a location.

"Minneapolis," Kristina replied tersely, her eyes never leaving Max's infuriating face.

June nodded, as if the city's name had been on the tip of her tongue. "Five-hour flight. Bound to make you tired." If she had been a bird, she would have been chirping. "Sydney!" She raised her voice, letting it carry to the rear of the inn. The last time she saw the young woman, Sydney had been on her way to the kitchen to see about getting lunch.

Kristina wasn't tired, but she did appreciate the value of retreating and regrouping. Shouting at this numbskulled cowboy wasn't going to get her anywhere. She needed a few minutes to freshen up.

And to get a better grip on her temper. She rarely lost it, but this man seemed to have an ability to wrench it from her with breathtaking speed.

"All right," she agreed. "I can unpack a few things, and then we can get started. I have a lot of notes and sketches I want to go over with you."

"I can hardly wait," Max muttered under his breath, just loud enough for her to hear.

Kristina refrained from answering. This was going to be more difficult than she'd thought. But not impossible. Nothing, she firmly believed, was ever impossible if you were determined enough. And she was.

Sydney appeared, moving in the same unhurried gait that seemed to be prevalent here, Kristina thought. Maybe Frank hadn't been wrong in his assessment of life in southern California. It was just too slow and laid-back for her.

But she had no intention of moving here. Just of moving things along.

June noted the curiosity in Sydney's eyes as the young woman looked at Kristina.

"Sydney, this is Kate Fortune's granddaughter, Kristina," June said. "She'll be taking Kate's place. This is Sydney Burnham, the baby of our group."

Sydney had been working at the inn for only the past four years. Coming to work during the summer between her junior and senior year at college, Sydney had joined the staff permanently after graduation, preferring the unhurried pace in La Jolla to the frantic life of a stockbroker.

Sydney looked around for luggage and noticed the two suitcases off to the side, by the desk. She picked up one in each hand and nodded at the newest guest. "Nice to meet you, Kristina."

The greeting was entirely too informal to suit Kristina. There had to be distance between management and employees in order for things to run smoothly. "Ms. Fortune," she corrected.

Max rolled his eyes as he turned his back on Kristina.

June waited until the two women had disappeared up the stairs before saying to Max, "I think I just bought you a little time."

"I have a feeling a century wouldn't be enough when it comes to that woman. She's spoiled, self-centered and pig-headed."

June laughed at the assessment. "And those are her good qualities." Time for a little pep talk. "But you'll find a way to pull this out of the fire, Max. I know you will."

Max thought of his foster father. The man was a born arbitrator. He could use him now. Max shook his head.

"I'm not John Murphy."

June had always liked Max's modest streak. A man as good-looking as he was could easily have been conceited. "No, but he taught you well. You'll find a way to get along with her, and get her to ease up those grand plans I see forming in her head."

He had his doubts about that. "At times I think you give me too much credit."

"At times, I don't think you give yourself enough." June looked up the stairs and shivered in spite of herself. There was a lot at stake here. "You've got to do something, Max. I get the definite impression that she wants all of our jobs."

That made two of them. Max frowned. He'd never seen the advantage in lying. "So do I, June. So do I."

There had to be a way to make Kristina Fortune see reason. The magic question was, how?

Three

Kristina curled her legs under her on the double bed, keeping the telephone receiver tucked between her shoulder and her ear. She made a mental note that the bed needed a canopy to give it a more romantic flavor.

Just outside her window, the Pacific Ocean was having the beginnings of a turbulent discussion with the shoreline. The recessed trees that fringed the perimeter of the grassy expanse just behind the inn were shaking their heads in abject disagreement. A storm was brewing, albeit in the distance.

It was romantic settings such as this that would make the inn's reputation, Kristina thought. Or at least part of it. The rest would be up to her, since Cooper obviously didn't seem interested in her ideas. But Cooper could be worked around, she silently promised herself. She was nothing if not resourceful and determined. This place was begging for guidance.

Her aunt's voice brought her mind back to the conversation. She'd placed a call to her as soon as she got to her room. As always, just the sound of her voice made Kristina feel better.

"I tell you, Rebecca, you just wouldn't believe this place."

Rebecca Fortune was her favorite aunt, the one who reminded her most of her grandmother. They were so close in age, Kristina thought of her more as an older sister than an aunt. Even as a child, Kristina had never been about to wrap her tongue around the word *aunt* when it was in reference to Rebecca. It just wouldn't have felt right.

"It has such possibilities," she enthused, warming to her subject and her own ideas. "But right now, it's all completely mired in a horrid Ma and Pa Kettle look." Rebecca loved old movies. Kristina knew that the reference to the movie series would get the idea across to her far faster than a whole string of adjectives.

"With a moose head hanging over the fireplace?" There was amusement in Rebecca's voice.

Maybe she had gone a little overboard in her assessment, Kristina thought. But it was hard not to have that reaction, when the staff reminded her of people straight off some unproductive farm. "Well, not quite that, but close."

Rebecca laughed with a touch of longing. "Sounds delicious."

Kristina could see that her aunt relished the image. Rebecca probably found the idea of a secluded house inviting. Maybe it was, but not if that house looked as if it was falling apart.

"That's only because you're thinking like a mystery writer, not like a guest."

There was no argument forthcoming on that count. Rebecca laughed softly at the observation. "Sorry, dear, force of habit."

There was a momentary pause. Kristina could hear the transformation in her aunt's voice when Rebecca continued. "I suppose that my thinking like a mystery writer is the reason I can't accept Mother's death." She sighed. "The whole thing just doesn't hit the right chord."

Kristina couldn't help wondering just how much of her aunt's response was due to her writer's instincts and how much of it was due to pure denial. It was a given that none of the family were really willing to admit that a force as powerful as Kate Fortune could actually be snuffed out so quickly, without preamble.

Still, she hated to see her aunt torture herself this way.

Her grandmother had been piloting the plane herself at the time of the crash. Kristina knew that Rebecca's hopes were tied to the fact that the body found at the site of the wreck had been burned beyond recognition. But who else's could it have been? There'd been no one else on the flight. And after all this time there was no other possibility.

"Rebecca..." Kristina began, her voice filled with affection.

"I know, I know. You're going to tell me to accept it, but I can't." There was neither apology nor defensiveness in Rebecca's voice. She was stating a simple fact. "I want proof, Kristina. Something to absolutely close the book for me. Right now, I feel that it's just a serial. Like in the Saturday matinees in the forties and fifties. 'To be continued.'"

Kristina knew there was no arguing with Rebecca. In her own fashion, Rebecca was as tenacious as Kate had been. It was something Kristina had in common with them. "Well, has that detective you and Father hired found anything?"

"Gabriel Devereax is doing his best, but it's just not enough. He's also been involved in a lot of the other investigations, including looking for proof of Jake's innocence. I know he didn't kill Monica Malone, and soon we're going to prove it. And then we'll get back to Mother's death. I'm not giving up yet." The change in topic was abrupt. It was a signal that Rebecca didn't want to discuss Gabriel or her mother any further. "You certainly sound like you've got your hands full." She paused, obviously thinking. "Mother never really talked about the inn."

Kristina looked down at the quilt beneath her. While still attractive, it had definitely seen better days. A lot of better days. Like the inn, it was worn in places.

"I don't wonder." Kristina laughed. "If I owned something like this, I wouldn't exactly broadcast it, either."

"But you're going to change all that," Rebecca said knowingly.

Kristina sat up a little straighter, as if bracing herself for the battles she knew lay ahead. She thought of Max and immediately frowned. "As fast as I can, provided Cowboy Max cooperates."

"And that would be—?"

Kristina realized that she had skipped over that small detail when she told Rebecca about the inn. "The other owner."

"Wait a minute, I thought it belonged to a couple named Murphy."

"It did." The phone slipped, and Kristina grabbed it, tucking it back. "But they retired, handing their interest over to their foster son." She fairly snorted. "I guess they didn't care what happened to it."

What was left unsaid spoke volumes. "Sounds like you and he aren't getting along."

Kristina caught herself grinning. She could have said the same thing about Rebecca and the detective she'd hired. "There's that witty understatement at work again." She thought of their first encounter. "We're more like a couple of junkyard dogs fighting over a bone."

"That doesn't sound too good. Make sure you take care of yourself," Rebecca cautioned.

Kristina dismissed Rebecca's concern. "Not to worry, this junkyard dog's got clout."

And Kristina meant to use every bit of her pull. She could get the advertising department to mount a campaign for the inn once she had it fixed up the way she wanted. The way it *should* be. She'd already drawn up a tentative schedule for the renovations. If things got rolling immediately, they would be concluded in six to seven months— just in time for the middle of summer.

"All Cowboy Max has is a sexy smile and cotton for brains. I can certainly handle that," she said with confidence.

The telephone slipped again when she heard the knock on her door. Kristina glanced at it impatiently.

"I've got to go, Rebecca. There's someone at the door. I'm going to be very busy, so I probably won't call often. Let the family know I'll be in touch, okay?"

"Sure, but I've got a little snooping of my own to tend to. We've got to get Jake free."

"Yes." And she didn't believe, for one minute, that her uncle had killed that dreadful woman. Uncle Jake, austere, reserved, was a rock. He would never be capable of killing anyone.

"Well, things are going to be rather hectic around here for a while. We're all doing what we can to get to the bottom of this. Everyone knows that Jake wouldn't hurt anyone."

Kristina heard the knock again, and her impatience mounted at the interruption. "Everyone but the law. Do they have a trial date set yet?"

"Beginning of March."

That would cut her time here short, but she knew the importance of a show of unity. She was just going to have to speed things up, that was all.

"I'll be back by then," she promised. "Good luck, Rebecca. I'll see you in a few weeks."

A third knock echoed, this time more insistent. Probably that big oaf. It sounded like his knuckles banging on the door. She had no doubts that they had gotten large and callused, dragging around the ground like that.

Hanging up the telephone, she leaned over to the nightstand and replaced it beside the lamp. A hurricane lamp should be there, she thought.

Kristina gathered together the notes and sketches she'd spread out on her bed and deposited them beside the phone. "Come in."

Curbing his annoyance, Max turned the knob and walked in. He'd caught a piece of Kristina's conversation before he knocked. Cotton for brains, was it? He was going to enjoy showing her just how worthy an adversary cotton actually was.

As soon as Max entered, Kristina felt a wave of discomfort enter with him. There was something about his presence in her room that made her feel uneasy.

Swinging her legs off the bed, Kristina stood up. Without her heels on, the top of her head barely came up to Max's shoulder. It gave him an unfair advantage. Nudging her shoes upright with her toe, she quickly slipped them on.

What was he doing here, anyway? She hadn't sent for him. Though she tried, she couldn't read anything in his expression.

She hazarded a guess. "Afraid I'd get started without you?"

Max hooked his thumbs on the loops of his jeans and gave her a long, studying look. Patience around this woman seemed to be in short supply, but for everyone's sake, he tried to exercise it.

"The thought did cross my mind." *Cottony though it is.*

There was something unfathomable in his eyes that contributed to the uneasy feeling wafting through her. The same kind of feeling she would have experienced by sticking her hand into a hole in the ground, not knowing if she was going to be bitten, or just find the hole empty.

"So why are you here?"

June's words of caution rang in his ears. He chose his words carefully. "I thought maybe we got off on the wrong foot."

Was he trying to apologize? Was that what she saw in his eyes? Discomfort? It didn't look like discomfort.

"Wrong foot? That's putting it rather mildly." Kristina waited for him to continue, anticipating an apology. It made sparring with him earlier almost worth it.

She had an irritating air about her. Max had come up to her room hoping to start over, to get her to understand how he felt about the inn. Strangling her wasn't part of the plan, though it would have been a definite bonus. He could always claim she had bitten herself and died of poisoning instantly.

Max forced a smile to his lips. "I'd like to ask you to dinner."

Well, he had certainly done an about-face. She eyed him warily. "Where?"

The woman looked as if she expected him to jump her bones. "Here."

"All right. I was planning on sampling the food anyway." Kristina decided to make the best of a bad situation. "We might as well discuss business while I do it."

The idea was to get her to relax a bit, to mellow out. If all they did was talk business, he could see another argument erupting. That wouldn't help to smooth anything over or generate the right atmosphere.

Max moved closer to Kristina, cutting the distance and, inexplicably, the air supply between them, at the same time. "I was just thinking more along the lines of us getting to know each other."

A crack of thunder made her jump. She looked at the window, fully expecting to see that it had shattered. Lightning streaked the sky like the mark of an expert swordsman. Kristina let out a breath and turned, only to find herself brushing up against Max.

Lightning of a different sort jolted her.

It took her a moment to refocus her mind on the conversation. She pressed her lips together and asked, "Why?"

He hadn't been prepared to be challenged over such a simple suggestion. "Don't you get to know the people you do business with?"

He was up to something—she could smell it. She could also smell his cologne, which was musky and male and would have clouded her mind if she let it. She didn't like distractions.

"If I have to."

It was obviously something she would not do by choice. "You make it sound real inviting," he commented dryly.

David had been exceedingly charming. She had trusted him, believed his words. And he had taken advantage of her. Nothing like that was ever going to happen to her again. Romantically or otherwise. Unless she missed her guess, Max Cooper probably fit into the same category, only the junior league.

"I didn't come here to socialize, Cooper. I came here with a purpose."

Riding on a broom, no doubt.

He wondered if she enjoyed irritating him. Trying another approach, he brusquely took her arm and ushered her out of the room.

Surprised, Kristina tried to yank her arm away and found that she couldn't. "Hey."

Max ignored her protest and tightened his hold. His voice was polite, if strained. "I think that once you become familiar with the surroundings, with the people, you'll see that—"

She knew what he was going to say, but it wouldn't change anything. She'd already made her plans, and she was going to see them executed. "I'm sure all the people you have working here are lovely, but this isn't their home. It's a place of business. And I intend to see that it's run like one."

He didn't want to create a scene. Releasing her arm, he waited until an elderly couple had made their way down the stairs, then continued what he knew was an argument in the making.

"You're wrong."

Of course. He had to say that. Men like Cooper were contrary about everything. "About what?"

Taking her arm again, he politely but firmly marched her down the stairs. He hadn't wanted to really get into an argument yet, but he should have known better than to think he could avoid it.

"This *is* a home. Their home. The staff lives on the premises. And it was my home, too, when I was growing up."

Well, that would explain some things. Kristina was unaware that her voice had taken on a patronizing tone. "And I'm sure that to the boy you were, it was a great place, but—"

Max felt his temper flaring. This wasn't why he had sought her out. Not to argue, but to convince, and if that failed, to compromise. It didn't look as if it were heading in that direction. Max surprised her again, this time by abruptly placing his finger to her lips.

"Why don't we table this for a while? Let's just go to dinner. We can continue negotiations over a good steak." He saw a smug, superior look enter her eyes. They would have been beautiful eyes, but for that. *Think it's all settled, don't you? Well, think again.* "Or are you a vegetarian?"

By the way he posed the question, she knew he didn't think very highly of that persuasion. Kristina was tempted to say that she was, just to annoy him. There was something about him that pushed all her buttons in a perverse way. Maybe it was his attitude toward her, as if she were a little girl, playing games. Or maybe it was just that he was so damn good-looking, the way David had been.

Actually, if she was to be impartial, Max was better-looking than David. But that wasn't going to get in the way of anything. All it would do was solidify her resolve. If he thought he was going to use his looks to get her to change her mind, he was in for a surprise, she thought confidently. Her mind was made up.

Kristina's eyes held his. "No, steak'll be fine. Rare." It was what she considered one of her few weaknesses.

It was his turn to be surprised. Her answer coaxed a smile to his lips. "Finally, we agree on something."

It was a very sensual smile. Her own lips seemed to tingle where he had touched them.

Kristina tossed her head. It was an action depicting arrogance and defiance. Yet, just for a brief moment, Max thought it was tinged with an element of insecurity. Probably his imagination.

"We'll agree about this," she told him, gesturing about the front room as they walked through it. "Eventually."

He smiled at her without saying another word. *When pigs fly jet planes.*

Out of the corner of his eye, he saw June watching them. Like a mother hen, he thought, concerned that the wolf was going to eat the chicks. Not this wolf. Not if he could help it. He nodded at June as they entered the dining room.

The spacious room, with its polished wooden floor and knickknack-lined shelves, was at the rear of the inn. It had a fantastic view of the ocean through large adjacent bay windows. Though the meals here were excellent, they were considered secondary to the scenery.

Kristina had made note of the view as she took her quick tour of the inn. Now, as a brooding storm hung over the distant sky, it struck her as magnificent.

Max saw the look on her face and interpreted it as a point in his favor.

"Like the view? Or would you like to improve on that, as well?" he couldn't help adding.

Her jaw tightened. She had developed her present sharp-tongued way of dealing with people because she'd discovered that no one bothered to listen to her opinions or follow her suggestions if she voiced them politely. They thought of her as "Kate's granddaughter," or "Nathaniel's little girl." She was that, but she was so much more. She was her own person, and if it took a heavy hand to make her point, then a heavy hand was what she had to use.

"Only by making sure the windows were cleaner. They could stand a washing," she attested casually.

Max wondered if killing her now would make the other guests lose their appetite, or if they would wind up applauding him.

Sydney approached their table. Sydney, like Antonio, doubled as a waiter during meals. Max nodded toward her. "Tell Sam we want two filets mignons. Rare."

"Anything to drink?" Sydney asked, placing an order of bread in the middle of the table.

He could do with a Scotch, a double, right about now. But he knew he was going to need a clear head to take on this woman fate had seen fit to saddle him with. "Just water. Two."

Kristina bristled at his presumption. "I can order for myself, Cooper."

He raised his hands, as if pulling them away from a sacred artifact he shouldn't have touched. "Sorry. Didn't mean to tread on your territory. Go ahead."

"Iced coffee, please," Kristina told Sydney as she took her seat.

"How appropriate," Max muttered under his breath. Their eyes met and held. He saw a flash within hers, and felt a measure of satisfaction. "Given the warmer turn of the weather," he added.

For the moment, Kristina said nothing. Sydney turned toward Max. "Will there be anything else?"

"No, just see if Sam can hurry it up." The chef had a tendency to let guests linger over their drinks. Now that he was sitting opposite Kristina, he wanted this over with as soon as possible.

Sydney gave Max a wide smile. "Sure thing, Max." The smile turned frosty as she nodded politely at Kristina. "Ms. Fortune."

Kristina spread her napkin across her lap. Not waiting for Max, she cut a slice from the loaf. The bread should have been warm, she noted. She glanced up at Max, then thought better of bringing the fact to his attention. Minor details like that would be lost on him.

Others, however, had to be made known. "You know, you really shouldn't let her call you Max."

He tore off an end of the loaf, a little abruptly, though his tone remained mild. "Funny, I was just thinking that you shouldn't insist on being called Ms. Fortune."

Kristina's eyes narrowed. She didn't take criticism well, especially if, in her opinion, it was unwarranted.

"Why?"

He would have thought that it was self-evident. But maybe not to someone like the ice princess. "Puts distance between you."

She still didn't see what he was driving at. Delicately she pushed aside the bread. Never a big eater, she wanted to leave room for the main course. "That's exactly my point."

Max took a deep breath. He was stuck with her. That meant he was going to have to try his best to educate her. She obviously had no experience in dealing with people who didn't have silver spoons in their mouths.

"You want them doing their best for you, not just thinking that it's a job."

His reasoning was so flawed, it took her breath away. "But it *is* a job. And their incentive is their paycheck— and bonuses if they perform well." After all, she wasn't heartless—she knew it was difficult to make it in this world.

He dropped the bread, and with it, the last of his appetite. "That makes them sound like trained seals." Leaning forward so that his face was inches from hers, he observed, "You have a very strange way of putting people off, Kristina. Is it a gift, like everything else you own?"

No, she wasn't going to enjoy working with this idiot. Kristina squared her shoulders. "You don't like me very much, Cooper. Fortunately for me, no pun intended, that doesn't matter. We can work together without liking each other."

He didn't have to read between the lines to know what she was saying to him. "As long as I do things your way."

"If my way makes sense..." Kristina let her voice trail off, leaving him to reach the conclusion that her way *did* make sense on his own. *If* the man had any brains at all.

His mouth quirked in a humorless smile. "As in 'Dollars and—' Correct?"

She didn't care for the way he was talking down to her. If he didn't like the idea of turning a profit, why was he hanging on to the inn? "Most people go into business to make money. This is a business."

Sydney returned with their meals before he could respond. He waited until Sydney receded again. He didn't miss the sympathetic look in her eyes as she left.

He nodded toward the plate in front of Kristina, taking advantage of the small diversion. "Eat your steak, Kris."

She hated nicknames. "The name," she told him, enunciating every syllable, "is Kristina."

The name is Pain, he thought, resigning himself to a very arduous evening. "Eat your steak, 'Kristina,'" he said deliberately.

Looking as if she had won a small victory, Kristina cut a piece of the thick steak on her plate. She had to admit that it did look appetizing. But the serving itself could be improved upon. Smaller portions, more artistically arranged. Honeymooners weren't all that interested in food, anyway.

She looked up and saw that Max was watching her. "Just look around you. The inn has sixteen bedrooms. Only five of them are filled." All five couples were in the dining room now. The room fairly echoed with her voice, reinforcing her point about the poor attendance.

The steak was done to perfection, but his appetite had completely waned. "And what you propose would fill them."

"Yes." Her eyes fairly glowed as she leaned forward, energy vibrating through her affirmation. "We'll have bookings two months in advance."

She knew nothing about the business. How could she be so certain of her ideas? "Sure of yourself, aren't you?"

There was no hesitation in her voice. "Yes."

He pinned her with a look. "Why?"

Hadn't he been listening? "Because I've got a good sense of business."

She was unbelievable. Had anyone bothered checking her for a pulse? "Is that all it is to you, just business?"

"Of course it is." She looked at him incredulously. "What else could it be?"

Patiently, like a teacher talking to a backward child, Max began again. "I mentioned earlier that it was a home—"

Did he really think she was being taken in by his smoke screen? "Spare me the sentiment, Cooper. It's just another excuse you're using not to do anything. I'm sure you're very comfortable this way. Well, you don't have to worry. I will handle everything. I'm accustomed to that. You can go on just napping." Disgust filled her eyes. "We'll try not to make too much noise for you, especially not when I slip you your share of the profits."

He'd tried it June's way. He'd tried being polite. This woman wouldn't understand anything but a show of force. "Tell me, because I'm new at this—does walking around with a wallet where your heart is supposed to be require any extra care on your part?"

Her head jerked up. How dare he! "I can't talk to you if you're going to be abusive."

That was a laugh. "Talk to me? Lady, all you do is talk *at* me, not to me." He raised his voice, for once unmindful of the people in the dining room. "I don't think you know *how* to talk to a person so that he'd listen of his own free will."

Kristina rose, throwing down her napkin. She didn't have to listen to this, and she certainly wasn't going to sit here trading insults with him while others listened.

"Tell the chef that the steak was delicious. The company, however, was not. It left a great deal to be desired."

With that, she walked out of the dining room.

Like the others in the room, Sydney had been looking on. She came forward now to clear away Kristina's plate. "Don't let it get to you, Max. If I'd been in your place, I would have decked her."

Max sighed. Sydney meant well, but that didn't alter the

fact that he was going to have to find some way to work with this infuriating woman.

"Thanks, but you're not in my place, and decking her wouldn't have helped, anyway."

Max looked down at his plate. It was a damn good steak. He wanted to finish his meal, but he knew there was damage control to attend to. With a sigh, he rose, leaving his napkin on the chair.

"Tell Sam this is nothing personal. The steak is great."

He went after Kristina, aware that the other guests were all looking at him. God, but he wished he was back at the construction site. Steel and concrete were things he knew how to handle. Stuck-up, gold-for-blood rich witches were in a league all their own.

A league Alexis had been quick to join, he recalled, jilting him and running off to marry that fancy executive of hers. When he thought of it, the man Alexis had described to him was a male counterpart to Kristina. No wonder he didn't like her, he thought.

Max passed June at the front desk. Instead of saying anything, the older woman just pointed toward the door. He sighed and hurried out.

He was in time to see Kristina heading toward the beach. Good. With any luck, she'd drown herself.

Not that he could let her.

Cursing roundly under his breath, he rushed after her.

Four

Damn stupid woman. With his luck, she'd probably walk straight into the water and get pulled under by a strong riptide. Then he'd be stuck explaining the situation to the local police.

"Hey!" Max called after Kristina as he hurried to catch up.

She made no effort to stop, and didn't give any indication that she'd even heard him. If anything, she seemed to quicken her pace.

Max swore as he broke into a run. The wind stole his words away, scattering them over the water. As if he didn't have enough trouble on his hands already with construction deadlines, now he had to deal with a rich, spoiled brat set on doing everything her way.

"Hey!"

Catching up to her, he grabbed Kristina by the arm and swung her around to face him. Even in the limited moonlight, he could see the storm clouds passing over not just the face of the moon, but her face, as well. It was a sensual face, a face he might have been attracted to. If it didn't belong to Kristina.

But it did, and he had less than no use for someone like her.

"Don't you know that it's dangerous to run off in the dark when you're not familiar with the area? The surf's heavy this time of year. Some of those waves could wash you out to sea before you had sense enough to scream for help."

As if that actually concerned him, she thought, annoyed at being manhandled.

"I can take care of myself," she retorted. "And for your information, I'm not about to wander into the water like some dazed Ophelia. I always know exactly where I am."

And so do I. In hell.

"What is it with you?" Max could only see one reason for her acting so unreasonably—that something had hurt her to the nth degree. He remembered the way he'd felt after Alexis. But that still didn't give her an excuse for wielding her bad temper like a sword, slicing away at everyone within range. "Did somebody dump you or something?"

The assumption made her jerk her head up and glare at him. That hadn't been the case, of course. It was she who had left David. But it was David who had never really wanted her in the first place, only her money. Only her position.

Kristina's eyes narrowed to tiny slits that glinted with anger. "Why? Don't you think a woman can be angry unless there's a man involved?"

"Well…" He pretended to seriously consider her question. He saw that the thought annoyed her. Maybe someone had walked out on her. Not that he could blame him. A guy would have to be crazy to be involved with the likes of her. "No."

She blew out a breath, dragging her hand through her hair. The pins that had held it so securely in place were scattered now, victims of her quick pace and the wind. The latter plucked away the last of them.

He was watching her, waiting. Looking at her as if he could see something beneath the lines of her face.

Making her uncomfortable again.

"In this case," she conceded, "you're right, but no one's 'dumped' me, as you so eloquently put it. But there is a man involved. You." She saw a hint of surprise enter his eyes. The egoist probably misunderstood. Well, she'd just squelch that misunderstanding. "I just wanted to get away from you." She frowned at him, the same way she might have at a stain that refused to respond to treatment and remained embedded in the weave of a favorite dress. "I didn't seem to succeed very well."

He wasn't going to let her draw him into another argument. He refused to allow that to happen—but it damn well wasn't easy, not when he wanted to wring her neck.

Putting out his hand to her, he made the ultimate sacrifice. "How about a truce?"

She looked at his hand. It was a strong hand with calluses on it. A hand that belonged to a man who wasn't afraid of working and getting dirty. So maybe he wasn't all that lazy, she conceded. Just pigheaded.

Still, she ignored the offer, looking directly up into his eyes.

"How about talking reason for a change?" she countered. Kristina raised her voice to be heard above the sound of the pounding surf. She held up her index finger. "Fact— the inn isn't making money." Another finger joined the first. "Fact—you have a very valuable piece of property." A third bounced up. He had the uncontrollable urge to shove her hand down to her side. Another urge, far less sensible than that, was beginning to surface, as well. He ascribed it to the fact that she had churned up his emotions. "Fact—I have the money that's necessary to make this into something unique. And fact—"

She stopped abruptly as Max closed his hand tightly over hers and pushed it to her side. Undaunted, she said through gritted teeth, "I am half owner."

"And fact—you are one hell of a pain in the neck." Max let go of her hand, curtailing the desire to give it one extra, hard squeeze.

Very gingerly, she flexed her fingers. She wasn't going to give him the satisfaction of wincing. He wasn't just pigheaded, he was a Neanderthal.

"With the money this place will make once I'm through

with it, you can afford to buy yourself an electric massager—or a masseuse, if that's too complicated for you to operate.''

He was standing toe-to-toe with her on one of the most beautiful spots in the state. It wasn't a place meant for shouting, or for escalating tempers. Why couldn't she just shut up and let the place work its magic on her? It already was on him, and he didn't even want any part of it.

Or her.

He tried again. ''Why don't you try to enjoy this place for a little while before deciding to make any changes?''

He didn't get it, did he? *Progress* was obviously a dirty word to him. Lucky for him she'd come along when she did.

''I don't have to enjoy it,'' she insisted, ''to know that this place has potential that is not being utilized.'' Frustrated, she gestured around at the beach, as if he'd never seen it before.

Max shoved his hands deep into his back pockets and began walking along the shoreline. She fell into step beside him. He felt a little like Lee on the eve of Appomattox, facing the inevitable and trying to come to grips with it. If nothing else, he wanted to make certain that his soldiers retained their swords.

''If there are changes, there's one thing I want to make perfectly clear at the outset,'' Max warned her. ''I don't want any of the staff 'outplaced,' or whatever the popular term for being fired is these days.''

His concern did soften the edges of the image he projected, but cold facts were cold facts. ''If they're not doing a good job—''

Max stopped walking, his eyes riveted to hers. ''They're doing a good job.''

The rugged face looked almost malevolent, she thought, startled by the intensity of the feeling she saw there. But not startled enough to back down. She intended to do everything she had planned to do on the plane. She couldn't allow sentiment, or a stubborn, sentimental half owner, to get in the way.

"But if—"

"This isn't negotiable, Kristina," he informed her harshly. "I gave my word to my foster parents when I took over the inn that no one who worked for them would be released. They would all have a job for life, if they wanted it."

This man did not belong in business. She was surprised that he hadn't been eaten by the sharks yet. While the attitude he espoused sounded noble, in reality it was just another excuse for not taking control.

"Yes," she allowed patiently, "but surely your foster parents wouldn't want you to—"

He didn't want to hear any more of her work philosophy. It wouldn't make any difference.

"My word, Kristina," he said, cutting in. "My word. Do you know what that means?" His eyes pinned her. "That means I made them a promise, and I always keep my promises."

Max felt the last of his temper fraying as he looked down into her stubborn, unrelenting face. How could anyone so beautiful be so damn heartless?

And then he remembered Alexis and had his answer.

"Not ever," he emphasized. "And certainly not for spoiled brats who come riding in on their brooms, ready to sweep everything and everyone out of their way." He drew himself up, and he was a good foot taller than she was. "That might be the way you do it in Minneapolis, but that isn't the way it's done out here."

Oh, puh-leeze. She rolled her eyes. "Oh, right—Californians are the last word in truth and fair play."

He had sounded pretty high-and-mighty, Max thought, annoyed with himself for giving her something else to ridicule. He raised his voice, shouting above the growing howl of the wind.

"Maybe not, but I am." He lowered his mouth to her

ear, so that his words wouldn't be swept away before she heard them. "Now, if you have any sense in your head, which I doubt, you'll go back to the inn." He clamped a hand on her shoulder and turned her roughly around to face the darkening sky. "There's a storm coming. We wouldn't want to take a chance on having lightning strike you, now, would we?"

His tone told her exactly how he would feel about it.

With that, Max turned and walked away with long, hurried strides, as if he couldn't wait to get away from her.

Frustrated, angry, Kristina looked around for something, anything, to throw. There was a piece of driftwood sticking up a few feet away from her. Yanking it out of the sand, she hurled it at Max before she could stop to think what she was doing.

The small piece struck him squarely in the back. Surprised, Max swung around just as the driftwood landed beside his foot. He spared it one look, then strode back to where Kristina was standing.

The look in his eyes was dark and forbidding.

Surprised at the level of her outburst, uncertain of what to expect from him, Kristina still refused to back down. Instead, she lifted her chin, daring him to retaliate.

Max grabbed her by the shoulders and gave her one strong shake that very nearly rattled her teeth. "What the hell's wrong with you?"

"You," she shot back. She blew out a shaky breath, refusing to tell him to release her, even though he was hurting her. "You make me lose my temper faster than anyone I've ever met."

He realized that he was holding her too hard. Letting her go, he saw the dark prints of his fingers on her upper arms. Damn it, he wasn't a savage, even if she was a shrew.

Annoyed with himself, with her, he scowled. "Well, we've got that in common, too. Steak and tempers. A hell of a combination." He shook his head. "This isn't going to work out."

Her bravado escalated to a fever pitch. "It's not a marriage, it's a business arrangement."

"It's more than that," he replied. "It's hell, right here on earth." And he was smack-dab in the middle of it, thanks to her.

A string of curses ran through his mind as he looked down into her face. Without fully realizing he was doing it, he pulled her back into his arms.

Emotions churned within him like the sea caught in the grip of a typhoon. Max felt himself on the verge of giving in to the almost overwhelming magnetic pull he felt when he looked into her eyes. It didn't make any sense to him, but then, pure sexual attraction probably never did. And that was what this was. Pure, raw sex.

In the moonlight, with the wind whipping her hair to and fro, making her look like some kind of siren, wrapping her scent around him, he felt a gut-level reaction that he hadn't experienced in a very long time.

He wanted her.

Whether to make love with or to strangle was a toss-up. But he did want her.

Kristina's breath caught in her throat. She wasn't nearly as sure of herself now as she had been a moment ago. With Max's steely fingers holding her in place and his brooding eyes on hers, she could feel her very insides quaking.

She had no idea what he was capable of. And no idea why the danger in his eyes fascinated her so. But she knew she didn't like the power it had over her.

His head inclined, and now his mouth was only a breath away from hers. Kristina could feel her heart pounding against her rib cage, bruising it as surely as his fingers had bruised her arms.

Like a cornered animal, she dug deep for courage and attacked. "You kiss me," she swore, "and I'll make you pay for it."

She would, too, he thought. And he didn't know if the price would be worth it. Maybe it would.

He laughed at her threat, and made the situation all the more worse.

"I bet you would, Kristina. Well, don't worry, I won't risk it. I haven't had my shots yet." With that, he let go of her, releasing her a bit more roughly than he had intended. He felt shaken, as well, and had no way of hiding it from himself. "Now walk ahead of me."

She didn't trust him. "Why?"

He gave her a little push to get her on her way, and she stumbled backward. Swearing, he grabbed her arm. The woman was wearing heels—a damn stupid thing to do, since she was on sand.

Max was quick to release her this time. He suddenly wanted very little physical contact with her. Because he wanted it too much.

"Because I don't have eyes in the back of my head, Kristina, and I don't want to get walloped with another piece of driftwood, that's why."

Uttering a few ripe curses of her own, Kristina strode in front of him. Her gait was long and measured as she hurried back to the inn. Because of the sand, she wobbled with each step she took. It didn't cut into the speed she maintained.

She didn't stop until she was back in her room, with the door locked.

Only when she'd finally stopped trembling did she place a call to her family lawyer. Since it was after hours, she called him at his home.

Her frustration mounted when the man's answering machine picked up in his place. He was obviously out. Though he was as independent as anyone in the Fortune family, Sterling Foster still knew better than not to pick up if he was within earshot.

Angry, she slammed the receiver down on its cradle. It

bounced off, and she replaced it, this time making an effort to calm down.

She was going to have to wait until morning to find out what it would take to buy Cooper out. But, one way or another, she intended to. There was no way she was going to be able to work with that man, not after tonight.

Without thinking, she ran the tip of her tongue along her lips. Just where his breath had touched them.

Kristina stared out into the inky blackness outside her window. Clouds had blotted out the moon completely now, and she saw nothing but her own reflection staring back at her.

Her own reflection, and a shadow of his. It was mocking her.

With an annoyed cry, she yanked the curtain into place.

Max opened his eyes slowly. Each lid felt as if it weighed a ton. The buzzing in his head registered a moment later, protesting his early rising, reminding him of what he'd imbibed last night.

Focusing, he saw the uncorked bottle of Scotch he'd left standing on the desk in his room. The early-morning sun caught the amber liquid in its palm, making it gleam like newly scattered semiprecious stones.

Making him remember.

He groaned, then sat up and scrubbed his hands over his face as the events of last night returned to him in reverse order. He'd felt compelled to have a couple of shots to wash the bad taste of desire from his mouth and blot the entire experience from his mind.

He'd succeeded in doing neither.

It wasn't a nightmare. It had happened.

Kristina Fortune had descended, in all her malevolent glory, upon the inn, and his life. And he was going to have to find a way to deal with her that met with the approval of the La Jolla Police Department.

Sighing, Max reached for his jeans at the foot of the bed.

Pulling them on, he rose to his feet. As an afterthought, he tugged on a shirt, but for the time being, he left it unbuttoned. As a concession to where he was, he put on his boots, instead of remaining barefoot.

If he was lucky, Kristina liked to sleep in and he could at least get some breakfast before having to face her again. He figured the odds were pretty good in his favor. After all, vampires and their kindred spirits liked to avoid the daylight.

He'd remained at the inn last night, instead of going home to his apartment in Newport Beach. At the time, he'd thought to try to work things out with Kristina in the morning. Maybe he'd have better luck in the daylight.

It had seemed like a reasonable idea then. Now, he wasn't so sure. It would mean having to deal with her again, a prospect he didn't relish in the slightest, no matter how physically attractive the woman was.

Max walked out into the hall, closing his door behind him. Maybe, having slept on it, she'd be more approachable.

Yeah, and the tooth fairy lives down the lane.

He'd spent the night in the room he occupied while growing up at the inn. It was located on the first floor, just behind the office. In order to get to the dining room, he had to pass the front desk and the main sitting room. Which he did.

And then stopped dead.

Kristina, perched on the next-to-the-top step of a ladder she must have commandeered from Antonio, was leaning over as far as she could. She was attempting to take down the tapestry from over the fireplace.

The tapestry he'd specifically told her he didn't want removed.

Damn her, the little witch was blatantly disregarding everything he'd said to her.

Incensed, he yelled at her. "Hey, what the hell do you think you're doing?"

Furious with herself for letting emotions get in her way last night, Kristina had made up her mind to get down to work this morning. The first thing that had come to mind was the portrait of Kate she wanted to have put up. It had occurred to her that the brickwork behind the tapestry might need work. It would have been just like Cooper to put the tapestry in place to hide a defect, rather than fix it.

His angry demand startled her. With a yelp, Kristina lost her balance.

Max saw the ladder wobble. In another second, it would be on its side, taking her down with it.

He rushed over in time to catch Kristina. His hands tightened around her waist, breaking her fall. But she hit her forehead against the corner of the fireplace.

She screamed in surprise, and in anticipation of the pain, a second before it claimed her.

Horror wafted through him. Kristina was slumped in his arms, unconscious. Turning her so that he could examine her forehead, he found no blood. Just a rapidly darkening bruise.

"Kristina?"

She made no reply. He knew she wasn't playing this out for effect. Her pride would have dictated that she jump up and dust herself off with a smirk on her lips.

Concern seized him as he checked her pulse. It was fluttering, but her breathing was regular. "Damn it, woman, you've been nothing but trouble to me since the minute you walked in."

June hurried over to them. The rest of the guests, mercifully, weren't within earshot.

"I heard the scream." June saw the overturned ladder and peered at the unconscious woman in Max's arms, gnawing her lower lip. "Did you kill her?"

He shook his head. This wasn't anything to joke about.

"No, she fell off the ladder and hit her head on the fireplace." With Kristina in his arms, Max walked toward the stairs. "Get Daniel Valente on the phone, June. If you hurry, you'll catch him before he leaves to make his rounds at the hospital." One foot on the stairs, he turned to look at the older woman, who was already at the desk, looking for the telephone book. "Tell him it's an emergency and that I need him." Daniel would know he wouldn't ask him to come if it wasn't serious.

"Leave it to me." June's calm voice helped soothe the jagged edges off his nerves.

Max carried Kristina to her room. Once inside, he gently placed her on her bed. She looked so small and helpless lying there. Max shook his head, refusing to let panic seize him. Just deceptive packaging. Beneath the smooth, pale skin and long blond hair was an anaconda.

Because there was nothing else to do but wait for Daniel, Max dragged a chair over to the bed. Before sitting down, he examined the bump that was rapidly swelling on her head, adding height to the bruise. He didn't like the looks of it, but Daniel would tell him if it was anything to be concerned about.

"Nothing but trouble," he repeated under his breath. Straddling the chair, he settled in to wait for Daniel to arrive or Kristina to wake up, whichever happened first.

If neither happened soon, he thought, he was going to take her to the hospital.

Max and Daniel Valente had played on the grounds of the inn during their childhood. Except, as young boys of thirteen, they'd referred to it as "hanging out." No matter what the term was, they had spent a great deal of time in each other's company and had grown up as friends.

The friendship had remained intact even when Daniel went away to medical school on the East Coast, while Max remained here, to put himself through a local college. Daniel had earned his degree and fulfilled his family's ambitions for him. Along the way, he'd discovered that he had a natural aptitude for being a doctor. He enjoyed it.

Max and he got together once every few months or so. Sometimes less. But no matter how much time had passed, their friendship was the kind that always seemed as if the threads had only been dropped just yesterday. They were always at ease in each other's company.

Daniel arrived ten minutes after June called him, just when Max had made up his mind to take Kristina to the hospital.

Max waited in silence as Daniel examined Kristina. When his friend said nothing, Max felt as if he couldn't take it any longer. "So?"

Daniel paused to push his large rimless glasses back up his short, angular nose. "So, she has one hell of a bump on her head."

Max snorted. "I didn't need someone with a medical degree to tell me that."

"No, but you need someone with a degree to tell you that there doesn't seem to be a concussion. Her pupils are both normal and the same size." Daniel replaced his stethoscope in his case and rose. "My advice to you is to watch her." He smiled at his friend. "Given what she looks like, I don't expect that will be much of a hardship for you."

This was where the adage that appearances were deceiving came into play, Max thought.

"Believe me, Daniel, you'd change your mind if you could see her in action once her eyes are opened."

Daniel laughed. "I'd like to take that chance." He closed his case and rose. "She might seem a little disoriented when she wakes up. If there are any problems—any at all," he said emphatically, growing serious, "call me. And if she's not conscious in, say, another hour, bring her over to the hospital. Give my office a call and I'll meet you there. But that's a big if," he added. "I don't expect anything serious." He gave her one final look. "Still, you never know."

"No," Max agreed softly, taking his seat again after Daniel left the room. "You never do."

Well, another day shot to hell, he thought. He couldn't just leave her when she was like this. With a sigh, Max pulled the telephone from the nightstand and onto his lap. Tapping out a series of numbers, he called Paul at the construction site.

He listened to the telephone on the other end ring, silently counting the number of times. Max knew that he could very easily just leave June to watch over this nuisance for him, but he felt responsible. If he hadn't yelled at Kristina when he did, she wouldn't have fallen off the ladder.

"Of course—" he was addressing the unconscious woman "—now if you had listened to me to begin with, you wouldn't have been on that damn ladder in the first place."

Moot point.

"Hello?" The question in Paul's voice told Max he had picked up on the tail end of his one-sided conversation with Kristina.

Quickly Max explained the situation to him. Paul listened, then told Max not to worry. For once, things at the site were going smoothly. Supplies were actually showing up on time.

Nice to know, Max thought as he hung up. He only wished he could say the same about things on the home front. He made himself as comfortable as he could, anticipating Kristina's first words to him when she woke up. She would obviously be ticked off, and twice as difficult to deal with.

He couldn't wait.

The unexpected low moan had him jumping to his feet. God, but she looked pale, he thought. Max was directly over her when she finally opened her eyes.

He smiled. "Hi. Welcome back."

"Hi," she murmured. Kristina pressed her hand to her head, then sucked in her breath as the tenderness registered. She bit back a groan. The pain continued, but in slower beats. She tried to sit up, but couldn't. "Where have I been?"

"Out." Daniel had said she'd be a little disoriented. She certainly looked it. "You hit your head."

"I did?" She turned her wide blue eyes in his direction. "When?"

That must have been some blow she'd gotten, Max mused. Even her voice was softer. Almost sensual. "When you fell off the ladder."

She paused, thinking. The staccato beating in her head became stronger, and she winced. "What was I doing on the ladder?"

Max narrowed his eyes, studying her expression. "Don't you remember?"

"No."

She *was* different. There was something in her manner that hadn't been evident before. Genuine concern nudged its way forward. "Just what do you remember?"

She paused a moment, trying to frame an answer. Her eyes were huge as she looked up at him. Where there should have been thoughts, ideas, impressions, there was nothing. Only a huge void.

"Nothing," she whispered hoarsely. "I remember nothing."

Five

Max stared at Kristina as he sank into the chair beside her bed. She couldn't mean what he thought she meant. "When you say you remember nothing, you mean nothing about the accident, right?"

Very slowly, Kristina moved her head from side to side. But even the smallest movement had instant repercussions. Pain immediately shot along the perimeter of her skull, threatening to shatter it.

Try as she might, she couldn't penetrate the wall of pain.

But she had this awful feeling that even if she could, there would be nothing waiting there for her. No memories, no anecdotes, no experiences to look back on, either with sentiment or with embarrassment. Nothing.

The stark realization drove fear deep into her heart.

She felt alone, isolated, and so terribly cold. She huddled, drawing into herself.

"No, I mean nothing. Nothing at all. I don't know your name, or where I am. Or—'' She stopped abruptly, because the admission she was about to utter was so overwhelmingly bleak, it threatened to undo her. Gathering her courage to her, she forced herself to continue. "Or even who I am."

It took Max a moment to absorb what she was telling him. This had to be some kind of a hoax. He studied her face closely to see if, for some reason, she was toying with him. Max wouldn't have put it past Kristina to play on his sympathies, so that when she "recovered," his relief would be so tremendous he'd be willing to let her do anything she wanted with the inn.

That wasn't about to happen anytime soon, he thought firmly.

But the look in her eyes was not that of a crafty woman scheming to get her way. Instead, it was the look of a woman who was uncertain and afraid, and struggling very hard not to show it.

Max tried to put himself in her place, and couldn't conceive of how it would feel to be a stranger to himself. Moved by compassion, he took Kristina's hand in his and closed his fingers over it. Her hand felt very small. "Think, Kris," he urged. "Think."

"I *am* thinking," she insisted. A small trace of fear broke through in her voice. She looked at him, startled, mining the nugget of information that suddenly jumped out at her. "Is that my name? Chris? You called me Chris."

Why didn't that sound familiar? Why did nothing feel familiar, look familiar? She was afraid that if she saw her own reflection, the face looking back at her would be unfamiliar, as well.

Max started to tell her that she had haughtily informed him that she wanted to be called Kristina, not Kris. But then he thought better of it. A kernel of an idea was beginning to form.

"Yes," he said slowly. "Short for Kristina. With a *K*." Max watched her face, to see if hearing her name jogged her memory at all. Her expression remained unchanged. "You really don't remember, do you?"

"No," she whispered softly. "I really don't."

Max saw the shimmer of tears gathering in her deep blue eyes. A well of sympathy opened within him. Feeling awkward, he slipped his arm around her shoulder. "Hey, it's going to be all right." He hoped she wouldn't start crying. Nothing undid him more than a woman's tears. "You just got a little shook up, that's all. Everything will be back to normal before you know it."

She sniffed, forcing back her tears. Crying wouldn't help anything. "That's just it. I don't know what normal is."

"I'll show you," he promised, his arm tightening around her. "Leave it to me."

Kristina rested her cheek against his chest. And she believed him.

She might not know him, but there was safety in his arms. Safety and comfort that she clung to. All sorts of questions battered their fists against the blackened barrier that held them back.

She took a deep breath, trying to steady herself. The scent of his cologne came to her. It smelled familiar, whispering through her mind, a shadow of something that had been. Or might have been.

Familiar. She didn't know how, or why, but it *was* familiar. She found herself rallying around that tiny bit.

Kristina raised her head and looked at him. Who was this man? What were they to each other? She hadn't the vaguest idea. "What's your name?"

Her eyes reminded him of the ocean, blue and fathomless. It occurred to him that a man could lose his soul looking into eyes like that.

"Max," he told her cautiously. "Max Cooper."

Nothing. His name meant nothing to her. He was ruggedly good-looking and he was being kind to her. If his cologne was familiar to her, shouldn't he be familiar, as well? Shouldn't that trigger something for her? Why couldn't she remember him—or herself?

"And mine?" Kristina asked. Maybe if she just heard her whole name, it would mean something to her. "What's my last name?"

Truth warred with expediency. Expediency won. If nothing else, her memory loss had bought them a little time. Max cast about for a name to give her. He noticed the heart-shaped charm she wore on a chain around her neck.

"Valentine. Your name is Kris Valentine."

Kris Valentine. She turned it around in her head, ignoring the jarring pain. The name meant nothing to her. It might as well have belonged to a stranger. It certainly didn't feel as if it belonged to her.

She felt as if she were desperately trying to climb out of a deep, dark well. All the while, her fingers were slipping along the dank, narrow walls, sending her deeper into the abyss, away from the sunshine.

Kristina looked into Max's eyes, and the desperation within her abated a little. There was something about him that made her feel protected. That had to mean something, didn't it?

"Are we anything? I mean—" she licked her lower lip, searching for the right words, feeling incredibly awkward, incredibly inadequate to tackle this situation she discovered herself in "—what are we to each other?" She tried to relate the feeling he created within her to something tangible. "Are we married?"

The question caught him completely off guard. He stumbled through his answer. "No, we're not married. We're—"

The term *business partners* froze on his lips. Max thought of the changes Kristina was bent on implementing, of the way she had forged ahead, taking down the tapestry when he had told her he didn't want it removed. She'd be like that with everything, the staff included. She wasn't the type to let anything or anyone get in the way of her plan to "transform" the inn into a money-making business.

Whatever pity he had felt for her died.

Max watched her face as he replied, "We're employer and employee. I'm the employer," he added after a beat.

She nodded her head slowly, not agreeing or disagreeing, merely absorbing the information and trying vainly to process it. Frustration filled her when no images appeared.

She worked for him. Doing what?

Kristina looked to him for all her answers. This Max Cooper, with his kind eyes and his disturbing cologne, obviously knew her better than she knew herself. "And I am—?"

He thought of the demeaning way Kristina had treated Sydney. It would be poetic justice to have her walk a mile in the other woman's shoes. He was probably going to pay dearly for this when her memory returned, but Max couldn't resist the temptation.

"A maid."

"A maid?" It didn't sound right, but then, her name hadn't rung any bells for her, either. Only the scent of his cologne, of his nearness, nudged at something within her. Stirring a memory she couldn't grasp, hinting of a page she wasn't able to turn over to read.

"That's right. You work here. This is a bed-and-breakfast inn." As Max uttered each word, he studied Kristina's face for any signs that the haughty firebrand had returned. He saw only a confused young woman who was trying desperately to cope with the situation and not break down.

A sliver of guilt stabbed him, piercing him like a splinter beneath his fingernail. He managed to ignore it. "We've got sixteen rooms altogether."

"And I clean them?" She looked around. What he was telling her meant she must have cleaned this room, dusted that bureau, washed that window. Why couldn't she remember doing any of that?

"Yes. And you wait on tables at meals." He was getting into the scenario he was creating. "You do both along with Sydney."

Another name she didn't know. "Sydney?"

He nodded. "The other maid."

So Sydney was a woman. A woman she wouldn't recognize if she walked into her. Exasperated, Kristina attempted to rise to her feet. But as soon as they touched the floor, the room began to spin.

She was growing pale again. As she swayed, Max caught her arms and gently urged her down on the bed again. He sat down beside her, trying not to think about how helpless she must feel.

With a little whimper, Kristina sagged against him. A strand of her hair brushed against his cheek, stirring something within him and making him feel ashamed. But he was doing this for the good of the inn, for the good of the others. Buying some desperately needed time. It wouldn't hurt anything in the long run.

Kristina looked up at him, her face inches from his. Had they been like this once before? It felt as if they had, even though she couldn't remember.

"And we're not...involved in any other way?"

The question was softly whispered, as if she believed that, somehow, they were. Something distant, tender and protective rose to the fore. It wasn't easy for him to ignore, even though it felt completely out of place in reference to her.

"No, we're not."

She'd been mistaken. "Sorry." Kristina flushed. The pink hue on her cheeks made her looked exceptionally lost and vulnerable. "I thought that we were. I guess it's the way you're holding me."

Wanting to put a little distance between them, Kristina struggled to her feet. This time, she managed to make it all the way up. Letting out a slow, shaky breath, she crossed to the window seat.

The storm that had threatened all day yesterday had arrived during the night. It had passed through quickly, like a barreling freight train, leaving a trail in its wake. The trees and grass were a lush, vibrant green from their fresh washing. The sea beyond was calm now, gently playing with the shore.

She'd seen this before, she thought suddenly. She had no recollection of when or how, only that she'd sat here before, looking out this window, seeing just this view.

It gave her something to hang on to. That, and the scent of his cologne. It fastened her to a place, if not a time.

The rest, she supposed, she prayed, would come.

Until that time, she had to place herself entirely in his hands.

The idea scared her a little, and yet she felt that this was the thing to do. That she could trust him.

"It's beautiful," she murmured. She could feel the beauty, feel the tranquillity begin to slowly soothe her. "How long have I worked here?"

Max came up behind her. She even sat differently, he thought, not ramrod-straight, as if she were poised to enter into battle, but pensively, as if she were trying to work things out in her head.

She seemed softer, somehow.

Going with his instincts, he placed a hand on her shoulder. "Not too long. A couple of months. You're just learning the routine."

Disappointment washed over her. "So then, you don't know anything about me?" That meant that he wouldn't be able to help her fill in the blanks.

It would be best if he went along with that scenario, he decided. That way, it wouldn't seem odd if he couldn't answer her questions.

"Just what's on your résumé." He wasn't as hard as he'd thought he might be with her. The disappointed expression on her face had him adding, "And what you've told me, of course."

"Could I see it?" she asked suddenly.

Oh-oh, where had he slipped up? "See what?"

"My résumé." Maybe there was something there she could use, a number to call, an address to visit.

"Sure." His reassuring smile hid the discomfort he felt. He shouldn't have mentioned that. Now he was going to have to create a résumé for her to look at. "I'll see if I can find it. It might take a while. June leaves the front desk a bit of a mess."

Another name to add to the growing list of names that meant nothing to her. The ache in her head became more insistent. She passed her hand over her forehead and winced. There was a bump there, and it was very tender. "June?"

"The receptionist."

"Oh." Feeling a little wobbly, reluctant to leave her perch, Kristina leaned her shoulder against the windowsill. "Was I always a maid?"

It still didn't feel right. She looked down at her hands. She wore no jewelry, but there was a thin tan line on her left ring finger. Had there been a ring there until recently?

"Um, no."

Max sat down beside her, his mind racing as he searched for something plausible to tell her. By nature, he was an honest man, but fate and Kristina had handed him the perfect opportunity to buy some time for the inn. He'd wanted Kristina to take some time to get to know the inn and the people who worked there, hoping that when she did, she would feel the same way he did and come to the same conclusion. That she'd decide to leave well enough alone.

This seemed like a godsend to him. At the very least, it would keep her out of his hair for a while.

But what to tell her?

He took his cue from the fading tan line on her finger. "You arrived here right after your divorce became final."

"I'm divorced?" she asked in wonder.

There had been someone in her life who wasn't there anymore. The thought struck a vague chord, somewhere in the distance. She raised her eyes to his. Maybe she had confided in him. He looked like the type she would have trusted. Kind, understanding.

"What happened?"

"I don't know," he said, trying to sound sincere. "You didn't go into details, and I didn't prod." Kristina vainly attempted to mask her disappointment. "You just said that you wanted to get away. That you wanted to start a new life." He embellished where he thought it was safe. "You arrived here, looking very upset and unhappy. You told me that you saw our ad for a maid in the local newspaper while on vacation in La Jolla and decided that was the perfect opportunity."

The others were going to have to be told about this turn of events, he thought. And fast. Max rose. She looked at him, so many questions in her eyes. He nodded toward her bed.

"Why don't you lay down again for a few minutes and see if you can get some rest?"

She felt exhausted, as if she'd been running a long distance, with the road continuing to lengthen before her with each step. And her head was really beginning to throb again.

Still, she looked for some guidelines to her routine. "Don't I have any work to do today?"

She made him feel guilty. He felt as if he were taking advantage of her, rather than utilizing an opportunity. "We're very easygoing here." He forced a smile onto his lips. "We let you rest when you smack your head on the fireplace."

She tried to remember. It had to have been the last thing that happened to her. Why couldn't she remember? "Is that what I did? Smacked my head on the fireplace?"

At least here he could tell her the truth. "Yes."

Was she that clumsy? she wondered. "What was I doing?"

He thought fast. "Cleaning the tapestry. You're very thorough."

That sounded right. Not the cleaning part, but the part about being thorough. Somehow, she knew that about herself. Knew she liked to work, liked to accomplish things. But a maid? That part just didn't seem to feel right. It was like a sweater that was too small, the wrong cut.

But what reason would Max have to lie to her?

He didn't look like the kind of man who would lie. She had no way of knowing why she knew that about him. But she did.

Max didn't want to leave her just sitting here. What if she fell again? The same woman who had looked like a veritable, unshakable rock now looked terribly fragile to him.

"Why don't you lie down again for a while, and get a little rest?" he urged again. That way, at least she'd be out of the way and safe.

The first thing he had to do was alert the others. The next was to call Daniel and ask him about this unexpected turn of events. Maybe he should still take her to the hospital.

"All right," she conceded.

He took her hand as she rose. She didn't voice a protest. Instead, she wrapped her fingers around his and smiled, looking grateful for his help.

Now there was a change, he thought.

Leading her to the bed, Max held her elbow as she lowered herself onto the mattress. He felt like a heel, but he was helpless to do anything about it now.

"I'll look in on you later," he promised.

He was at the door when he heard her call him. "Max?"

He turned and looked at her over his shoulder. He couldn't have left the room if he tried. "Yes?"

"Would you stay with me?" She knew she was asking a lot. He was probably very busy. "Just for a little while? It would make me feel better."

She couldn't have explained why it would, not even to herself. But having someone here, someone who knew who she was, somehow helped negate the overwhelming helplessness she was feeling. It helped keep the dark at bay.

He knew he should be begging off. She'd undoubtedly accuse him of taking advantage of her once her memory returned.

"Sure."

How could he refuse her? She looked so lost, so completely different from the woman she'd been only a couple of hours ago. Though not a hair on her head had changed, there was something different in her expression, something different in her eyes. It had transformed her from the shrew she was into the lost, bewildered woman who was lying here before him.

The woman he felt compelled to remain with.

He sat down on the side of the bed. With a hint of shyness, she took his hand in hers as she curled up toward him.

He felt his mouth grow dry. She really was very beautiful. The fact struck him even more intently now that her haughty go-to-hell manner was gone. He reminded himself that all this was temporary, both her amnesia and his lie. He caught himself thinking that it was a pity.

"Want a bedtime story?" he asked wryly.

Her smile was sad as it curved her mouth. "Only if the princess regains her memory at the end of the story."

Max shook his head. "Sorry, my repertoire is limited. The only ones I know are about princesses kissing frogs or eating poisoned apples."

"Too bad," she said softly, as her eyes drifted shut again.

Yeah, too bad, he thought.

Too bad she wasn't like this normally. There was something very likable about Kristina Fortune, when she didn't look as if she were ready to go a full ten rounds with him.

He slowly extracted his hand from hers. Satisfied that she was asleep, he pulled the edge of the quilt over her, then stood for a moment, just watching her.

"What the hell am I going to do with you now?" he muttered to himself under his breath.

Kristina was three-quarters asleep, and far too tired to answer him. But she'd heard him. She thought he meant that she couldn't do any work in her present condition. She vowed to show him otherwise. Just as soon as her headache went away.

He waited until he was sure she was asleep before he rose to leave. Just as he opened the door, Max noticed

Kristina's small black leather purse lying on the bureau. His pulse quickened. Damn, that had been an oversight on his part.

Max could see Kristina's reflection in the small black-trimmed oval mirror hanging over the bureau. She was curled up on the bed, breathing evenly. His eyes on her, Max quickly snared the purse and went out into the hall.

The room next to Kristina's was empty. He entered, shutting the door behind him. With an economy of movement, he went through her purse.

There were no letters or bills inside addressed to her. But there was a personalized memo pad, which he removed, along with her wallet.

Flipping through the latter, Max took out Kristina's driver's license and her credit cards. For safekeeping, he slipped them into his own wallet. He didn't know how long this charade he'd fashioned would last, but he didn't want to take a chance on Kristina inadvertently stumbling across the truth before he was prepared for her to do so.

As if he ever would be, he thought cynically, slipping back into Kristina's room. Watching her for any sudden movements, Max replaced her purse and silently closed the door behind him. If she asked why she had no form of identification, he'd come up with something when the time came.

He hoped.

Max shoved his hands into his pockets as he made his way down the stairs. For better or for worse, the die was cast.

Max decided that an impromptu meeting with the staff could wait. He wanted to hear Daniel's reassurances first. Cutting through the protests of a receptionist/nurse who insisted, "Dr. Valente will call you after his office hours are over," Max finally managed to get Daniel on the telephone.

"This better be important, Max," Daniel warned.

"It is."

Quickly he related the conversation he'd had with Kristina.

Daniel listened quietly. When Max finished, there was a long, thoughtful moment of silence before he said, "Sounds like amnesia to me."

Max blew out an annoyed breath. "I know it sounds like amnesia. I figured that part out by myself. What am I supposed to do about it?"

"Nothing you *can* do about it. Just wait it out."

That wasn't the answer he wanted to hear. Though he had laid the groundwork for an elaborate charade, Max couldn't help feeling guilty about what he proposed doing, even if it was for everyone's good in the long run.

"How long?" he asked impatiently.

Daniel's voice, in contrast, was measured and steady. Max had never known him to get excited or upset about anything. That was what made them such good friends. There was a spectrum of feelings between them. "However long it takes. A day, a week—"

Max figured the situation would make for a good movie of the week, but he had assumed that in actuality, medicine had found a way to remedy this kind of thing.

That it hadn't left him with a very real dilemma. "Could she remain like this forever?"

Daniel sighed heavily. "She could. It's highly unlikely, of course," he hastened to add, "but there have been cases where the patient never recovered his memory. Try to surround her with familiar things. You never know what might trigger her memory. It could be something relatively insignificant. A mood, a scent, a certain look. A photograph, a song. In the meantime, I'll swing by tonight and look in on her, if you'd like."

Yes, he'd like. Though he could rationalize the charade, he wasn't about to take chances with her health. If Daniel assured him she was fine, then he would continue with what he had already set in motion.

"I'd appreciate it."

Max hung up the receiver and then looked thoughtfully at the telephone. Daniel's words played themselves over again in his mind.

Surround her with familiar things.

There were no familiar things around here to surround Kristina with. Everything was new to her.

Which, he thought, might not be that bad a thing. She seemed grateful to him, the way shipwreck victims were grateful to those who rescued them. The situation had a great deal of potential. Now she would be exposed to the redeeming qualities of the inn. She could see, without prejudice obstructing her judgment, the way the inn was operated. Since Daniel had assured him that there was no way to deliberately restore her memory, he would make the most of this unexpected break.

Who knew? When Kristina recovered, her experience here might make her decide not to remodel the inn. More important than that, if she became friendly with the others, she wouldn't insist on their being let go. After all, her attitude could hardly get worse.

"June," he called as he walked out of his office, "get everyone together for me, will you? I've got a little announcement I want to make."

June looked up from the romance novel she was reading. Placing a coaster between the pages to serve as a marker, she went to find the others.

And so the plot thickens, Max thought, glancing toward the stairs and Kristina's room. He only hoped he wouldn't live to regret it.

Six

Max leaned a hip against his desk as he looked at the semicircle of people gathered around him in the small office that had once been occupied by his foster mother. It was she, rather than John Murphy, who had actually run the inn. John had found that the part of the glad-handing greeter suited him far better. He'd been more of a host than a businessman. And Sylvia had been happy to let her husband do what he did best.

They had both loved this place, and it showed. Both in the atmosphere and in the people they had employed. Max intended to see that neither was tampered with.

Three of the staff, June, Sam and Jimmy, he'd known ever since he was taken in by the Murphys. June had been here since the inn had opened under the Murphys' management, rechristened the Dew Drop Inn. Sydney and Antonio were relatively new, in comparison, but had quickly fit into the fabric of the inn and were now regarded as as much a part of the "family" as the others. It was a family that had a right to remain intact if it so chose. And Max already knew that it did.

If he felt a little guilty about what he was proposing, he had only to remind himself that what it all boiled down to was a matter of them against a new partner who saw dollar signs where people stood. He owed a great deal more to them than he did to a partner who would disappear back into her conglomerate once the damage was done.

Still, even as he explained his idea to the five people he'd had June gather for this impromptu meeting, Max couldn't help feeling like a man who was doing something inherently wrong.

Sam Beaulieu sat in one of the two available chairs in the office. Listening, he laced his long fingers together before him. "And she does not remember *anything?*"

"No," Max answered.

"Nothing?" Sydney looked at him in wonder. "I can't count the number of times my little brother smacked his head as a kid, and he never forgot anything." She smiled as she thought of him. "Except to do his chores."

"Nothing," Max said emphatically. "She's a total blank. Now, I don't know how long this is going to last. I called Daniel about it—" he addressed his words to June, who had mothered both of them in her time "—and he says it's anyone's guess. A day, a week." He shrugged and spread his hands. "Something in between, or longer."

"The poor kid." June clucked sympathetically. She could only imagine how horrible it would be to wake up and not recognize anything or anyone.

To Max, June was the grandmother he'd never had. June was everyone's grandmother, as long as grandmothers came with tinted blond hair, lusty laughs and a weakness for romantic old movies. And could play pool until the wee hours of the morning.

He laughed shortly. June could save her pity. "Yes, well, that 'poor kid' wanted to get rid of all of you, if she had her way." Max got to the crux of his idea. "This is a perfect opportunity to have Her Royal Highness see life from your side." Kristina Fortune had probably never put in a real day's work in her life. Not like his foster parents, or the people in this room. This would be payback, he thought. "Especially yours, Sydney." Max looked at the younger woman.

Sydney blinked. "Me?"

He nodded. "I want you to show her the ropes."

It didn't make any sense to her. "Why?" Sydney exchanged a look with June. The latter shrugged.

"Because right now, I've got the esteemed Ms. Fortune thinking that she's Kris Valentine, a newly divorced woman who's trying to mend her life while she works here as the other maid."

Sydney frowned. She'd been at the inn for four years, and in that time, there had never been anyone else to help with the housekeeping chores, except when she went on vacation, and then it had only been temporary. She didn't particularly like this turn of events.

"What other maid?"

Max grinned, pleased with himself. "The one we've 'hired.'" He became serious. "If Kristina Fortune gets to know the routine, starts to think of the inn as more than just something pertaining to lines on an IRS form her accountant fills out, maybe we stand a chance of convincing her to leave the inn the way it is."

He looked from one face to another, waiting for their input. The inn might have his name on the deed now, but he left the operation of it up to the others. They were far more attuned to it than he was these days.

Sam nodded slowly, like a sage giving his permission. "Sounds good to me."

"Count on my help," Jimmy agreed eagerly. He couldn't begin to bring himself to imagine life without the inn. Way past the age of retirement, he'd always thought that he would live out his days puttering in the inn's garden, tending to his beloved rosebushes.

Sydney and Antonio both nodded, inclined to go along with whatever Max suggested. Only June looked a little distracted.

Max raised a brow. "Something you don't like?"

There were too many loose ends that needed tending. "What are you going to do about the Fortunes if they decide to call?"

If the rest of the family was as warm and loving as Kristina, he had a feeling no one would ever call. They probably estimated that her stay here would run well into two months. That was the way she'd made it sound to him when she began talking about her plans. There was no reason to believe they'd miss her before then.

"We'll take that as it comes." He shrugged. "My guess is no one will call. They're probably glad to be rid of her."

"Amen to that," Sydney murmured. She hadn't liked Kristina's high-handed manner from the moment she met her, and didn't care for the idea of working with her in any capacity now. She frowned, looking at Max. "Couldn't you have her working with Sam in the kitchen, or pulling weeds for Jimmy or something? I really don't want her working with me."

Max grinned. A small dose of the woman went a long way. "Don't worry, Syd. We'll make proper use of the lady. I intend to use her throughout the inn. Tell her that's how we break in a new member of the staff." He paused, considering. "Actually, she seems rather nice right now."

Sydney laughed shortly. "I'll believe that when I see it."

Antonio added his agreement to Sydney's assessment. Jimmy muttered something under his breath about her haughty dismissal of his landscaping.

"She waltzed through my kitchen and started telling me that I could organize it more efficiently. I did not even know who she was," Sam grumbled. The offense was still fresh in his mind.

"That's easy," Antonio quipped. "She's the dragon lady."

Max had no idea why he felt compelled to defend a woman he considered the last word on irritation and snobbery. Maybe it was because she was unable to do it herself. Or maybe because he felt that he owed it to Kristina for lying to her.

Whatever the reason, he cut the discussion short. "Well, at any rate, she's behaving like a changed woman. At least for now. Maybe someone should have hit her in the head a long time ago."

Sydney's mouth spread in a broad grin. "I'll drink to that."

After the others left his office, Max checked his watch. It was too late to get in any useful work on the construction site. He eased his conscience by reminding himself that Paul could competently manage the crews. He might as well remain here until tomorrow morning.

Max put in a call to him. The phone rang a total of nineteen times. He almost hung up before Paul picked up. "Took you long enough," he said impatiently.

"Hey, some of us have got better things to do than to hang around a phone all morning, waiting for calls," Paul joked. It was difficult to hear him, with all the background noise. "The cement trucks were delayed, but they finally got here at seven-thirty."

"Thanks for shouldering all this on your own." The construction was where his heart really belonged. Max wasn't accustomed to letting someone else do his share, but there was nothing he could do right now. "It doesn't look as if I'll be coming in today after all." He paused, dragging his hand through his hair. As a rule, Max hated complications. "I've got what you might call a situation here."

Paul picked up the tension in his voice. Max didn't get ruffled easily. "Is it more serious than you thought?"

"In a way." With a minimum of words, Max filled Paul in. But there was no way to minimize Kristina's apparent bout of amnesia. Paul listened quietly, then let out a low whistle.

"What are you going to do with her? Can you get someone in her family to fly out and pick her up?"

Max felt like Pinocchio on the phone to Jiminy Cricket. He deliberately blocked his conscience. "No, not just yet." He remembered a fragment of the telephone conversation he'd overheard. "I think most of them are busy with business or something. That's all these people care about. Nobody's going to miss her."

There was the sound of a loud boom on the phone before Paul answered. Max missed the noise of the site already. "I don't think it's business," Paul fairly shouted into the receiver. "Don't you read the papers, Max?"

Max held the phone away from his ear until the echo faded. "Not lately. Why?"

"Seems one of them's on trial for killing a woman. That old actress Monica somebody-or-other. Made the tabloid rounds for a couple of weeks. Maybe the rest of them are running out while the running's good."

That was the way his real family had operated, Max thought. Discarding whatever wasn't to their advantage to keep. That would give Kristina and him something in common, he mused.

"Well, whatever the reason, they're not around. That makes her my problem." He knew he was sugarcoating the situation, but Paul didn't have to be drawn into his charade unless it was necessary. "While I'm dealing with it, I figure to show her how the inn operates."

Paul's laugh was deep and insinuating. "And how you operate?"

Max thought of last night on the beach. What he thought he'd felt was probably just in his imagination. The last thing Max would have wished for himself was to get personally involved with the likes of Kristina Fortune.

"No danger there. This woman has men for breakfast. Chews them up and spits them out." He thought of the look in her eyes when she'd come to. "At least," he amended, "she did before she forgot how. She's almost docile now. You know, it's kind of funny."

"What is?"

"Well, to see her now is like looking at the before-and-after photos of Dr. Jekyll and Mr. Hyde, except the personality switch is in reverse."

Despite the fact that he'd been married for ten years— or maybe because of it—women had always confused Paul. The older he got, the more the point was brought home.

"Well, good luck, Max. I sure hope you know what you're doing."

Max laughed to himself. "That makes two of us." He glanced out the window, watching the waves calmly stroking the shore. **He** had the same view that Kristina had. It occurred to him that his office was directly below her room. He lowered his voice, even though he knew she couldn't hear him. "I'll see you on the site tomorrow. Promise."

"Not that I don't welcome your expertise, but don't feel you have to hurry back, buddy. Everything's under control. We've just poured the foundations on lots 3A and 3B today. For once, we're actually sticking to the schedule."

"The revised schedule," Max reminded him pointedly. He knew that Paul had a tendency to let things slide a little. Just as he did with the inn, Max reminded himself. Pot calling the kettle black. "See what you can do about getting ahead of it. That penalty clause is a big sucker."

"Don't I know it! Okay, I'll drag out the whip, bwana."

Max laughed. "See you tomorrow." Paul hung up, and Max replaced the receiver in the cradle. He glanced up, toward the ceiling, wondering what she had to be feeling right about now.

Restless, Max walked out to the front desk in time to see the Abbots check out. The elderly couple, who made a practice of returning to the inn each year the last week in January, promised to be back, "Same time next year."

"We look forward to seeing you," June told them with a warm smile.

"We'll be here." Mrs. Abbot exchanged a look with her husband. It was a promise to each other, rather than to anyone else.

"Bet we will," Mr. Abbot echoed. "Last night's storm was particularly romantic, wasn't it, Edna?"

Mrs. Abbot laughed and blushed. "He thinks he's sixty-five again," she confided to June.

Max watched the couple walk out, arm in arm. Sydney accompanied them out the door as Antonio carried their bags. In their eighties, they still looked as if they were in love. With an unabashed surge of envy, Max wondered how some people got to be that lucky.

June noted his expression. "Makes you feel good about the world, doesn't it?"

He roused himself. "You're an incurable romantic, June."

She saw no reason to apologize for it. "Guilty as charged."

With the Abbots gone, only four rooms at the inn were occupied. Twelve were empty, if he didn't count the one Kristina was in. He frowned, looking at the old-fashioned ledger where guests were still asked to sign in and out. His foster father had been completely computer-illiterate, intimidated by the very thought of putting data into a machine that might be judged to be brighter than he was. Max hadn't gotten around to putting one in yet, despite the fact that he depended on one in his construction business. He didn't see the need.

He studied the sparse sign-in column. Business could be better, even if it was the off-season.

God, now he was thinking like her. With an involuntary shake of his shoulders, he dismissed the thought.

June raised a brow in amusement. It was particularly warm for the first day of February. "Chilly?"

He pushed the ledger back in her direction. "Just flexing my shoulders."

June pretended to flutter her lashes as she placed a well-manicured hand with hot-pink nails across her heaving chest. "My, my, but you have turned into a really good-looking boy."

Boy. The last time he had felt like a boy was when he was twelve, just when he was arrested. "I'm thirty-two, June."

"And I'm—" She almost slipped and gave him her age. With a smile that made her look years younger than what her birth certificate attested to, June said, "Older. So, to me, you're still a boy. Or a hunk, as the popular term goes."

He laughed and shook his head. "Has Kris come down yet?"

"Not that I've seen." She looked at her watch. "Want someone to take a tray up to her? It's getting close to lunchtime."

He remembered that he hadn't eaten anything himself yet today. The situation with Kristina had robbed him of his appetite, but now a trace of it had returned. He'd grab something from the kitchen.

"No, I'll do it," he decided out loud. If nothing else, it would give him a tangible excuse to look in on her.

"I kind of thought you'd say that," June murmured under her breath. She smiled knowingly to herself as she picked up her book again.

"Don't mind me," Max told Sam as he took a tray from the table in the corner.

It was one of the trays they used when a guest requested breakfast in bed. Made of oak, it had a place on either side for newspapers and magazines. There was an indentation in one corner for a bud vase. Jimmy raised tea roses to be harvested just for this purpose.

Max helped himself to a handful of grapes before taking a plate down.

Sam didn't care for puttering in his kitchen. "If you are hungry, Max, I could fix you—"

"It's not for me. I'm taking up a tray to Kris."

Sam turned his back on the tray and began dicing unpeeled potatoes with a vengeance. "In that case, the rat poison is in the back of the storeroom."

Max grinned as he put together a salad plate. "I'll keep that in mind."

As an afterthought, he placed a silver pot of coffee on the tray, then angled in a cup, turned facedown on the saucer, and a small creamer. He grabbed a couple of packets of sugar and shoved them into his pocket.

"Nice touch," Sam commented. "I will see if I can find a way to package the rat poison in little pink packets next time."

"You do that, Sam." Sam was not a man who forgave easily, Max mused.

Balancing the tray carefully, Max made his way out of the kitchen and up the service stairs at the rear of the inn. He came out in the hall, directly in front of Kristina's room.

Resting the tray on the antique side table, Max knocked softly on her door. When there was no response, he tried the knob and found that it gave in his hand. She hadn't gotten up to lock it. He wondered if she was worse. Picking up the tray again, Max pushed the door open with his elbow and peered in.

Kristina's eyes shifted toward the door. She'd been lying here since he left, searching her mind for something, anything, that had shape, dimension, depth. But there were only fragments of shades that floated through, hinting of something, but were gone before she could catch them.

"I'm awake," she said softly.

So she was. Carefully Max placed the tray next to her on the bed. "You didn't answer when I knocked."

"I didn't hear you," she confessed. "I was thinking. Or trying to."

Kristina sat up on the bed, pulling her legs to her. She waited for the dizziness to come, but it didn't. A small victory.

She laced her hands together around her legs and looked at the tray. He watched as her hair floated along her face like a silky blond curtain and tried not to think of how sensual she looked.

There were small servings of three kinds of salads on a plate, beside a pot of coffee. Did she like salads? Did she like coffee? She didn't know.

"Do you know what it feels like not to have anything

real to think about? I mean, there's nothing in my head. No pictures, no images, no feelings." She looked up at him, her helplessness in her eyes. "I feel like an empty canvas."

The image appealed to him. "An empty canvas, just waiting for someone to paint on it," he remarked. And he was going to be that someone.

She smiled at him then, and if it hadn't been Kristina, Max would have called it a shy smile. But the last word he would ever have associated with Kristina Fortune was *shy*.

Still, he mused, she didn't know she was Kristina Fortune. Maybe this was a side of her she normally kept buried.

Kristina toyed with the fork on her tray. "Do I like salad?"

He turned the chair beside her bed and straddled it. "Why don't you try it and see?"

She did and then nodded, pleased by the discovery. "I do." Her eyes rose to his before she took another bite. "This is very nice of you—bringing me lunch like this," Kristina explained when she saw the question in his eyes.

Max would have preferred that she not be so grateful to him. He shrugged uncomfortably.

"Can't have you starving up here." He was silent for a moment, looking out the window. It was easier than looking at her. "I sent for the doctor to check you over. He'll be by later."

She'd had no idea she was so hungry. "The inn has a doctor?" she asked between mouthfuls.

"No, he's a friend of mine." Max was relieved to be talking about something besides her condition. "Daniel kind of grew up here with me, at the inn."

Like a sponge, she absorbed the information. Anything to fill this gaping hole. "You grew up here?"

"Yeah." As far as he was concerned, his life had started when he walked up those wooden steps and entered through that doorway.

Kristina thought she detected something in his voice and cocked her head, trying to pinpoint it. Wistfulness? Happiness?

"This must have been a wonderful place for a small boy to grow up in." Had she grown up in a place like this, with a lovely view outside her window?

His mouth curved as his eyes met hers. "I wasn't that small. I came here when I was thirteen."

Finished, she turned the cup upright on the saucer. Max leaned over and poured the coffee for her. Her eyes thanked him.

"Is that when your parents bought the inn? When you were thirteen?"

He had no idea why he told her the truth. He supposed that it was just simpler that way. "No, that's when social services sent me here as a final alternative to juvenile hall."

She saw the somber look in his eyes and forgot about her own situation. "I don't understand."

The tray tottered unevenly on the bed. Max rose and placed it on the bureau. "The couple who owned the inn are my foster parents."

"You're an orphan?" She could relate to the way he must have felt. Right now, as far as she knew, she was an orphan herself.

He turned and looked at her. Was that compassion he heard in her voice? Under normal circumstances, it would have turned him off. He'd never been comfortable with any form of sympathy or pity. It had a way of emphasizing his neediness. But hers warmed him, slipping softly under his skin.

"In a manner of speaking."

She didn't understand again. "Isn't that usually a black-or-white situation? You either are an orphan, or you're not?"

There was another alternative. "I felt like an orphan." Especially when he was being shuttled from one home to another, always unwanted, except for the monthly check his presence assured. "But technically I'm not. My parents are probably still alive someplace." The small laugh that escaped his lips was bitter. He hadn't meant it to be. "I wouldn't know either one if I tripped over them, which, I'm sure, is just the way they'd like it."

Without thinking, she reached out to cover his hand. How sad, she thought. How very sad. "How did you wind up with social services?"

Because her voice was soft, coaxing, because her touch was gentle, the words came as if of their own volition, drawn to the concern he heard, like a soaked dog to the warmth of a fireplace.

"I remember waking up one morning in a motel room." It was from that point on that his memories of life began. He'd been four or so at the time. Maybe five. "Looking back, I realize that it wasn't nearly as big as this one, but it felt huge to me. Huge and empty. There was a reason for that." He recited the story as if it was something that had happened to someone else. "My 'parents' had just taken off in the middle of the night, leaving behind whatever they didn't want to take with them." He shrugged. "I was one of the things they didn't want to take."

Kristina's eyes were huge. He looked at her, taken back by the emotion he saw there.

"Oh, Max, I'm so sorry."

He cleared his throat. He had absolutely no idea how they had gotten to this juncture. He'd only meant to exchange a little casual conversation with her, to see how she was feeling. He'd had no intention of rehashing something he hadn't thought about in years. Something that he hadn't allowed himself to think about in years.

"Nothing to feel sorry about." His tone was matter-of-fact. "I was better off without them. And if they'd stuck around, I would never have wound up with the Murphys. Or here."

And he would have regretted that. Deeply. For the Murphys had saved his soul, turning a kid hell-bent on living on the wrong side of the law into a decent human being, not by platitudes, but by example.

They would be thrilled with him now, he thought cynically, looking at Kristina.

"I guess everything turns out for the best," she murmured. She placed the empty cup aside on the nightstand. "I hope that applies to me, as well."

"It will."

She wished she could believe that. Wished she could believe in something. Just before he entered, she had been lying awake, staring at the ceiling, wondering how many times she had done that before, if ever. It was awful not to be able to remember *anything*.

"You sound a great deal more confident than I feel right now."

He felt compelled to offer her a little hope. "The doctor's confident that this is just temporary. He told me that anything might trigger your memory and make it return."

"That's comforting." She only hoped the doctor was right. Kristina sighed and stretched. "That was good." She nodded at the tray on the bureau.

"I'll be sure to tell Sam." Maybe he'd decide not to repackage the rat poison.

So many names she didn't know. "Sam?"

"The cook."

Sam. That could be a man or a woman. "Samantha?" she guessed.

"Samuel," he corrected.

The name failed to bring a corresponding face to her mind. She tried not to be dejected. "I feel like there's just so much to learn."

It was time to leave her, before he did something stupid, like tell her the truth. If she remembered who she was, that would blow the one chance he had. Kristina hadn't struck him as a woman who could be reasoned with. She had, however, struck him as someone who could find a way to take the inn from him if she so chose.

"Don't let it worry you. We'll all try to help you when we can. You take today off, and if you feel up to it, you can start working again tomorrow."

She felt tired now, but the prospect of work filled her with eagerness.

"I'd like that," she said. "The sooner I get back to a familiar routine, the sooner things might start coming back to me."

"Absolutely," he agreed. *But with any luck, not too soon.*

Seven

When she opened her eyes the next day, a sliver of hope that this had all been a dream shot through Kristina. But when she searched her mind, all she remembered was limited to the day before.

The doctor Max brought to see her had been kind and reassuring. He and Max had taken her to the hospital to run a few tests, but in the end, he had returned to the same conclusion. There was no sign of any physical damage. In all likelihood, the amnesia was temporary.

All she could do was wait.

So she did.

There had been dreams during the night, formless shadows of things that might or might not have had significance in her life. When Kristina awoke the next day, she was aware that she had dreamed, but not of what, not of who.

Frustration ate away at her. She felt so helpless, so exposed. Did she have secrets? Was there someone important in her life she was just getting to know? Would there be someone to worry if she didn't call them?

There was no one to tell her.

She let out a shaky breath and forced herself to be calm. She couldn't allow herself to fall apart. Right now, her own strength was all she had. She didn't know how she knew she was strong, but she did. It was a feeling, and she built on it.

Kristina threw back the covers, too wound up to remain in bed. She glanced at the clock. It was still fairly early. She wondered if she was normally an early riser, or if it was anxiety that was rousing her, forcing her out of bed. That was the worst of it, not knowing anything about herself.

Not even the way she wore her hair.

Kristina looked at her reflection in the mirror, toying with the ends. Did she wear her hair up or down? Parted on the right? In the middle? What?

Curious, she tried them all, and decided she would leave her hair down for now. Somehow, it looked more natural.

She felt like a baby taking its first uncertain steps. Not knowing whether it could make it across the room, or if it would wind up sitting smack on its bottom.

She supposed babies didn't have those kind of thoughts. But for now they were the only kind she *did* have. And all the steps she could make were tiny ones.

She'd just finished dressing when she heard the soft knock on her door. Kristina was eager for company, for someone to talk to. For someone to begin helping her fill this void inside.

"Yes?"

"It's Max."

Max was surprised when the door flew open. Kristina looked genuinely happy to see him. If she only knew, he thought.

"I thought we'd get you started this morning." He searched her face, making his own judgment. "Unless you're not feeling well."

"Oh, I'm fine," she said quickly. "Or as fine as I can be, given the circumstances." She looked down at the clothes she'd just put on. "Is this all right to wear? I didn't find a uniform or anything."

Max congratulated himself on his foresight. He'd had Sydney come into Kristina's room last night to take out all her notes on the inn. Sydney had also hung up Kristina's clothes while he and Daniel took her to the hospital. If she'd found all her clothes still packed in a suitcase, it might have raised questions he couldn't have readily answered.

She had on a denim skirt and blouse. He wouldn't have thought she was the type to even own denim. Simple, but undoubtedly designer-stamped with a high price tag, he guessed.

"You look fine. And we don't have any uniforms here. I like to keep things uncomplicated." *Yeah, right,* a little voice nagged him. "If you're ready, why don't you come to the dining room with me?"

Kristina followed him down the front stairs. "I dreamed about you," she remembered suddenly. "At least, I think it was about you." But even as she reached for that simple memory, it eluded her, dissolving right before her. She sighed, frustrated again. "Seems like I can't remember anything."

He stopped at the landing. As befitted a benevolent big brother, he slipped an arm around her shoulders. "You will, Kris, you will." *Just, please, not too soon. Not until I can figure a way out of this with my skin on.*

Max guided her to the dining room. Given the time, he knew Sydney would be there, setting places for their guests. Occasionally, a few people who lived in the area dropped by for breakfast, as well. But that was generally on the weekends.

There was no one in the dining room yet, only Sydney. She looked up when she heard them enter. Her friendly expression froze when she saw Kristina.

"Good morning," she said crisply as she set the last place.

"Good morning, Sydney." Max noted the frosty glance she spared Kristina. "Kris says she's feeling better today."

"That's good," Sydney murmured without looking up. She elaborately straightened the place setting in front of her.

His hand on Kristina's back, Max gently pushed her forward. He detected the tension in her shoulders. Max could almost have felt sorry for her. Almost.

"I'm afraid that you're going to have to show Kris the ropes all over again."

Kristina looked around the room, with its wide adjacent bay windows. They faced the morning sun and gleamed a warm invitation to anyone who chanced to walk by. Sydney's frown as she listened to Max's instructions cast a gloom upon the room.

Sydney squared her shoulders and nodded. "Sure, Max, if that's what you want."

She had no memory, and thus no experience to gauge by, but Kristina would have bet that more heartfelt invitations had been extended to people awaiting their fate on death row.

Kris started. Where had that come from? Did she know anyone who had ever been accused of murder? Or perhaps even convicted? The thought made her heart begin to pound, but nothing else followed. No moment of truth, no revelations.

Her reaction was probably just generated by nerves and uncertainty, she told herself. Her mind was a blank slate, so every thought became amplified.

Max noticed the change in her expression. "What's the matter?"

Kristina shook her head. "Nothing. I just thought I remembered something." She sighed. "But I didn't."

"Don't try too hard," he cautioned. "Maybe whatever you were trying to remember will come back on its own, when you least expect it." He felt Sydney's eyes on him. Looking up, he saw a trace of a smile on her lips. At least one of them was being entertained by this, he thought. "I'll see you tonight," he promised Kristina.

She looked at him in surprise, a shaft of panic shooting through her. "You're leaving?" She had expected him to be around somewhere on the premises. Right now, he was her only real anchor in this uncharted sea she found herself in.

The note of anxiety chafed his conscience. He reasoned himself out of it again, but it took more effort than the last time.

Max began easing away, toward the doorway. If he didn't leave now, he had a feeling that he wouldn't make it out at all. He couldn't afford to neglect his company indefinitely.

"I have to," he told her. "I've got a construction company to run."

More confusion, she thought. Kristina looked from Sydney to Max. She *really* wanted him to stay. "But I thought you said you owned the inn." At least that was what she thought he'd said. Or had he? Everything in her head felt as if it were cast in Jell-O.

"He does," Sydney interjected. Taking her arm, she drew Kristina farther away from Max. "But the construction company is something he's built up on his own." Sydney spared Max one last glance, this time accompanying it with a warm smile. It contrasted severely with the look she spared Kristina.

"I'll see you all tonight," Max repeated.

Sydney merely grinned in response. The grin faded as Max walked out. Making the best of the burden she'd been saddled with, she turned toward Kristina.

"C'mon, we've got sixteen rooms to clean before lunchtime." And she sincerely doubted that Kristina would be much help with any of them.

"Sixteen?" Kristina followed Sydney out of the room. "Are there that many people here?"

She hadn't seen anyone in the halls when she came down, except for June at the front desk. Realizing that she had managed to associate a name with a person, Kristina smiled to herself. It was a small triumph, but a triumph nonetheless.

"There're four couples here right now." Sydney led the

way upstairs. "But the dust doesn't stay out of the other rooms just because people aren't in them. We clean every room every day."

She turned to look at her as Kristina came to the landing. Sydney had a feeling this had the makings of a long day. With a long-suffering shake of her head, she led the way to the small walk-in closet that served as the utility room.

It didn't take a lifetime of recollections to know that this was not one of her better days, Kristina thought miserably. Or a good day at all. Her feelings of frustration and inadequacy mounted as the day, and everyone's tempers, wore on.

It began under Sydney's tutelage. She hadn't a clue what hospital corners were, so when Sydney sent her into room 4 to strip and remake her first bed, she had failed to do an acceptable job.

"You've short-sheeted them," Sydney pointed out in exasperation. "Here, let me do it." She elbowed Kristina out of the way. "See if you can dust right. I don't think there's a wrong way to do that."

Neither did Kris.

Until she broke a figurine in one of the unoccupied rooms.

"Oh, God."

Heart hammering, she quickly scooped up the pieces. One of the jagged edges caught the tip of her finger. Dabbing at the blood with her handkerchief, she wrapped the pieces of the figurine in it.

Moving out cautiously, she checked the hall to see if Sydney was around. She wasn't. Kristina hurriedly deposited the pieces in her room. With any luck, she'd be able to glue them together and restore the figurine before anyone noticed it was missing.

That is, if I *have* any luck, she thought ruefully. So far, it didn't look as if she were the lucky type.

Sydney found fault with everything she did. Admittedly,

Kristina knew she did everything poorly, but she felt completely out of her element no matter what she did. When she vacuumed the rooms, she felt as if she'd never done it before. The upright, with its high suction power, needed constant supervision. Preoccupied for just a moment, she found the bottom of the drape being wrapped around the machine's bristles as the attachment greedily consumed the material.

Sydney heard her cry of distress and came running into the room to find her trying to tug the fabric out. Sydney grabbed the vacuum out of her hands.

"I'll handle the rest of it," she told her curtly. "You've made enough work for me today." Sydney looked at the bottom of the frayed drape. "This is going to have to be mended. Why don't you go see what you can do for Jimmy for a while? The gardener," she added impatiently, when Kristina looked at her blankly.

Dejected, Kristina headed for the doorway, then stopped. "Where would I find him?"

"In the garden," Sydney snapped, then shook her head.

Jimmy was on his knees in the back of the house. Kristina watched him lovingly planting daisies. White, to help bring out the other vivid colors in a garden he treated more like a well-kept mistress than like landscaping.

She cleared her throat, but he seemed oblivious of her presence. Finally, she said, "Sydney sent me out to help you."

Jimmy glanced up at her then, squinting as he tried to make out her face. Anything beyond eighteen inches was a soft blur that blended into the background. He saw no reason to wear glasses, since all his work was close, unless he was taking a stroll around the perimeter of the building.

"Remind me to thank Sydney for her thoughtfulness." He neither smiled nor frowned. Instead, he appeared wearily resigned. Jimmy gestured toward a hand shovel. "Well, you might as well make yourself useful. You can do the weeding for me. Mind that you're careful around her.''

"Her?" She thought he was warning her about Sydney, and found it odd. Appropriate, but odd.

"The garden. Treat her like a lady," he cautioned. "She'll know it if you don't.''

A gnarled hand pointed in the direction where he wanted her to begin weeding. It was a good distance away from him. Kristina wondered if that was coincidence.

The sun felt hot about her shoulders as she squatted, pulling weeds out. The pile beside her grew as she sacrificed nail after nail. She'd had no idea that there were that many different kinds of weeds. Some pinched her fingers, some gave easily, still others struggled for dear life. She thought she was doing rather well until she heard the high-pitched squeal of protest directly behind her.

She looked up to see a distressed Jimmy hovering over her, glaring accusingly. He pointed at the pile beside her. "What's the matter with you, girl? Don't you know weeds from ground cover?"

Apparently she didn't. Kristina jumped to her feet. "I'm sorry.''

He didn't appear to hear her. Instead, he picked up a plant and held it up, making her come face-to-face with her crime. "Do you have any idea how long it's taken me to coax this into growing?''

Kristina winced inwardly. "No.''

He remembered how she'd looked down her nose at his beloved flowers when she arrived. "No, your kind wouldn't. Go back inside. See if you can turn Antonio's hair white. He's young. His heart can stand seeing something he loves butchered.''

She tried to apologize again, but he turned a deaf ear to her, mumbling something about inept help and murdered plants. Tears stinging her eyes, Kristina hurried back inside. She had no idea where to find Antonio, or even what he looked like.

As it was, she didn't have to look for Antonio. She ran into him. Literally. He was a tall man, built like a solid brick wall. The toolbox he was carrying was not. It went crashing to the wooden floor, flipping tools out every which way.

"Oh, I'm sorry." Kristina dropped to her knees, quickly gathering the tools together and replacing them in the box.

"It's okay." Antonio picked up the toolbox, and he was making good his escape when Kristina called after him.

"Are you Antonio?"

Uneasy, he turned around. "Yes, why?"

"Jimmy said I should help you."

"Oh, he did, did he?" After a moment, a good-natured smile bloomed. Shrugging, he beckoned her forward. "All right, come on. I guess it can't hurt to have someone pretty to look at while I'm working."

Antonio found out otherwise. Kristina misunderstood his instructions when he was fixing a showerhead in one of the downstairs bathrooms and turned the water back on too soon. Antonio was soaked in a matter of seconds.

Dripping, he'd gone off to change and told her to see Sam in the kitchen.

Sam looked far from delighted when she walked in, and made no effort to hide it. His reaction, added to that of the others, was completely undermining the tiny shred of confidence she was trying to nurture. She couldn't understand why she remained working with these people if they didn't like her.

Why didn't they like her? Had she done something to them? She was going to have to ask Max about it when she got the chance.

Determined to make the best of it, she applied herself to the job Sam gave her.

But peeling potatoes wasn't something she did naturally, either, she discovered. She had no idea how to hold the knife, how to make the peel come off smoothly or evenly.

She tried her best, even after she nicked herself twice, but it was no use.

Her best wasn't good enough. Sam uttered an oath in a language she didn't understand and dramatically took the knife away from her. With his other hand, he gestured at the potatoes she'd deposited in a bowl.

"Look what you have done to them. You have taken healthy, plump potatoes and made marbles out of them. What am I to do with marbles? Go into the dining room, set places for dinner. Leave me in peace to make amends here. Sydney!" he called. "Take her out of here before I am forced to quit!"

Resigned, Sydney took Kristina back under her wing. "You're making quite a name for yourself, Kris," she commented with a shake of her head. "Let's see if we can find something safe for you to do."

But she doubted they would.

Max arrived at the inn at seven, exhausted. The drive from the Woodbridge East construction site down the 5 freeway had been particularly taxing. A big rig had jack-knifed, snarling traffic at the El Toro Y intersection for miles. Beyond the accident had been no better. Cars had moved along as if their wheels were dipped in glue.

Halfway there, Max had debated getting off and turning around to go home. A combination of conscience and curiosity wouldn't let him. He wanted to find out just how "Kristina the maid" was faring.

It was the first question out of his mouth when he finally walked in that night.

June was seated behind the desk, reading. She looked unruffled, and that gave him hope that maybe things had actually progressed smoothly. No one had placed an emergency call to him. At the very least, that meant that Kristina still didn't remember who she was. They were still in the ball game.

"Hi, June. How's she doing?"

Before June could answer, a loud crash was heard from the dining room. June placed a fingertip between the pages to mark her place. "That would be her."

"Great." He knew by her tone that this was an indication of the way the day had gone. Max sighed. "I'll be in my office if anyone needs me."

Sinking into his chair, he allowed the weariness that had been dogging him all day to catch up. Max stretched his legs out before him and shut his eyes. Maybe having her think she worked here wasn't such a good idea after all, he mused.

Right now, nothing seemed like a good idea. It had been a long day for him, as well. Two of the workers had failed to show, and the day laborers he hired had turned out to be inept at the tasks they claimed to be able to do "with their eyes shut." It would have gone better if they had done them with their eyes open. There would have been fewer mishaps.

He could use a vacation, he thought. Too bad he couldn't take one for the next ten years or so.

His back to the door, Max heard someone entering the office. Turning around, he expected to see one or all of the staff standing there, up in arms. Instead, it was Kristina.

She reminded him of a lost waif. She stood just shy of his doorway, shifting from foot to foot. "Max, could I see you for a minute?"

"Sure." Rising in his chair, Max gestured for her to come in. "Take a seat."

"Thanks, but I'd rather stand." She continued to look uneasy and he couldn't help wondering if some of her memory *had* returned. Kristina twisted her hands together and looked away. "This just isn't a good idea."

There was agony in her face, tugging at his sympathy. "What isn't a good idea?"

"My working here." She waved her hands around, taking in the entire area. It was obvious that she was not comfortable with what she was saying. Not comfortable, he thought, in her skin. That was because he'd given her someone else's, he thought. This wasn't who or what she was, and that was bound to make her stumble.

Kristina blew out a breath. It pained her to go over the details of the day, but as her employer, he had the right to know, and she'd rather tell him herself, before the others had the opportunity.

"I can't seem to make a bed right. I can't tell a weed from a ground cover, and I take too much off the potatoes when I peel." As she recited each infraction, they all sounded incredibly insignificant. But they weren't. Not to her. Not to the people she worked with.

She held up her hands for his inspection. The polish on her nails had been chipped, some of her nails were broken, and there were cuts on several of her fingers.

Her first honest day's work, Max thought. The satisfaction he'd thought he'd feel wasn't nearly as strong as he had expected it to be. It felt rather hollow.

She sighed, adding, "Plus, I dropped a tray full of glasses."

He struggled to hide the smile that rose to his lips. "I heard."

He wasn't yelling at her, she realized. Didn't he understand what she was saying? "I'm a liability here."

He was surprised that she actually seemed upset by her shortcomings. Surprised and oddly touched.

"Don't worry about that," he said softly.

But she did worry about it. Worry about the way her ineptitude made her feel. She didn't like being a liability. She didn't understand why Max seemed so calm about it.

"You don't mind?"

He rose and rounded his desk to stand next to her. "People take time to fit into new niches. For you, right now, this is a new niche. We allow for that." This time he didn't bother hiding his smile. "I just hope you'll keep the glass-breaking to a minimum—"

"It was an accident," she was quick to point out.

"I was hoping it hadn't been on purpose."

She stared at him. "Why would I throw anything on purpose?"

Max thought of the driftwood Kristina had thrown at him. He shrugged nonchalantly. "Oh, because you were angry or frustrated about something."

That was no excuse. "I wouldn't do something like that." She looked at him, wondering if he was trying to gently hint at something. "Would I?"

"No, I guess you wouldn't." At least, this Kristina wouldn't, he judged. It amazed him that within that sharp-tongued woman who arrived here on the 2:15 broom there had been this sweet person who actually cared about the impression she made and the things she did. Maybe Kristina Fortune hadn't been all bad.

Kristina weighed her words carefully. "I think I should leave, Max. I'm just not any good at this."

He couldn't just turn her loose. Not like this. And if he tried to call her family, who knew what sort of liabilities he'd be leaving himself open to? This was something he was going to have to ride out, for better or for worse.

"Of course you are," he said quickly. "Just give yourself a little time, that's all. Besides, everyone messes up. Everyone," he said emphatically. He saw the gratitude enter her eyes. "Cut yourself a little slack, Kris. We all are." He saw something in her face he couldn't fathom. "What?"

She felt like a little kid, complaining. But this mattered to her, and she wasn't complaining, she reasoned, so much as sharing. "I don't think the others like me very much."

And it bothered her, he realized. Who would have thought it? He needed to have a word or two with the staff. For now, Max dismissed her observation.

"That's just your imagination. Don't forget, you've just been through a very stressful ordeal. You don't know who you are, where you are. It's only natural that you might be experiencing a little paranoia."

She knew it wasn't that, and she didn't want to stay where she wasn't wanted. But the idea of actually leaving here made her uneasy, as well. Where would she go? Wavering, she looked at Max.

"I don't know." She chewed on her lower lip. "You're sure you want me to stay?"

Right now, he'd never been so sure of anything in his life. The other alternative produced too many complications.

"Sure," he said firmly. "Besides, where would you go?" He kicked himself for it, but he had to say this in order to get her to remain. "You don't have anyone."

That felt so awful. She didn't remember anyone, but to know that even if her mind came back, there would be no one to turn to, felt devastating. "I don't?"

He turned away. Looking at her made this too difficult to say. "No, that's what you told me. You came here to get away from painful memories. Your divorce," he added, in case she'd forgotten. "While you've been here, June said you didn't place any personal calls. She thought that was strange," he added.

"I guess that means I'm a loner." Kristina turned the idea over in her mind as she said it. It didn't sound quite right, and yet, somehow, it did. Instinctively she knew that she was a loner, someone who did things on her own. "I just don't remember." And it was driving her crazy.

"Patience," Max counseled. "It'll all fall together for you soon enough."

She was beginning to have her doubts about that, but she knew she was being unfair. Having him here, reassuring her, helped negate the loneliness that hovered along the perimeter of her soul.

Warmed by his concern, Kristina smiled at Max. "If you say so."

He wished her faith in him didn't seem so secure. "I say so. So, no more talk of quitting?"

"No more talk of quitting," she echoed. "Thanks for taking the time to talk to me." Turning, Kristina began to leave, then stopped. She looked at him over her shoulder. "Can I get you anything?"

He'd just begun to go through the papers June kept piling on his desk. The papers he hadn't had time to look at in about three weeks, he thought ruefully. Max looked up at her. "What?"

"You haven't eaten yet," she reminded him. If he'd come in to the dining room, she would have seen him. "The kitchen's about to close. I thought maybe you'd like something. Provided Sam hasn't permanently banned me from there," she added ruefully. "I think he hates me."

Max laughed. "Sam doesn't hate you. He's just temperamental. I'll tell you the secret to working with Sam. He needs some coddling, but it's worth it. He's a really great chef."

That didn't make sense to her. She would have thought that a man like that would want to go on to bigger things, not remain closeted in a little out-of-the-way inn.

"Then what's he doing here?" She flushed, hoping that hadn't come out the way she thought it had. She hadn't meant to insult Max. "I mean, wouldn't he rather be working in some fancy restaurant?"

So, maybe a little of the old Kristina was returning, Max thought uneasily. It had certainly sounded like something she'd say.

"No, he likes it here. June tells me Sam came here one summer to recuperate after some minor surgery. The cook we had then didn't live up to Sam's standards. Sam took to going in and offering suggestions. He even cooked a few meals, called it a busman's holiday. As he was checking out, he remarked to my foster mother that he was going to miss the tranquillity of this place. On a whim, she offered him a job. He never went back to his old one."

"What about the cook you had?" She had already gotten the impression that no one was fired around here. Not if he was talking *her* out of quitting.

"They kept him on as an assistant." Max thought for a moment. Phil had been gone three years now. Since just around the time the inn became his. "He went to live with his daughter a few years ago. Sam's been the sole tyrant of the kitchen ever since. Won't even go on vacation." He grinned. "Says that maybe another chef'll come here on vacation and take his place while he's gone."

She laughed softly, then looked into Max's face. It was a kind face, she thought. A strong face. The face of a man you could depend on. "You're making this up."

Elaborately he crossed his heart and then held up his hand. "It's too hokey to make up. The inn attracts people like that. People who tend to think of this place as home. At least, it used to," he remarked. Of late, he supposed probably due to his lessened interest, business had slackened off.

She knew she should go, but she hesitated. She liked being here, with him. Did he have someone else? "Does everyone have a story like that?"

Max thought for a second. "Pretty much." He was getting too comfortable with her, he realized. "You mentioned getting me something to eat?"

"Oh, right." He probably thought she was getting too friendly, she told herself. After all, he was the boss. "I'll bring you the house special."

He nodded as she went out, pretending to be busy. He only raised his eyes after he was sure she was gone.

Damn it, she was likable, he thought. Really likable. That made her easier to work with, but harder on his conscience.

Max reminded himself of the story he had just told her. For the sake of Sam and the others, he was going to have to stick to this charade he'd set in motion.

He was beginning to feel a little like a man who had a tiger by the tail—or rather by the tale.

Kristina hesitated in the doorway of the kitchen. Everything within the large room was immaculate and orderly. "Sam?"

Sam was bent over the worktable, putting the finishing touches on a soufflé he intended to try out on the staff. There were advantages to living on the premises. He always had a ready-made audience to practice on.

He looked up at the sound of her voice and scowled. "Oh, it's you. Looking for something else to break?"

She wanted to turn around and run, but she remained where she was. Running wasn't going to solve anything. She'd still have to face this man, and the others, tomorrow. And the day after that. "No, Max is back. He'd like to have dinner."

Sam nodded curtly, taking a tray from the stack. Carving fresh slices from the ham he'd baked for dinner, he arranged them on a plate, adding a helping of home fries and steamed broccoli. "There, ready."

"I'm sorry about before."

Sam raised a tufted gray brow in her direction. "Hmm?"

She'd started this, and she was determined to see it through. "The dishes and the potatoes and all." She took a chance and confided in him. "Sam, I really don't feel as if I've ever done this sort of thing, but everyone tells me that I have, so I guess this amnesia thing has not only wiped out my memory, but made me a bumbling, inept klutz, as well." She shrugged helplessly.

Sam sighed, relenting. She'd taken the edge off his anger with her apology. He hadn't meant to make her feel that bad.

"You are not a bumbling, inept klutz. You are a little clumsy, that is all." He put down the soufflé cups he'd been arranging and nodded at the plate. "Why don't you take Max his dinner and then come back here? Maybe I can show you a few things, so you won't feel so lost around the kitchen tomorrow."

"I'd like that." Picking up the tray, she hurried out.

The smile on her lips had Sam humming as he poured out his soufflé. Perhaps, he mused, as Max had said, she was not so bad after all.

Eight

It wasn't until much later that Kristina was finally able to slip back into her room. From her pocket, she took the small, half-empty bottle of all-purpose glue June had given her, then spread the pieces of the figurine out on her desk.

It didn't look as bad as she'd first thought. It wasn't in a dozen tiny pieces. There weren't even any slivers that refused to match. The cherubic-looking shepherd had lost his staff and his arm, and half his hat was missing. But the jaunty red feather in the hat was still intact.

Kristina reasoned that if she looked at it as a kind of jigsaw puzzle, it might even be fun putting it together. The thought nudged another question forward in her mind. Had she liked jigsaw puzzles as a child?

She paused, looking out the window into the darkness beyond. What had she been like as a child? Who had loved her? *Had* there been anyone to love her, or had she been like Max, abandoned at an early age to make her own way in the world, as best she could?

"Keep asking yourself questions and you're never going to get this put together," she muttered.

She sat down at the desk and got started. As she squeezed the bottle, a large white blotch oozed out, overflowing the edge of the piece she was holding. Instant mess.

So far, this wasn't going very well, she thought with an inward sigh. Kristina dabbed at the excess glue with a tissue, taking care not to get stuck. The knock on the door startled her and she dropped the piece on the blotter.

Oh, great.

She wiped it clean just as another, louder knock came. Now what?

Opening the door just a crack, she saw Max standing in the hall. She was usually pleased to see him, but not right now. Not with the pieces of the figurine spread out all over her desk.

"Something wrong?" she asked.

She was holding the door as if she didn't want him to come in. Something was definitely up. "I was going to ask you the same thing. June said you borrowed some glue."

Max thought he noticed a trace of guilt passing fleetingly over her face. She kept her hand tightly on the door. "I did."

"Why would you need glue?"

Kristina debated for a second. With a reluctant sigh, she opened the door all the way. "You might as well know. I broke a figurine dusting today." Something else to add to the litany of transgressions.

Crossing to the desk, she gestured at her aborted handiwork. "I was trying to glue it back together before anyone noticed."

Max picked up the severed arm, pretending to look it over. It masked his surprise. The difference in attitudes was enormous. "Kristina" had blatantly disregarded his request to leave Sylvia Murphy's tapestry alone, while "Kris" felt responsible for something as inconsequential as a dime-store knickknack.

Kristina sat down at the table again and resumed working with the pieces. Max shook his head. "Don't bother. I can get another one in town. They're not expensive."

Maybe they weren't, but she had broken it, so she was going to fix it. Stubbornly she applied the glue to the same piece. This time, it spread more evenly. "I know, but I shouldn't have broken it."

Amused, he watched her as she concentrated on matching the jagged edges just so. She looked so serious, she might have been working on something vital to national security, not a broken shepherd.

"You're very conscientious."

She glanced up at him before picking up another piece. "No, I'm very clumsy. I keep knocking things down, or sucking them up, every time I turn around."

Max perched on the edge of her desk. "Sucking them up?"

She shrugged ruefully, pressing the brim of the shepherd's hat onto the piece that was still on his head. "I ran the vacuum cleaner too close to the drapes."

Max laughed and held up his hand. He wanted to spare her the embarrassment of reciting the details. "Say no more, I get the picture."

Gingerly she pried her finger from the statue. A telltale residue of glue remained, like a rough white halo, on her fingertip. She rubbed her thumb over it, trying to peel it off. "Change your mind yet?"

"About what?"

Finished, she set the figurine down and raised her eyes to his. "About keeping me on?"

But if he had changed his mind, if he fired her, where would she go? Did she have enough money saved to get along until she found another job? Even if she did, could she find her bankbook? So many questions crowded into her mind, and there were no answers for them.

For the present, until things were at least sorted out, she wanted to remain here. But that was up to Max.

He'd like that, Max thought. To keep her. Just the way she was. He found this new Kristina infinitely preferable to the one he'd met before. She was sweet, conscientious, and determined to do things right.

Kristina struggled not to lower her eyes from his. She could feel herself fidgeting inside. He had a way of looking at her that went clear down to her toes and unlocked doors she hadn't known, until this moment, were closed.

Maybe it was just the vulnerable state she found herself

in. Or maybe it was because, when she opened her eyes, his had been the first face she saw. For whatever reason, there was something about Max that made her want to discover just how close they could become.

After a beat, she twisted the top on the glue clockwise, closing it. She studied her handiwork and realized that, though mended, the cracks were vividly apparent. So much for that.

"Maybe I could go with you?"

She was the one with amnesia, he reminded himself. So how come he was the one who kept feeling confused? "Go where?"

"Into town. To replace the figurine." She held it up for his inspection. "I'll pay for it out of my paycheck," she added quickly. "If there's anything left after I finish paying for the glasses I dropped this afternoon and the drape I almost ruined."

She was being too hard on herself. He would never have believed it if he hadn't heard it.

"I think there might be a few pennies left over." He knew he was on shaky ground, but he took a few more steps forward. "All right, the next time I go, you can come with me." He liked the idea of going somewhere with her. Not just into town, but somewhere intimate, where dim lights flickered on round little tables and people talked until the wee hours of the morning. "I'll even let you treat me to a beer."

"A beer." She could easily imagine him sitting in some smoky place, nursing an amber-filled glass while the sounds of a throaty love song wafted from the jukebox, cutting through the low din of voices. "You like beer?"

The innocent way she kept plying him with questions stung his conscience. "I've been known to down one or two." Especially his first year in college, before he had decided to buckle down and make something of himself.

She wondered if the scenario she'd just sketched in her

mind was one she'd ever experienced firsthand. "Do I drink beer?"

Max shoved his hands in his pockets and studied her face. He sincerely doubted Kristina Fortune had ever tipped back a brew. But Kris Valentine might. "I really don't know."

Drawn by need, Kristina moved closer to him. Her breath skimmed along his face as she asked, "What do you know about me, Max? Did I ever talk about my family?"

Getting a grip on his thoughts took concentrated effort. They were clearly going where they had no business venturing. Not in this case. Not with her.

"You never mentioned them." That much was true. "You gave me the impression that if there was someone, you were estranged."

She looked around the bare bureau and nightstand. "There are no photographs in my room."

"No," he agreed cautiously, wondering where she was going with this.

"So I guess you're right. If I had any family left, there would be photographs around." She looked up at him. "It's like my whole life was a blank before I came here."

Though he knew better, he couldn't help relating to the sentiment she expressed. "That's the way I always felt. Nothing counted until I came here."

She wanted him to hold her, she thought. To hold her and make her feel safe, the way he had yesterday, when she woke up to nothing.

He wished she wouldn't look at him like that. Like a cool vanilla sundae. Not when he had a craving for ice cream.

Kristina lifted her chin, her eyes on his. Her voice was low, silky. "That gives us something in common."

He could almost feel her skin sliding along his. It made his mouth water, and his mind yell, *Retreat.* "I guess it does." He had no business getting close to someone who actually didn't exist. Someone he was fashioning in his own mind.

Abruptly Max turned, walking toward the door. "You'd better get some sleep, Kris. You've got an early day tomorrow."

She nodded, following him. Her eyes skimmed along the broad set of his shoulders, taking in the way his body tapered to his hips. She felt her stomach flip-flop.

"Max?"

In his heart, he knew it was a mistake. He should just go out the door and keep on going. But he turned around to look at her. "Yes?"

Impulse took her where courage failed to. Her fingers embedded in the fabric of his work shirt, Kristina rose up on her toes and kissed him lightly on the lips.

It took him completely by surprise, both the kiss and the sweetness he detected beneath it. Max looked at her, more stunned than when she had thrown the driftwood at him. For one thing, her kiss had more of a wallop to it.

"What was that for?"

Her smile was slow, spreading from her lips into her eyes. And then into him. "Just to say thank-you. For being kind. For being you."

Kristina looked into his eyes, searching for a place for herself there. The vulnerability he saw in hers was more than he could resist. Gathering her in his arms, Max kissed her. Really kissed her. Kissed her with a passion that slowly unfurled, wrapping its ends around both of them and holding them tightly within its fabric.

Pulse racing, Kristina felt alive for the first time since she had opened her eyes in this room and found herself lost. She tilted her head back, drinking in the varied flavors of his mouth like a sparrow drinking rainwater that gently fell from the heavens.

Something soared within her. Kristina felt reborn. Or perhaps born for the first time.

This was the first time he had kissed her. She would have

known if it wasn't. She would have remembered if this had happened to her before. Amnesia or not, she would have known somehow. Something this mind-numbing wasn't erased by a blow to the head.

Only a blow to the heart.

Her hands tightened around his neck as her body pressed against his, taking comfort from the heat that surged between them. She could easily have given herself up to this sensation rushing through her, claiming her, without another thought or even a whisper of hesitation.

The protest that escaped her lips turned into a moan when Max gently removed her hands from around his neck and pushed her away from him.

Dazed, confused, she looked up at him for an explanation.

Max held her hands in his to keep them still. To keep them from touching him again. He was trying to do the right thing, but he knew his limits. If she touched him again, if she feathered her fingers along his neck, he knew that the noble fight he was waging would be lost.

"I think we'd better stop right now."

Bereavement pierced her, as sharp as any arrow. Kristina came to the only conclusion she could. She'd made a mistake. An awful mistake. "Max, is there someone else?"

Yes, he thought, there was. There was someone else. But the someone else was her. The other her, the one whose memory was gone. He had no doubts that it was only a temporary condition. Someday, probably very soon, it would return. Until it did, he couldn't allow himself to take advantage of the woman she was now. It wouldn't be fair to either of them. Especially her.

If this savage sweetness that licked over his body made him ache, well, that was the price he had to pay for the deception he was pulling off. He might be doing something underhanded, but he was doing it for the right reasons. There were no right reasons for allowing something to flower between them.

He didn't answer her question. Instead, he released her hands and backed away. "Get some sleep, Kris."

And then he let himself out, leaving her to look at the closed door and wonder.

And feel even more lost.

Sydney regarded Kristina warily. This morning, Kristina had come down herself, looking for her. There was a spark in her eyes today that hadn't been there yesterday. She looked vibrant, ready to take anything on. This wasn't the timid, awkward woman Max had foisted on her in the dining room. There was a confidence to her. Had her memory returned during the night?

But if it had, Kristina would be issuing orders or, like as not, looking for vengeance. She wouldn't look as if she were eager to get started cleaning rooms.

"Ready for another day?" Sydney asked her cautiously.

"Yes." Kristina fairly announced the word. If she had felt lost yesterday, today she felt like a pathfinder, determined to forge a new road for herself.

Kissing Max had made all the difference in the world. There might not have been anything between them before, but there would be. She couldn't explain it, it was just a feeling she had.

Something was up. There had to be a reason for this change. Sydney cocked her head and peered at Kristina's face. "You okay?"

"I'm great."

Taking the apron Sydney offered her, Kristina tied the strings around her waist. God, but she felt good. Happy, she realized. She wondered if it was a new experience for her. It certainly felt like it was.

Sydney was still staring at her. "And I'm sorry about yesterday," she said. Arming herself with window cleaner and paper towels from the utility closet, she was ready to roll. "I think I was just overwhelmed by everything. I didn't mean to make more work for you than you already had." There was no way to describe the feeling dancing through her. She felt ready to tackle the world. "Just point me in the right direction, and I'll see if I can do better."

If Kristina was willing to make an honest effort, the least she could do was meet her halfway. Sydney put aside the hard feelings she'd been harboring. They had to do with the rich snob who had swooped down on the inn, not this woman next to her.

"All right. You can get started on room 5 this morning. June wants it ready by eleven. The Hennesseys are arriving around then. They're coming in with their daughter, Heather." Sydney sighed, getting her own cleaning tools together.

"You don't sound like you're looking forward to their arrival."

"I'm not." Sydney tried not to dwell on the last time the Hennesseys had been here. Sticky handprints all over the wallpaper. This time, June was booking them into a room where the walls were painted, not papered. "The little girl is five and runs completely wild. They refuse to discipline her. As for them, they're snobs like—the rich tend to be," she amended at the last minute. She'd almost slipped and compared the Hennesseys to Kristina.

Kristina took no note of the hesitation. "Maybe they've changed," she suggested hopefully.

"Maybe, but I wouldn't place any bets on it."

To her relief, Kristina found her second day progressing far better than her first. She got through cleaning the rooms quickly, and this time there was no figurine to sweep away, no breakage of any kind. And she only vacuumed what she was supposed to. Kristina felt rather pleased with herself.

As did Sydney. Letting her guard down, Sydney discovered that Kristina was very easy to talk to. As they worked side by side, Sydney slowly opened up to her. It felt good to talk to another woman close to her own age. She even confided to her about her crush on Antonio. Kristina listened and made sympathetic noises. And thought of Max.

* * *

The afternoon found her in the kitchen. The dishwasher had died that morning, just before breakfast was served. Unable to repair it with what he had on hand, Antonio had gone into town to buy new parts. Without the machine, Sam was left with a mountain of pots and pans, as well as dishes from two meals. Kristina volunteered to wash them, forever ingratiating herself to Sydney, who had narrowly avoided being drafted for the job.

Both she and Sam were surprised that Kristina didn't mind being up to her elbows in greasy suds.

"Sam?"

"Hmm?" Cocking his head in her direction, he didn't bother looking up from the pot he was hovering over as closely as the steam that floated above it.

She wasn't sure just how to phrase this. "Do you know if Max is, um, taken?"

Sam spared her a quick look. "You mean, is he married? No."

There was a lull in the conversation as she wrestled with a large broiler pan and Sam debated between two ingredients in his spice rack. He finally selected one and added just a pinch to the pot.

Kristina tried again. "Is there someone special in his life?"

Sam laughed to himself as he thought of the string of women he had seen pass through the inn's doors. And Max's own. He had no doubt that that was just the tip of the iceberg. After all, Max spent most of his time in his apartment in Newport Beach.

"So many 'special' someones that I think we have all lost count." Sam turned to look at her, the long aluminum ladle suspended above the pot. "He likes relationships short and sweet, like a good meal that does not repeat on you." For Sam, everything always boiled down to food.

It wasn't what she had wanted to hear. With a sigh, she

turned the water on high, rinsing off the saucepan she was scouring. "Oh."

Her response was almost lost in the surrounding noise, but he had heard it. And more. Sam softened. "Why? Are you smitten with him?"

The word didn't mean anything to her. It sounded insignificant, somehow. "Smitten?"

He didn't know if she was playing coy or not. In either case, he had no patience. "Do you like him?" he asked.

Kristina had a feeling that Sam was the type who brooked no evasion. You either trusted him or not, and she needed someone to trust. "I think I do. When he kissed me—"

The tufted brows rose halfway up on his head. This was Kristina, after all. The one Antonio had referred to as the dragon lady. The one they had all found so easy to dislike. "He kissed you?"

Maybe she'd better start at the beginning. Sam wouldn't appreciate being misled. "Actually, I kissed him first, just to thank him, and then—" her grin was wide as she flushed "— well..."

Sam nodded. "Yes, 'well.'"

So, Max was taken with her. And she with him. This had all the signs of becoming very interesting. Sam paused for a moment, knowing his loyalty lay with Max. But this wasn't really Kristina Fortune right now. He found himself liking this woman who had emerged. Maybe a word or two of caution wasn't entirely out of place.

"Max is a good man, but he has itchy feet. I think it is because there were no stable relationships for him as a boy." That sounded too philosophical for his basically simple taste. His meals were elaborate but, as he often said, he had the soul of a peasant. "Or maybe he just feels that there are so many beautiful women, so little time."

That *really* wasn't what she wanted to hear. Kris began to furiously scour the large pot. "I see."

Sam returned to his creation, wondering if she actually did.

Kristina and Sydney stood beside the reception desk as June welcomed the couple who had arrived at eleven right on the dot. The much-anticipated and dreaded Heather was between them.

One look told Kristina that the word *precocious* had probably been coined with the little redheaded girl in mind. Her mother was holding her tightly by the hand, and neither of them looked very happy about the union.

Heather's eyes bounced about the room in anticipation. An accident waiting to happen, Kristina suddenly thought. The next moment, though it seemed physically impossible, Heather managed to knock over the lamp on the end table as she passed it.

The smile on June's face never changed as the lamp crashed to the wooden floor. "That's all right, we'll clean it up."

"Of course you will," Mrs. Hennessey retorted crisply. "I don't want Heather hurting herself."

It annoyed Kristina that neither parent had the decency to apologize for the child or to scold her.

"Sydney," June said, "could you show the Hennesseys to their room, please?" She took out a key from one of the cubbyholes and placed it on the counter. "You'll be staying in room 5."

Elaine Hennessey looked at the key as if it were tainted. "I thought we were going to stay in the one we had before. Room 4. I specifically asked—"

"It's being renovated," Kristina quickly explained, before June could offer an excuse.

Her expression never changed, but there was a grateful look in June's eyes.

Heather tugged her hand free from her mother's as her parents began to follow Sydney to their room. "No, I want to see the ocean now."

Mrs. Hennessey sighed, clearly worn out. "Later, dear," she said between clenched teeth.

Heather stamped her foot, her eyes narrowing. "Now. You said I could. You said I could as soon as we got here. You did," she insisted.

At a loss, the woman tried to reclaim her daughter's hand. "Yes, but now I'm saying later."

Heather raised her hands over her head, dancing out of reach.

"Heather," Mr. Hennessey warned, "behave."

This had all the makings of a scene. Kristina stepped forward, between mother and child. "Mrs. Hennessey, I'd be glad to take Heather for a walk on the beach while you and your husband settle in."

Suspicious, the little girl looked at Kristina uncertainly. She wasn't the only one. June and Sydney exchanged glances, surprised by the offer.

Mrs. Hennessey didn't hesitate. Her dour expression, softened by relief, lessened considerably. "That would be wonderful."

Kristina bent down to the little girl's level. There was something in her antagonistic attitude that struck a distant chord within her. Instinctively she understood that Heather felt the only way she would get attention was to make noise.

"Heather, my name is Kris. I'd be happy to take you for a walk along the beach, if you'd like."

Heather appeared to weigh her options. The ocean won. She placed her hand in Kristina's.

Though she couldn't have put into words why, Kristina felt a deep sense of satisfaction. They walked toward the front door. "We'll be back in about an hour," she promised Mrs. Hennessey.

For the first time since they'd entered, Mr. Hennessey appeared to relax. "Thank you." He looked at his wife. The glance they exchanged was not hard to read.

Kristina smiled as she left. "Maybe two."

"Well, would you look at that?" June murmured to herself as Sydney took the Hennesseys to their room. "There actually is a real heart in there after all."

"She's outside, in the back," June told Max as he walked in that night.

He groaned. "That bad?"

"No," she answered cheerfully. "That good."

He was in no mood for riddles. "Come again?"

"Go see for yourself." The urge was accompanied by a broad wink.

He didn't have time for this, Max thought. He'd done some real figuring last night. In order to keep everyone at the inn, the place was going to have to start showing a larger profit margin than it was. Otherwise, he couldn't afford to keep on paying the staff's salaries.

It didn't make him happy.

Bracing himself for anything, Max went outside and circled to the back of the building.

He heard Kristina before he saw her. She was reading something aloud about a miller's daughter and her talent for spinning straw into gold. Now there was a woman who'd come in handy, he thought.

Max found Kristina sitting beneath the coral tree, her long legs tucked under her comfortably. There was a large book spread out on her lap and a little girl of about five lying on her stomach, captivated, beside her. Charmed by the picture they made, he stopped and listened for a moment.

She was doing different voices, he realized, and throwing herself into the story as if it were a classic rendition of Shakespeare, instead of a fairy tale.

She sensed him. Even with her back to him, with Heather looking up at her with rapt attention, Kristina sensed Max's presence. It was the way her skin tingled, and the happy glow that took over her countenance.

Pausing, she looked over toward him. "Hi."

Heather shot the intruder a look, annoyed that the story was being interrupted.

"Hi." Because she made it look so inviting, Max sat down on the grass beside Kristina. "What are you doing?"

"She's reading me a fairy tale," Heather said importantly.

Kristina held up the book for his inspection, turning it so that he could see the cover. "This is Heather." She nodded at the girl. "And this—" she nodded down at the open book "—is 'Rumpelstiltskin.'"

She said it as if she were familiar with the story. Maybe some things were coming back to her. "I don't know that one."

They were almost finished. She could read another. "Which ones do you know? This book seems to have them all."

After their walk, Heather had run into her parents' room and emerged a few minutes later with the book under her arm and a request on her lips: "Read."

Max looked off at the horizon. The sun was beginning to dip low in the sky. They had a few minutes of daylight left at best, he judged. It was getting chilly again. "None."

Kristina cocked her head. "No one ever read you fairy tales?"

She made it sound so sad, he thought. It wasn't one of the things he particularly felt was missing from his life. The love of a family, Christmas morning as a little boy, those were the things he regretted not having. Not fairy tales.

"No."

There had been a definite sense of familiarity when she began reading to Heather. Someone had taken the time to read aloud to her. She knew it, she just didn't know who. That no one had read to him saddened her more than she could have put into words.

"Why don't you stay here, and I'll read one to both of you?" Not waiting for an answer, Kristina began to read.

It was a preposterous suggestion. But her voice was lyrical, and she did make the words come alive. And he was tired, he told himself.

What would it hurt, to linger just a little while?

So he did.

Nine

"What's all this?" June moved out of the way as Max deposited a large carton on her desk. She slid her ledger to one side, a moment before a second carton joined the first.

"We're entering the computer age." Max tossed the words over his shoulder as he walked back to his car to get the box that contained the keyboard.

"I thought you didn't think we needed one." June shook her head as she regarded the unopened boxes before her. Even their size was intimidating.

"I thought wrong," he said, returning.

Balancing the last box on top of the others, Max took out his Swiss Army knife. It had been his first gift from John Murphy, and it was his most prized one. Before then, no one had ever given him anything.

"What's going on?" Sydney asked coming into the front room.

"Max is kicking us into the twenty-first century." It was obvious from her expression that June had her doubts about the journey being a pleasant one.

Sydney watched as Max opened the cartons. She had just assumed that they would hold out indefinitely. They'd done fine up until now, and there didn't seem to be a need for a change. It wasn't as if business had tripled at the inn. "Not that I'm against progress, but why?"

Max glanced at Kristina as she joined the group. It had been her idea, actually. Something she said to him in passing had made him think that maybe he had been resisting change for all the wrong reasons. He owed it to his foster parents to do the best he could with what they had given him. The inn represented years of their hard work.

"I just thought it was time, that's all." He took hold of the monitor by its sides and attempted to lift it out of the box. It didn't budge. Kristina grabbed the carton to keep it steady as Max pulled. He nodded his thanks. "With this, we can keep track of our guests."

June laughed softly under her breath as Max placed the monitor on the counter. "Right now, I can keep track of them on my fingers. With one hand tied behind my back."

Drawn by the sound of their voices, Antonio and Sam came out into the front room. Sam stared at the computer as the disk drive and keyboard joined the monitor on the desk. His tufted brows drew together in a wiggly gray line.

"What is all this?" he wanted to know.

"Max just spent our raises on a computer," June told him.

"We are getting a computer?" Sam grumbled.

"We were getting raises?" This was news to Antonio.

Max frowned over the cables. They reminded him of gray snakes. Which went into what port?

"No, I didn't spend your money on a computer, and yes, maybe you'll have raises. Once business picks up," he added carefully. There was no point in letting them think otherwise.

The communal groan told him that no one had much faith in that happening anytime soon. No one, he noted, but Kristina, who hadn't uttered a sound. In the past two weeks, she had come along far better than he could have ever hoped possible. Between June and Sydney, he had full progress reports each evening. Kristina was becoming involved in every facet at the inn, absorbing everything thrown her way, like an insatiable sponge, and slowly adding a piece of herself to the formula.

He found himself looking forward to returning each evening. To seeing her, even though he knew he was on dangerous ground.

Max looked at the plastic-wrapped instruction booklets nestled in the bottom of the main carton and handed them over to June.

She frowned. "What am I supposed to do with them?"

"Read. Learn," Max told her encouragingly.

"I'll help you," Kristina volunteered, moving next to the older woman. Slitting the plastic, she took out the manual and flipped through it with the ease of someone who knew her way around the pages. "The computer will be a great help," she enthused. "It might help us get more bookings. There's a program that can track the different tastes, preferences, age groups, of our clients. Things like that."

Kristina blinked as she suddenly realized what she was saying. "And I have no idea how I know that." The words left her mouth slowly as she searched vainly for their origin.

"You told me that you'd taken some adult-education courses on computers before you came here." Max supplied, exchanging glances with the others. "They must have mentioned the program."

In the past two weeks, as Kristina embedded herself more and more in the daily life of the inn, he'd managed to field every one of her questions with an explanation that satisfied her. He wondered how much longer his luck could hold out.

"Must have." There was no other explanation. Politely she elbowed him out of the way and took the cable from his hand. He was attempting to push it into the wrong port.

With an expertise that surprised her even as it pleased her, Kristina attached the different components of the computer. She had it up and running within a matter of minutes.

"Maybe you'd better handle it," June suggested, eyeing the computer doubtfully. "I'm too old for this kind of stuff."

"Never too old," Kristina told her coaxingly. "It's easy. I'll show you."

"Can you show me?" Antonio asked. Stretching out his

fingers, he tapped a few words on the keyboard. "There's not much call for computers when you're fixing a stopped-up drain, but I always wanted to try my hand at those games."

"After she teaches June," Max told him pointedly.

This transition was going to take time, he thought, seeing the dubious expression on June's face. But he had faith that Kristina would live up to her word. She took on each task with an enthusiasm that was infectious. And it certainly beat having to make June take classes.

He turned toward June. "So how do the bookings for this month look?"

June was relieved to turn the conversation away from the computer.

"Right now, we've got twelve reservations Valentine's Day weekend." That was the good news. "But so far, the rest of the month isn't shaping up nearly as well." June glanced at the computer as if it were the enemy. She stroked the ledger's leather cover as she continued. "It pains me to say this, but we're going to have to do something, Max. I don't know what, but something." She looked at the others, and they all nodded their heads in agreement. "The inn can't continue, if this is the best it does."

Max sighed, frustrated. June was putting into words the same thought he had been wrestling with ever since Kristina arrived with her list of changes. Whatever else he might think of her, she had made him think.

Kristina piled the instruction manuals beside the computer. "What'll happen if it does continue this way?" Even as she asked the question, she had a sinking feeling she knew the answer.

Max hooked his thumbs in his pockets. "We'll have to close our doors." He had his own business, and it was fairly booming. Closing the inn would mean the end of a lot of headaches.

But it would mean other things to him, as well. The end of an era. And he didn't want to see it happen.

Kristina looked around the room, with its vaulted ceiling and its wooden beams. There was much to be said for the rustic flavor.

"That would be terrible, to lose a beautiful place like this." And then another thought struck her as she looked at the rest of the staff. "If the inn closed, where would we all go?"

Sydney shrugged. It seemed silly to get so attached to a place at her age. This was the time of her life when she should be traveling, exploring, finding herself. But all she could think of was what it would feel like to get up each morning and not see the ocean fifty feet from her window.

"To other jobs, I suppose." The very thought made her sad.

June shook her head. "Not me." She sighed dejectedly as she thought of the possibility. "Who would hire a woman my age?"

Jimmy had entered unnoticed during the beginning of the debate and sat down on one of the wicker chairs. He coughed, drawing attention to himself. "You're a spring chicken compared to me."

Kristina looked from one face to another. For all she knew, this might be the only family she had. She didn't want to think about it being broken up and scattered. "Max, you have to do something. This just can't happen," she insisted.

Kristina was uttering the very sentiments he had hoped she'd acquire. So why did he still feel as if he'd done something wrong?

He shook off the thought. "My sentiments exactly." He turned his attention to the others. "We're going to have to look into revamping the inn, find a way of competing with what's out there."

Again, a disembodied voice that had its source in a world she wasn't privy to seemed to whisper in her ear.

"No," Kristina said slowly, her mind racing, forming thoughts that didn't seem to be her own. "Wouldn't you have to do something different than what's out there?'' As she spoke, her excitement increased. "Different, yet appealing to a large group of people?''

Sounded good. June nodded at Max. "What's the largest group of people out there?''

Antonio shrugged.

"Baby boomers?'' Sam suggested.

"Good answer,'' Kristina said suddenly, "but not on target.'' Where were these words coming from? Why did they feel so comfortable on her tongue? She was going to have to think about that later. "Even bigger than that,'' she said to Max. Didn't he see? This was perfect. "Newlyweds, or people trying to recapture that magic they felt when they were first married.''

"You know—'' Sam looked at Max "—you might have something there.''

"Yes, but what?'' Jimmy asked. He liked everything clearly spelled out before he voted for or against it.

"We'll work on it,'' Max said.

He thought of the papers Sydney had taken out of Kristina's suitcase that first night. The papers with Kristina's plans for the inn. He was going to have to give them more than a cursory look.

"In the meantime—'' June's voice brought him back to the present "—we need to get some decorations for the upcoming weekend.'' Now that the subject had been broached, she wanted to give the inn a definite shot in the arm. "Maybe something that'll make these people want to come back more than just once a year.''

They celebrated Valentine's Day at the inn every year. He'd kissed his first girl here on Valentine's Day, under the staircase. He remembered that there had been a bold drawing of a cupid on the wall opposite them. He hadn't been around last year, but he assumed that decorations had been put up, as they had been each year. "Don't we have decorations?''

June and Sydney exchanged disparaging looks. "Yes, we

have decorations," June agreed. "If you count tired-looking hearts and sagging cupids who are just about ready to collect social security checks."

Kristina was vaguely aware of what they were saying. She was studying the area, envisioning the walls decorated with pink and white streamers, balloons and vases of fresh-cut flowers in the right colors, strategically placed. There were such possibilities.

She turned on her heel, accidentally brushing up against Max. A jolt of electricity passed between them, singeing them both. For a moment, she forgot about the others. She could see from the look on Max's face that he was feeling the same thing.

Excitement wove its way through her.

"Why don't I go into town and see what I can find?" she suggested haltingly, trying to focus on the ideas she had just thought of for the inn.

"How?" Max asked, drawing back. He could still feel her body curving into his despite the space between them. "You don't have a car, and you don't drive."

She shrugged, nonplussed. "Could you take me?"

The smart thing would have been to say no. Or to hand her over to Antonio. Being alone with Kristina wouldn't be the wisest move he'd ever made, not when he wanted it so much.

Yet he couldn't quite get himself to just hand her over to someone else, either. So he stood like a fool, not saying anything.

June shook her head. Plain as the nose on his face, and he couldn't see it. "Go, Max. We haven't got that much time." She shot the others a look, warning them not to contradict her as she added, "And we're all going to be busy here."

Antonio had never been quick on the uptake. "We are?"

Sydney threaded her arm through his. "Yes," she insisted pointedly. "We are."

Slowly, Jimmy rose. Kristina could almost hear the

creaks as he set his body in motion, heading toward the front door. "Well, I've wasted enough time, listening to all of you. I've got the garden to spruce up."

Sam was already leaving the room. "And there's a new menu to plan. One that will have them begging for more." He said the words with obvious relish.

"What about you and Sydney?" Max suggested. It was his only attempt to save himself.

"Hey, we're going to be busy. Sydney and I are going to be locking horns with this new monstrosity you brought in." June nodded at the computer. She pursed her lips, frowning, as she shook her head in disbelief. "Imagine, having to learn something at my age."

Max surrendered to the inevitable and went to get his Jeep.

Max brought his vehicle to a stop in the strip mall's parking lot and turned to look at Kristina. He still didn't completely know how he'd gotten here. Shopping was something he viewed as an ordeal. He only shopped for clothes if his old ones were on the verge of disintegration.

"All right, this is your idea. Where do you suggest we get started?"

She'd probably come here dozens of times, Kristina thought. Yet nothing looked familiar to her. Slowly she scanned the area, hoping to see something that would give her a clue, an inkling. She would hate to think she had dragged Max here for nothing.

"There." She pointed to a quaint party-and-gift store that was housed between a pizza parlor and a shop that carried bathroom furnishings. A triumphant grin curved her lips. "It's a start."

Yes, it certainly was, he mused. It took him a long moment to stop looking at her mouth and remember why they were there in the first place.

Once she was "started," Max learned, it was very hard to stop Kristina. Her memory might be gone, but there was nothing to get in the way of her instincts. They had remained unaffected. She picked and chose with an unerring eye.

The list of things they "needed" grew with each store she dragged him to. As did the paraphernalia he wound up carrying to the Jeep. The only way to stop her was to plead exhaustion, which he did around one.

"Aren't you tired?" he demanded incredulously as he dumped the latest load of things into the back seat of the car. A back seat that was getting very crammed. If he never saw the inside of another store, it would be too soon. He might enjoy building malls, but walking through them was another matter entirely.

It was a beautiful day, and Kris felt wonderful. Because she was spending it with him. "No, I'm just getting my second wind."

He raised a hand up in defense. "Don't. Your first one is costing me a fortune." Damn, he'd slipped. Max cast a sidelong glance to see if the sound of her name had stirred something.

But it didn't appear to have. "It takes money to make money." As soon as she uttered the phrase, Kristina looked at Max, dumbfounded. "I feel like I'm this hollow dummy and there's this ventriloquist hiding in the wings somewhere, putting words into my mouth. I have no idea that they're coming until they're out."

That would be the old Kristina trying to emerge, he thought. Certain things she'd said in the past couple of weeks, certain suggestions she'd made, were rooted in the way she'd looked at things before she got amnesia. He knew it was just a matter of time before the rest of her emerged.

"Is that why you kissed me the other night? Because a ventriloquist told you to?" The words were teasing, but he really wanted to know if something had prompted her behavior, or if it was the new Kristina who had touched her lips to his.

She wondered if she had ever known how to be coy. She certainly didn't now. All she had at her disposal was honesty.

"No, I told me to. Because I wanted to," she added. She was going out on a limb here. "Something tells me that I go after what I want."

This was the part where he should say something gallant and retreat. He should have, but he didn't. Not when he wanted an answer. "And what is it you want?"

She ran her tongue over her upper lip. She hadn't a clue what that did to the pit of his stomach, he thought. "Lunch," she answered, her eyes teasing his.

He laughed. Lunch it was. There was a fairly decent restaurant just on the next block. Max took her arm, careful to direct her away from any more stores.

"I suppose I'll have to pay for that, too," he said in a long-suffering voice.

He wasn't fooling her with his complaints. Max was having just as good a time as she was. She sensed it. Funny how she could know things about him, when she didn't know anything about herself.

"Fringe benefits," she said flippantly.

They reached the Wayward Pelican. Max held the door open for her. "I thought it was 'fringe' enough when I didn't make you pay for the glasses and the drapes."

Kristina looked around as they entered. Beyond the reservation desk was a large communal room with small tables scattered about. Two walls were glass from floor to ceiling, looking out on the harbor. The view wasn't nearly as nice as the one in the inn's dining room, she thought with a touch of pride.

"Two," Max told the receptionist.

"The drapes didn't have to be replaced, just mended," she reminded him as a young woman in a floor-length black skirt showed them to a table. "You said that was part of my learning curve."

Max helped Kristina with her chair, then sat down opposite her. Long, dark green menus with gold lettering lay on the table between them. "Yes, but that was when I didn't know you wanted to single-handedly restore La Jolla's economy."

She perused the menu, comparing it to Sam's. The entrées had fancier names. "We didn't buy that much."

He begged to differ. "One hundred red scented candles, new linens for sixteen rooms, towels with hearts on them and enough decorations to paper the walls of the White House comes under the heading of 'Much.'"

He didn't bother opening the menu. He'd been here several times before, and he knew what he wanted. Besides her, he thought ruefully.

Kristina set her menu aside. "We don't have that many decorations, and I think the lacy linens add to the romantic ambience we're trying to promote."

It was midday, but there was a candle in the center of each table. He watched as the light flickered, casting a warm glow to her face. Maybe she was right about the candles.

A smart man would have tried to distance himself from the thoughts he was having, and from her. Maybe he wasn't as smart as he gave himself credit for. "Right now, most of the people who book the inn are closer to retirement than romance."

Folding her hands before her, she leaned her chin on her laced fingers. "The two are not mutually exclusive, Max."

He could have sworn he smelled the shampoo she'd used in her hair. Something herbal. His pulse quickened, as if he were some adolescent on his first date. "And what makes you such an expert?"

"I don't know." She should be feeling self-conscious right now, she thought. But she wasn't. Instead, her confidence seemed to grow with each word.

"Maybe it's when I think of the way you held me that night." She grinned when she saw him shift in his seat. "You've been avoiding me, you know."

"No, I haven't." But he was avoiding her now. Or at least her eyes. And not doing a very good job of it, either. "I've seen you almost every night."

"Not alone."

The words skimmed along his mind, soft, seductive. God, this woman was lethal, and she didn't even know it. "No," he admitted. "Not alone."

Now or never. With elaborate movements, she spread her dark green linen napkin on her lap, then raised her eyes to his. "You never answered my question when I asked you. Is there someone else?"

He could lie and bring an end to this. But something within him resisted. "No, there isn't." No one he could actually tell her about, at any rate.

That didn't change the fact that he felt guilty about leading her on when she wasn't really herself, wasn't really in her right mind.

Kristina took a long sip of water, her throat suddenly dry. Her pulse was hammering. Maybe she was nervous after all.

"You know, Sam told me that the women in your life could populate a small state." She hesitated a second before continuing. She might go after what she wanted, but this felt awkward for her somehow. "I've never seen you with one."

"It's only been two weeks," he pointed out. "And I've been busy. Right now, I'm between relationships." He broke the roll on his plate, offering her half.

She nodded her thanks. The smile on her lips told him that she didn't believe him.

She was one hell of a woman, he thought. "I would ask you if you're always this straightforward, but you wouldn't know, would you?"

"No, I wouldn't." Somewhere along the line, in the past week, she had stopped trying so hard to piece her life together. It occurred to her that she felt as if she were newly liberated somehow, free of restraints and shackles, but that those restraints were waiting for her just beyond, in the shadows. Remembering would make them reappear that much more quickly. So she tabled remembering. "But that doesn't really bother me anymore."

He cocked his head. "Why?"

It was simple, really. "Because you told me that there's no one in my life, except for a painful incident that I guess is better left where it is, in the dark." If she was divorced, then that relationship was over. Why drag it up again? Why drag up the pain that had probably been involved? It served no purpose. "I'd rather concentrate on what's here and now." Her eyes held his as she popped a piece of a roll into her mouth. "And ahead of me."

Wow, was he in trouble! And without the sense to turn tail and run.

"Ready to order?" the waitress asked as she approached their table.

Kristina glanced at Max before saying, "More than ready."

"Sam will be happy to know that nothing in town offers competition," Max said to her when they left the restaurant an hour later.

Kristina nodded. Sam was as chauvinistic about his cuisine as Jimmy was about his garden. She'd grown very fond of both of them.

Because it was chilly, she linked her arm through Max's. Guilelessly she moved her body closer to his as they walked. "It would be a shame if you had to sell the inn."

Max wondered if she knew what she was doing to him. Could she be as innocent as she seemed? "Who says I'm selling the inn?"

"Well, if you can't make it turn a profit, you said there was no alternative."

He'd already made up his mind about that. The computer was just the first step.

"We can make it turn a profit." He stopped by his Jeep

and looked at her. He'd been hasty in dismissing her suggestions before, but only because she had rubbed him the wrong way. "I've been thinking about what you said earlier, about making the inn into a Honeymoon Hideaway."

She tried to remember. "I said that?"

"Well, not in so many words." He upbraided himself for the slip. Because she'd become so easy to talk to, he'd gotten the woman she'd been confused with the woman she was. "But you implied it when you said the largest group we had to deal with were newlyweds." It was a nice save, he thought.

"Oh, right." Interested, eager, she urged him on. "So, what are you saying?"

He tried to remember what it was she had said. He'd been so busy resisting, he hadn't been paying attention. "Maybe we can do a little renovation, update the rooms. Put in more bathrooms. I can do the job myself." Very carefully, he studied her face, waiting for some sign of recollection.

But she only listened and nodded. "Sounds good to me."

It should. You said it, he thought.

For a moment, they just stood there. He watched the way the wind played with the ends of her hair. It reminded him of when they'd been on the beach that first night. That seemed like light-years away.

Did some amnesia victims remain that way permanently? He knew it was a terrible thing to wish for, but he couldn't help himself. He'd never been drawn to another woman like this, never felt this attracted before. Or this damn confused.

"Kris?"

She turned her face up to his. "Hmm?"

He almost kissed her then, but stopped himself at the last minute. He just wanted to enjoy her company, nothing more. Or so he silently insisted. "I don't want to go back just yet."

He'd almost kissed her. The thought warmed her. Her

grin was wide. Inviting. "Me neither." She thought of the inn. They'd been gone a long time. "But won't the others miss us?"

He laughed to himself. "Right now, the staff outnumbers the occupied rooms by one. I think they can handle it for a little while longer."

Who was she to argue with the boss? "What do you suggest we do?"

There was a multiplex theater not too far from here. He should know. He'd helped build it. It represented the first bid he'd ever won.

The idea of sitting in the dark with her for a couple of hours appealed to him. "How does a movie sound to you?"

"Wonderful." She would have agreed to just about anything, she realized, as long as they did it together.

It had been a while since he took in a movie. He had no idea what was currently playing. "What do you want to see?"

She drew another blank, but this one, at least, was far from painful. "I don't know—surprise me."

He did.

And surprised himself, as well. His preferences leaned toward action movies that were long on entertainment and short on plot, or buddy movies with witty dialogue said at improbable times.

He took her to see a love story. And found himself enjoying it.

Afterward, he treated her to an ice-cream cone. She chose vanilla fudge, after making him wait while she read all the flavors. He picked pistachio. And then they walked arm in arm through the streets, as evening wrapped itself around them.

The stars had obligingly come out. Looking up at the array, Kristina wondered if she had ever felt this happy before.

"That was pretty terrific," she commented, thoughtfully taking a bite out of her cone. "The way he gave up everything for her. Could you do that?'' she asked suddenly. She looked at him. "Could you give up everything for the person you loved?''

The thought had never occurred to him. It did now. "I don't know. Could you?''

She grinned, twirling the cone as she licked a complete circle around it. "Right now, I've got nothing to give up, so I guess the answer is an unqualified yes.''

"And if you had more?''

In a heartbeat, she thought. "Depends on how much I loved that person, I suppose.'' They were getting too close to something too fast. She was doing all the talking, not him. "How about you?''

"I've never been in love that way, so I don't know.'' But he could be. With the right woman, he could be. "It's possible.''

Kristina began walking again. "I don't think you have to worry. I doubt any woman would ask you to give up a place as special as the inn for her.''

But you already have. "You think the inn is special?''

How could he ask? "Absolutely.'' Her life had begun the moment she opened her eyes in her room that night. She'd only been around the inn for two weeks, and she'd fallen in love with it almost from the start.

"There's this wonderful aura about it. Once I stopped destroying everything I touched and the others stopped thinking of me as a walking disaster area, I got this, oh, I don't know, comfortable feeling about the place.'' Her eyes seemed to sparkle as she talked, he thought. "I can't see why you would have even wanted to start a construction company. I'd have wanted to hang around the inn all the time if I'd been you.''

His reasons were simple. "I wanted something that was mine alone. Something I had built up on my own. The inn belonged to my foster parents at the time.''

Something he said nudged at a feeling she couldn't grasp. "I can understand that, too, I guess,'' she murmured slowly, exploring the feeling. Something warned her off. And then it was gone.

"I guess we'd better be getting back."

"Yes." Finished with the cone, Kristina tossed the napkin into a trash can on the corner. "I guess we should."

Her scent wafted to him, enticing, sensual. There was moonlight, a star-filled sky above, and a beautiful woman at his side. A man could only resist the inevitable so long.

Max couldn't help himself. He didn't even want to try. Very gently, he turned her toward him. Cupping her cheek in his hand, he lowered his mouth to hers.

And did what he'd been wanting to do for the past thirteen days.

Ten

As soon as his lips touched hers, Max felt it. The mini-Fourth of July celebration erupting inside of him. He could hardly catch his breath, he wanted her so badly.

Wishing time could somehow stand still, he allowed himself to linger just for one more moment. The kiss deepened, taking him with it. Luring him further. His mouth drew in the sweetness she offered him, absorbing it. Savoring it.

How could something that felt so right be so wrong?

And how could he have let this happen in the first place? When had the situation gotten so out of hand? He was supposed to be the director, in control of the scenario he'd plotted. He wasn't even supposed to be part of the scenery. And he certainly wasn't supposed to be one of the featured players.

Blood rushed in his ears, stirring his heart, awakening needs that had never been fully dormant since the first night on the beach when, amid the yelling and the tension that hummed between them, he had unconsciously recognized this for what it was. Attraction so strong, so powerful, it had threatened to undo him.

It still did.

No, she wasn't just deluding herself. Max felt the same way about her that she did about him. Kristina could taste it, she could feel it. It wasn't just wishful thinking on her part. It was real.

She knew it.

"Maybe we'd better continue this somewhere else," she murmured against his mouth.

If he wanted to take her to his room tonight, she'd come willingly. There was no reason to deny what she felt, what they both felt. It should be allowed to follow a natural progression. Whatever that might be, wherever that might lead.

Kristina knew she was ready for it. Her body heated as she waited for his answer.

Oh, God, why couldn't he have been given an easier challenge? Maybe spinning straw into gold, like in that damn story she'd read. Why this?

His body ached for her, rebelling against him. But if he took what she was offering, without telling her who she was, Kristina would only wind up hating him in the end. A night's pleasure wasn't worth that.

But the night was just ahead, and the future was still so far away...

Like a spring snapping into place, his resolve returned, saving him.

Depriving him.

"Some other time." It was one of the hardest things he'd ever had to say.

Feeling suddenly very foolish, Kristina moved stiffly away from him. She avoided his eyes as she got into the car. Had she misread the signs? Jumped to the wrong conclusion, because it was where she wanted to be?

She glanced at Max.

No, damn it, she hadn't misread the signs. She might not know much, at this murky point in her life, but she did know what she felt. And what he felt. At least about her.

He wanted her, she wanted him. They were both decent, consenting adults. What was the problem?

Silence hung in the car like a thick, heavy cloud, growing as the miles to the inn decreased. It engulfed them and left them feeling awkward with each other.

* * *

The road back looked different at night, softer. More romantic. Very slowly, Kristina forced the tension from her body, instinctively knowing that it could rule her if she allowed it to.

Maybe she had once allowed it to rule her. The feeling was vague and she couldn't pinpoint it. No matter—she wasn't going to spend the remainder of the trip back nursing hurt feelings.

"Max?"

He didn't look at her. It helped not to look at her. If he did, he'd only wind up backsliding, the way he urgently wanted to.

"Yes?"

His voice was distant, like a stranger's. But he wasn't a stranger. Not to her. The man who had kissed her didn't want to be a stranger. Kristina chose her words carefully, wanting to build a bridge between them, instead of blowing one up.

"I get the feeling that there's something you're not telling me."

Now that has got to win the prize for the understatement of the century. Oh, did I forget to tell you that you're really this rich snob who owns half the inn you're slaving in? Sorry about that. By the way, you also have a financial empire at your feet. It must have slipped my mind. You're leaving? I understand. Would you mind making up room 10 on your way out?

His hands tightened on the steering wheel as he slanted a look at her. "What gives you that idea?"

Maybe she was wrong. She saw no reason why he would keep something from her. But then, she really didn't know all that much, did she?

She knew all she needed to know.

Kristina lifted a shoulder and let it drop carelessly. "I don't know. Every time we get close—" She turned in her seat to look at his profile. She curled her hands in her lap to keep from touching him. "Every time you kiss me, it feels like you want to, well, continue." This wasn't coming out right, but he had to know what she meant. "And then you pull back."

It's for your own good. It sure as hell isn't for mine. Max flipped on the radio to fill the empty space between them. "Just your imagination."

Very deliberately, she turned down the sound, until it was just a whisper in the background. "I don't think so."

Time for some fancy footwork. *Remember the inn.* "I'm not holding anything back." He'd said that a little too emphatically, and he lightened his tone. "It's only natural for you to feel that way when everything around you feels so strange, so different. But I've told you everything I can."

Can. It was a very telling word, she thought.

No, he was right, she was just being paranoid.

With a sigh, she dragged her hand through her hair and let it fall around her shoulders. "All right, have it your way," she agreed softly.

Right now, he thought, it had to be his way. She'd have hers soon enough.

Arms loaded down with decorations, Kristina gave Max an accusing look as she managed to snare the sleeve of his work shirt. She'd decided to put yesterday and its awkwardness behind her. Today was a brand-new day. With brand-new opportunities.

She grinned at him. "Just because you're the boss, that doesn't mean that you're excluded from the work." She'd deliberately saved some of the decorations, waiting for him to return home. She wanted to do this together with him, to include Max in what she perceived as a ritual.

She'd cornered him just as he was about to enter his office. After returning from the construction site, he'd had ten minutes to himself in the empty dining room, during which time he'd wolfed down a steak sandwich. Now he had all but psyched himself up to face the mound of accounts stamped Overdue that were piled up on his desk.

"I have work," he pointed out. "A great deal of work." Even as he said it, he felt himself weakening. And only partially because he didn't want to face the paperwork demanding his attention. "I've got the construction company to run and a mountain of bills to juggle for both places.

"And," he pointed out, "if I want to start making some changes around here, I'm going to have to budget my time strictly."

He thought he'd gotten his point across. Kristina certainly listened patiently as he talked. He found out differently when he was finished and she handed him a stack of cardboard decorations. Smiling as if he hadn't said a word, she dragged him over to where she had set up a ladder in the front room.

"And what—" he held the decorations up "—am I supposed to do with these?"

"Follow me around, and hand them to me one at a time, so I can tape them up on the walls." She began to climb up the ladder.

A feeling of déjà vu washed over him with astounding speed. Max dropped the decorations, grabbing both sides of the ladder.

On his way to the storeroom, Antonio glanced in their direction. He grinned at Max as he passed, giving him the high sign. "Seems to me as if you've been given the plum job."

Max blew out a breath. He didn't have time for this. Didn't have time to stand, holding a ladder, looking up, when the greatest pair of legs he could ever recall seeing were almost at eye level in front of him. There were better things to do.

He couldn't think of one.

In what spare time he had available, Max had pored over Kristina's sketchy plans. Without sentiment blinding his common sense, he had started to see the merit in her suggestions. It didn't take a rocket scientist to see that their best weekend since the beginning of the year was going to be the one that fell right before Valentine's Day. They'd gotten three more bookings, and all because of the little bit of local advertising Kristina had managed.

Kristina had been on target with her idea to turn the inn into a Honeymoon Hideaway.

Right after this weekend was behind them, he was going to tally up exactly how much it would cost to add private baths to five of the rooms. Right now, they shared adjoining bathrooms. Even with his contractor's discount and doing most of the work himself, it still added up. But Kristina was right. It took money to make money, and he had some put aside for emergencies.

This came under the heading of an emergency.

He mused, his eyes skimming along the long line of her legs. She was wearing shorts. He could feel heat rising, curling within him like smoke.

"Why aren't you wearing jeans?" And why couldn't he say no to her? It was such a small word. Why wouldn't he fit his mouth around it? He'd certainly said it often enough in his life.

The answer was simple.

Because he didn't want to.

Kristina spared him a look over her shoulder, down the line of her body. She made no effort to hide her knowing grin. "Why aren't you looking somewhere else?"

Not that she wanted him to. She'd already made up her mind to use every weapon at her disposal to help Max overcome this nameless obstacle that stood like a roadblock between them.

He let out a breath, and with it some of the tension lodged in his body. "Maybe because the view's pretty terrific right here."

Her eyes danced as she resumed taping the cherub into place. "Then don't complain."

The way he saw it, either way, he was lost.

When she stretched to tape the plump cupid's head, she brought visions of the accident back to him. "You really think you should be up there? I mean, you fell off one ladder, I don't want to see anything happening to you again."

She liked that, she thought, having him worry about her. Kristina decided to play out the line a little farther.

"Haven't you ever heard about getting right back up on the ladder that threw you?" she asked teasingly.

She might be in the mood to kid around, but he wasn't. Enough was enough. "That's for horses. Get down off of that."

Something bristled within Kristina, making her think that perhaps she didn't like taking orders. But he *was* the boss. After a moment, she began to climb down.

Not waiting, Max put his hands around her waist and set her on the floor himself. He took the tape out of her hand.

"Here, give that to me. You hold the ladder."

The quick flash of temper that had surprised her was gone in a heartbeat. A smile unfurled on her lips. "Yes, sir."

She stood aside as he climbed up to take her place.

Finding herself in the same position he'd been in a few moments ago, with close to the same view, Kristina grinned. The man had a phenomenal butt.

"Nice lines," she commented.

Max turned to look down at her. He had no idea what she was talking about. "What lines?" Then he saw just where she was looking. "Oh."

She laughed. "Turnabout is fair play."

Max wondered if she'd say that once her memory returned.

"A full house," June announced to Max as Sydney took the couple who had just signed in to their room. Though the computer was quickly becoming integrated into the way they did things, guests were still required to sign the ledger. It was a tradition they had all agreed to maintain.

This last couple was number sixteen. She'd even had to turn a couple away when they called earlier. It felt good to see the inn filled to capacity again. She turned the book around and looked at it. The page was crowded with different signatures, all current.

"Feels good," she said to Max. "Like the old days."

But they weren't the old days, he thought with a vague nod. And they never would be again. They had to make way for the new days. And new ways.

"I'm going ahead with the changes," he told her. "I can't get started on them until March, but we can begin planning the advertising for the inn's new look."

"Advertising?" June echoed. He hadn't mentioned anything about that. She knew that Max was funding all this out of his own pocket, not the inn's reserves. The inn was fresh out of reserves.

He nodded. "Print up some new brochures, things like that."

Carrying the fresh towels and scented bath salts room 12 had requested, Kristina overheard and paused. Ideas seemed to pop up in her mind like popcorn kernels shooting up over a hot fire.

"Why stop there?" They turned to look at her. "Why not take out some ads in the newspaper? Maybe even one of the local magazines?"

It sounded good, but he had to be cost-conscious, and at the moment he didn't have the money that having Kristina Fortune as a partner would have given him. Talk about a catch-22 situation.

"You're talking about a lot of money."

"I think you'll get a lot of money once this is under way." She had the oddest feeling of déjà vu again. Had she said this before? Thought this before? Passing it off, she laughed. "God, listen to me, I sound like some big ad executive." That somehow sounded familiar, too. But why?

"No need to apologize," Max said quickly. He didn't want the conversation to start her thinking. "They all sound like great suggestions. It's just that they're all going to take time to implement."

"Ads just require picking up the telephone," she countered matter-of-factly. Again, she had the feeling that she was on automatic pilot, somehow. "Of course, you don't want to get started too soon. Maybe just a word here and there, until you get the inn into the shape you want. How soon do you think that'll be?"

Not nearly soon enough, unfortunately. "I've got everyone I can get working on phase two of the Woodbridge development." He considered. "About the only one I can spare is me."

She shifted the towels, temporarily forgetting her errand. "How about day labor?"

Kristina knew all about the sad-eyed men, unskilled laborers and men who couldn't find other work, who hung around one of the city parks. She'd seen them, going into town for supplies with Sam. They gathered near the play area, hoping contractors would drive by and hire them for the day or the week.

"There's that," he agreed thoughtfully, then looked at her, surprised. "How do you know about day labor?"

She'd passed his office the other day. The door hadn't been quite closed. Kristina had eavesdropped, hoping to hear him say something about her.

Kristina bit her lower lip. "I overheard you talking to someone named Paul on the phone a couple of days ago. You mentioned hiring them."

"Paul's my partner in the construction company." He had an uneasy feeling as he tried to remember if he'd said anything that might have tipped her off about the ruse. "What else did you overhear?"

She shrugged. She'd come away disappointed. "Nothing much. Why?" Her eyes looked up into his. God, but he had beautiful eyes. Eyes that seemed to reach in and touch her soul. "Afraid I'll hear you talk about something private?"

He could feel June looking at him. "My life's an open book," he said innocently. "Just curious, that's all."

She looked exceptionally pretty this evening. Suddenly, forgetting caution, he wanted to be alone with her in the moonlight. And if the moon wouldn't oblige, they'd make their own light.

"Why don't you knock off early, and we'll go for a walk on the beach?"

Kristina remembered the towels, and the Shoenbergs, who were waiting for them. "This is our busiest time. I can't knock off now."

It seemed that any way you scratched her, Kristina was a hard worker. "I know the boss." He winked. "I'll make him go easy on you."

The smile bloomed from her lips into his soul. Everything else—June, the flickering candles, the inn itself—faded away. "Will you?"

He hardly knew what he was saying as he crossed his heart. "Scout's honor."

God, but he wanted her. Wanted her not just in his arms, but in his bed. He had to be careful. One wrong move, and he would pay for it dearly. She was Kris now, but he reminded himself that Kristina would be the one who made him pay. Miserably.

Torn between a sense of responsibility and desire, she compromised. "Okay, right after dinner. I promised Sydney I'd help serve."

He didn't want to wait. "What about Antonio?"

"Shh." She drew closer to Max, looking around to see if Sydney was in the vicinity. "He's gone into town to get her a bouquet of roses."

He could smell her hair. Wildflowers. And something arousing. Damn, but he was acting like a teenager, anticipating his first time.

There wasn't going to be a first time with Kristina, he reminded himself.

"Why would Antonio have to go into town for roses?" He looked at the vases on the coffee table and the front desk. "We've got roses right here."

She shook her head. "Not the same thing." She grinned impishly. "Besides, Jimmy would kill him if he caught Antonio plucking any of his children."

Max looked at her, amazed. Kristina had certainly gotten enmeshed in the lives of everyone at the inn. Just as he'd wanted. With one major exception.

He hadn't wanted her to get enmeshed in his life. But she had. So deeply that he was going to miss her like hell when she finally returned to her senses. And her life. Daniel had told him that her amnesia might continue for a while, but he couldn't keep Kristina away from her family indefinitely. One of them was bound to call and ask to speak to her eventually. Then what?

He didn't want to think about that. Not when she was standing here next to him, fresher than spring rain, more tempting than a woman had a right to be.

Kristina hugged the towels to her. "I'll be back soon," she promised, hurrying up the stairs.

June could almost read his thoughts. She'd known Max, both man and boy, ever since John Murphy brought him home from the orphanage. She'd never seen him quite so enamored-looking. Apparently he'd set out to make Kristina over, and he'd succeeded. Too well.

"Ever read *Pygmalion?*"

He shook his head. Max understood her meaning. "No, but I've seen *My Fair Lady*. I like that better."

"Me too." Affection sprouted in her eyes. You just never knew, did you? "Happier ending."

Maybe in plays, but not this time. "Not from where I'm standing."

A ring-encrusted hand covered his. "You've got to have faith, Max."

It was going to take a hell of a lot more than faith to get him out of this one, he thought. There was no way this situation could be successfully resolved. He'd set out to change her mind, and he'd wound up changing his. In the meantime, he'd deceived her, and probably messed up something that might have been the best thing in his life.

"What I've got," Max confided, "is one colossal headache."

June firmly believed that things had a way of working themselves out for the best. Sometimes they just needed a little helping hand, and she'd gladly lend hers.

"Take two aspirin and go wait for her on the beach." She nodded toward the dining room. "I'll see to it that Sam closes the kitchen early tonight. These couples aren't here to eat, anyway."

Max didn't need any more convincing.

Max stood at the rear of the inn, enveloped in the sensual darkness that had wrapped itself around the earth. Impatience feathered through him as he waited. Trying to reason with himself wasn't working. He wasn't paying attention.

This was all wrong. He was only getting more deeply caught up with her each time he allowed himself to be alone with Kristina.

But he really couldn't help himself.

Somehow, all the paths he took, whether by accident or design, just seemed to lead him to her sooner or later.

He liked sooner better than later.

Kristina walked carefully down the stone steps leading down to the beach, balancing a steaming mug of coffee in each hand. June had told her where to find Max.

He was waiting for her, she thought. The realization warmed her far more than the mugs in her hand.

She came around to face him. "Here."

Almost in a trance, Max took the mug she was offering him. "What's this?"

"Coffee. Sam thought you might want something to warm you up. It's chilly tonight." She cupped her hands around her own mug as they began to walk down to the beach.

He'd had all the warming-up he needed, just thinking about her. "I hadn't noticed."

The tide had come in, eating away at the beach, bringing the water closer. Despite the cold, she had an irresistible urge to take her shoes off and let the waves lap at her toes.

He'd probably think she was crazy. Maybe she was, at that. Crazy not to wonder any more about the life she'd apparently lost.

Being here with him was enough.

"The inn was really busy tonight," she commented, taking another sip.

"That I did notice. I guess you were right." *About a hell of a lot of things I can't tell you about.* "Romance is a big attraction."

She let her eyes touch him before she turned her head again. "Oldest one in the world."

He watched as moonlight danced along her hair. He longed to bury his face in it. "Kris, what do you remember?"

Kristina thought about it for a moment. "Bits and pieces."

He tried not to sound too wary. "Bits and pieces of what?"

Kristina took a long sip. The coffee was cooling rapidly. Unlike her. She slanted a look at him.

"That's just it—I don't know." She searched for a way to make him understand. "It's like when you're working on a big jigsaw puzzle and you get this tiny piece that looks like it might be part of a nose or a foot or maybe something in between. You hold on to it, hoping that eventually it'll fit in somewhere, once the picture begins taking on some kind of shape.''

It didn't sound as if he had anything to worry about yet. She was still going to be Kris for a while longer. ''And so far, nothing has?''

''No.'' She finished the coffee. Absently she dangled the mug from her fingers as they continued to walk. ''I still don't feel that this is what I was meant to do, although I am getting better at it,'' she told him proudly. She was beginning to feel like an asset, finally. Especially since Max had taken her advice about the computer and let her select the decorations. ''No more breakage.''

''You're getting better at it than just not breaking things.'' It amazed him how quickly the others had rallied around her. You would have thought she had been part of the inn all along. ''Sam thinks you have the makings of a great cook, June says she'd be lost with that computer if it wasn't for you, and I hear Jimmy is actually allowing you back into the garden.''

She watched as one wave christened her shoes. ''Just to bring in the bags of fertilizer.''

It didn't seem to upset her. She was a rare woman. ''It's a start.''

A start. She'd made a great many of them these last few weeks, she thought with satisfaction. ''Did you ever find my résumé?''

The question caught him off guard. His expression gave nothing away. ''No. Why?''

She lifted a shoulder, then let it fall. The wind was picking up. She should have worn a warmer sweatshirt. ''I just wanted to see it. See if anything jarred a memory. It would be nice to have one,'' she said wistfully. ''A memory of something that's older than a few weeks.''

He stopped walking and faced her. Their relationship was only a few weeks old. Suddenly, he felt protective of it, and her. ''Is that so bad?''

''No, I guess it isn't.'' She smiled up into his eyes as he

began to take her into his arms. "You're going to spill your coffee," she warned.

So he was. He didn't care. "What's life without risks?"

"Boring," she answered, her eyes never leaving his. "Very, very boring."

"I was never one who liked being bored."

She'd already figured that out for herself. "I'll try not to bore you, then."

God, but she felt good in his arms. "Couldn't happen. Not in a million years."

Because she wouldn't let it. "You're sure?" she asked innocently.

That much he knew, if nothing else. Kris Valentine did just the opposite. She heated his blood and made him yearn for things that couldn't be. "Never more sure of anything in my life."

She turned her face up to his. "Kiss me, Max. A woman should be kissed on a day that bears her name."

Heaven help him, but he was lost. "That was just what I was thinking."

And then he kissed her, knowing that the brakes had to be put on, knowing that he couldn't take it any further than this. So he put everything he had into it. His heart. His soul.

He kissed her as if there would never be a tomorrow for them.

Because, for all he knew, there might not be.

Sterling Foster frowned at the tall, statuesque woman in his den. The woman he'd given shelter to all these months, hiding her from the world. The woman who had been his employer, and the object of both his ire and his admiration, for more years than he cared to remember.

"I'm against this, Kate. Nothing's changed."

Kate Fortune narrowed her gaze until it was a bright blue laser beam aimed in his direction. "I'm not asking for your permission, Sterling. I'm being polite and letting you know what I intend to do.''

She was the most stubborn damn woman ever to walk the face of the earth. And, more than likely, the most fascinating.

"For your information, everything's changed. My son is going on trial for his life.''

She was fidgeting, he thought. He couldn't remember ever seeing her fidget. "You can't help him,'' he told her gently.

"Perhaps not personally,'' she conceded. "But I can be there for him.''

Sterling sighed. This was a mistake, but it was hers to make. All he could do was point it out to her. "I suppose there's nothing I can do to make you change your mind.''

The smile was regal. And warm. "It's taken you a long time, Sterling—but you're finally learning.''

With a prison guard at his back, shadowing his every step, Jake Fortune walked into the small, drab conference room. He saw Sterling Foster standing by the small barred window, his brown eyes watching him thoughtfully as he entered.

Now what?

Impatience drummed long, weary fingers inside him. Jake had no idea why his lawyer had asked for this meeting. They had already gone over everything connected with Monica's murder at great length, from every possible angle. If he had to recite the events that had brought him to this pass one more time, he was sure he'd snap. Prison had robbed him of the cool, calm edge that had been the hallmark of everything he'd done in his lifetime.

The door behind Jake slammed shut with a finality that Jake had come to dread. Every door that closed here sucked him that much further into the black abyss that was waiting for him.

Never an optimistic man, he'd found that the last shreds

of hope had been drained from him as he sat in his cell, waiting for his trial.

Waiting for the verdict that would make him permanently one of these gray-clad ghosts who haunted the cells and corridors of the prison.

"Anything new?" he quipped.

Sterling didn't answer. Instead, he raised his eyes toward the wall at Jake's back. Jake turned with a start, just as he heard the rust-and-honey voice.

"Hello, Jake. How are you?"

For a minute, he thought he was hallucinating. That the endless days and bottomless nights within the prison walls had stripped him of the last of his sanity.

"Mother?"

Kate Fortune's heart ached as she stepped from behind the door to touch her firstborn. Tears glistened on her lashes, and she blinked them away. What had they done to him?

"You look so thin, Jake," she whispered. It was even worse than she had thought. She could bear anything done to herself, but not if it was done to one of her own.

"Mother?" he repeated incredulously. Jake shook his head, trying to clear it, expecting to see her vanish. But the long, thin fingers that touched his face were real. Were warm. "How can you be here? You're dead."

A sad smile graced the aristocratic features. "News of my death has been highly exaggerated. Isn't that what Twain said?"

Jake's surprise gave way to anger. She was alive. Alive, while all of them had grieved for her. Was it a game? Had she been toying with all of them all this time, for her own reasons?

"The hell with Twain. How could you let us think you were dead?"

"Don't shout at your mother," Sterling ordered, his voice calm, his manner not.

Kate waved him into silence. "He has a right to yell, Sterling. This is a shock to him."

"A shock?" Fury entered the normally inexpressive brown eyes. "It's a hell of a lot more than that. Who are you going to parade in next?" he demanded of Sterling. "Monica?"

The silvery head moved slowly from side to side. "No, Monica is still dead."

"And you?" Jake asked his mother. "Why did you play dead?"

She wasn't accustomed to being spoken to this way by Jake. He'd always been the unemotional one. Kate raised her chin. "Because someone tried to kill me, and I wanted to find out who."

He couldn't believe what he was hearing, what she was alluding to. "And you thought it was one of us?"

She lifted her shoulders helplessly and let them fall. "I didn't know what to think."

Jake sat down then, burying his face in his hands. It took him a moment to pull himself together. "Thanks for the vote of confidence." He raised his eyes to her face. A thousand memories crowded his brain. "But then, you were never close enough to me to know me, were you, Mother?"

Words had never been easy between them. There had always been walls, limits. As if separated by a force field, they could see one another, but could not reach out and touch. Anger, guilt, shame, all of that had always gotten in their way. She regretted that more than he would ever know.

"If I was a little harder on you…"

"If?"

"…it was because you were my first, and my expectations were high." She'd never been one not to admit her mistakes. "I didn't know how to be a mother."

"But you're going to try your hand at it now?" The question mocked her.

He wasn't prepared for the look of compassion in her eyes. Or the way it affected him.

"Yes, I'm going to try my hand at it now. And support you any way that I can." She exchanged looks with Sterling. "That's why I'm here."

"You expect me to be grateful?" Jake asked her challengingly.

"No," she replied, in the crisp voice that was so familiar to him. "I expect you to be proven innocent."

Eleven

Paul found Max talking to the new electrician they had subcontracted on Monday. Both he and Max had been on the site since seven, the same as every day. It was almost noon, and this was the first opportunity he'd had to get together with him. They were shy one roofer, which in a perverse sort of way coincided with the fact that the last shipment of tiles had been delayed. As far as days went, this was one of their better ones.

Handing Max a can of soda he'd taken out of the small refrigerator in the trailer, Paul took a break. No matter what the weather, Max favored cold colas over hot coffee every time.

"Think they're going to be finished grading that last section in time?" Paul nodded toward the only open section left.

"With time to spare." Max smiled, popping the tab. It felt good to be on top of things for a change, at least in one area. "The foreman and his guys are handling those machines as if they were racing chariots."

Paul took a long sip of his own cola. He'd gotten hooked on this stuff himself since throwing his lot in with Max. "Whatever works. Speaking of working," he said, slanting a look at his partner. "How's Lady Fortune doing?"

Max winced slightly at the label he'd affixed to her. It wasn't a fair one. Not anymore.

"All right."

The answer seemed deliberately vague. It wasn't like Max to be evasive. Because they'd both been going nonstop all morning long, Paul allowed himself a minute to survey the site and blank out his mind. The thought led him to his next question. "She still doesn't remember?"

Max nearly drained the can in three long swallows. He stood, contemplating the container in his hand, his mind elsewhere. "No."

It had been at least a month now, hadn't it? Max hadn't talked about it, but they'd had other things on their mind. Paul had just assumed that things were progressing with Kristina. "Nothing?"

Max rotated his shoulders in a rolling shrug. "She claims to have bits and pieces floating around in her mind, but nothing she can pinpoint or put together." And he lived in dread anticipation of the day that she could.

Paul voiced Max's thoughts out loud. "How much longer do you think your luck can hold out?"

Max laughed shortly, crushing the can in his hand. In long strides, he walked back toward the trailer and the trash can they kept there for the sole purpose of collecting the cans they went through. Ecology was something he'd practiced before it became fashionable. When you had little, you were mindful of supply.

"I don't know."

Half a foot shorter, Paul had to lengthen his stride just to keep up. "You know, if it were me, I think I'd find a way to tell her the truth before she finds out herself."

Max tossed the can. It clinked onto the top of the pile. "That's very good in theory." He turned to look at Paul, his mind on Kristina. On what she would say if she knew. *Once* she knew. "But the execution might be a little difficult." Difficult, hell—it was impossible, no matter which angle he approached it from.

"Execution." Paul's mouth curved as he repeated the word. "Good choice. Freudian?"

The laugh was short and self-deprecating. Hell of a mess he'd gotten himself into this time, Max thought. And he had no one to blame but himself.

"Probably."

Paul studied Max's profile. His partner seemed oddly pensive today. He wondered if it had to do with the changes he was planning for the inn, or with the woman herself. Probably the latter. Max had sounded pretty gung ho about the new changes, once he made his peace with them. Caught up, Paul had volunteered to help out on weekends when he could. Ellen would complain, but sometimes a man had to do things for a friend.

"You know," Paul began thoughtfully, "since you are using just about everything she originally tried to force on you, maybe that could help you ease into telling her who she really is." He could think of only one stumbling block. "I don't think she's going to get rid of the staff. You said she likes them."

Like was a mild word. "They're practically one big, happy family." They were all ganging up on him, taking her side, even though she didn't know she had one. "June and Sydney are after me to tell her the truth."

Sounded like a good idea to Paul. "So?"

Max paused as his foreman presented him with a clipboard. Attached was the order form he'd requested for more wiring. He signed his name on the bottom, then handed the clipboard and the pen back to the man.

He hooked his thumbs in his pockets as he looked at Paul. "So just how do you tell someone you've taken advantage of their condition to lie to them, to make them pay for the way they've behaved, and not have them hate you?"

Paul nodded. He was relieved that it wasn't him. "Not easily."

Taking off his hard hat, Max ran his hand through his hair. "Exactly."

Something in Max's voice caught his attention. They'd been partners for almost eight years now. When they first started out, their office had been Paul's den. You got to know a lot about a man when you shared a nine-by-twelve space with him on a regular basis.

"There's more, isn't there?" Paul asked quietly.

There was no use in trying to hide it from him. Paul had the tenacity of a pit bull when he set his mind to something. "Yeah, there's more."

Paul looked at Max's face, then shook his head. "Oh, boy."

Max glanced at his partner sharply. "What 'Oh, boy'? I haven't said anything yet."

"You don't have to. The look on your face says it all." He'd never thought it would happen twice. Not after what Max had said the last time. "You've fallen for her, haven't you?"

He wanted to deny it, desperately, both to himself and Paul. But there really wasn't any point in it. It didn't change the truth. "Yeah."

"Bad?" It was a rhetorical question. He could see that it was.

A hint of an ironic smile quirked Max's mouth. "That all depends on your point of view." He watched in admiration as one of the roofers scampered along the unfinished terrain with the surefootedness of a mountain goat. Wouldn't catch him up there like that. Thank God Martinez didn't share his phobia about heights. "Personally, I think it's bad no matter which way I look at it." He glanced at Paul. "I haven't a prayer of making this work, not once she gets her memory back."

"She might not."

Paul was grasping at straws, and they both knew it. Besides, it wasn't a solution. "So what do I do, lie to her for the rest of her life? Even if she wasn't Kristina Fortune, with a large enough extended family to fill half a football stadium, I couldn't lie to her." He shoved his hands into his pockets. He knew he was being ill-tempered, but he couldn't help it. "Not forever.

"It started eating away at me almost from the beginning," he confessed. "As soon as she opened those blue eyes and looked up at me like some waif they draw on the cover of sentimental greeting cards.''

Max shrugged, wishing he could shrug off the guilty feeling as easily. ''I only did it because I thought I was saving myself a hassle and the others their jobs. Logically, she wasn't supposed to be able to do anything on her own, not as only half owner. But she's a Fortune, and they always get everything they want.''

Maybe that had been his reason in the beginning, Paul thought. But not anymore. ''Why are you doing it now?''

Max blew out a breath. He couldn't just stand here talking all afternoon. He had to get over to the first block of houses. They were near completion, and he wanted to conduct an impromptu inspection.

''I already told you.'' Impatience clawed at Max's throat. ''Because I can't find a way to tell her without getting burned.'' He backtracked. ''Sorry, didn't mean to bite your head off.'' Paul might as well know the whole reason. He probably suspected as much. ''As long as she doesn't know, she's still Kris Valentine, a sweet, spirited woman who smells like wildflowers, and...'' God, he was waxing poetic. What was the matter with him?

Paul answered the unspoken question for him. ''You're in love with her.''

''No, I'm not,'' Max told him flatly. ''I'm attracted to her.''

Paul stuck with his assessment. ''You're in love with her. I know damn well what you're like when you're just 'attracted.' I've been with you through enough women to know the difference.'' Concern took over. ''This is Alexis all over again.''

Paul was only saying what he'd been afraid to admit to himself. But there was no other explanation. The only difference in the situation was that he hadn't taken Kristina to bed. But he didn't have to, to know how he felt about her. How she made him feel.

''Yeah, with the same 'happy' ending waiting in the

wings.'' Max couldn't help the bitter note in his voice. ''She gets her memory back, and if she doesn't skewer me for lying to her all this time, she's still going to go back to a world I don't belong in.''

He frowned, remembering the picture of that world that Alexis had painted before she walked out on him. She hadn't wanted any part of him, but she'd kept the ring he gave her readily enough.

''Wouldn't belong in if you paid me,'' Max added firmly. ''A world with an army of utensils surrounding your dinner plate and not a genuine emotion in your repertoire. A world of phonies who count dollar signs every night before they fall asleep and forget about everything else.''

Max had led him to believe that Kristina was different. Paul looked at him, confused. ''She's like that?''

''Kristina Fortune is,'' Max explained. It had taken only five minutes in her presence for him to realize that. ''Not Kris. If I could keep her this way, I would. But I can't.'' There was no use trying to pretend. ''And any day now, someone from her family's going to pop up or call. They're all probably involved in this murder trial, but eventually, one of them is going to notice she hasn't called. I can't lie to all of them indefinitely. I wouldn't want to.'' He scrubbed his hands over his face, the inspection temporarily on hold. ''God, knowing their kind, they could haul me up on charges, for emotional kidnapping or something.''

Amusement flitted across Paul's face. ''Getting a little dramatic, are we?''

Maybe, but not nearly as dramatic as he knew Kristina Fortune would get, once her memory returned.

''Bulldozers,'' Max said with a sigh, crossing the newly graded field.

Paul hurried after him, wondering if Max was still talking to him, or just to himself at this point.

''I should have stuck to bulldozers.'' He thought of Kristina, of the way she'd looked that first afternoon. A hurricane looking to uproot an island before breakfast. "Mechanical ones," Max added, "not the human kind."

"My guess is that you wouldn't find them nearly as satisfying."

"Maybe," Max conceded, walking away. "But at least you know enough to jump out of their way before they flatten you."

Finished with her explanation, Kristina shut down the computer and turned to her pupil.

"June?" The older woman lifted a wary brow, waiting. "Did I like Max before my accident?"

June felt her way around the answer carefully. "You two traded words a time or two." June watched Kristina's face, waiting for a sign that something she said had stirred a memory. They all did, these days, holding their breath. "If you liked him, you kept that pretty well hidden from the rest of us." That much was gospel.

Kristina couldn't picture herself not responding to Max. She looked forward to each evening. When his work kept him in Newport, the disappointment she felt had a keen edge to it.

"I guess maybe I'm lucky, then."

June wasn't quite sure she followed what Kristina was saying. "How so?"

Idly Kristina moved toward the sofa and straightened the throw pillows on it.

"Not to remember. Not to let the past inhibit me." She turned to look at June. "I can't imagine not liking Max." If she was being a little giddy, maybe she'd earned the right. "There's something almost delicious about him." She could feel herself taking on a glow when she spoke. That was how he made her feel. As if she were glowing. Like a bright beacon in the dark. "When he looks at me, my stomach just flips over, like one of Sam's crepes when he's tossing them."

June laughed. There was nothing she enjoyed more than watching a romance bloom.

"We've got to get you out of the kitchen more, honey." She could read Kristina's feelings in her expression. "Yes, our Max is pretty terrific, I'll agree with you there." A twinkle entered June's eye as she added, "If I was a few years younger, I'd fight you for him."

June had probably been something in her youth, Kristina decided.

A restlessness pervaded her as she glanced toward the door. He was late tonight. And it was raining again. Maybe he wouldn't come again.

She sighed. "There're times when I feel Max is really interested in me, and there are other times when I think I'm just imagining all of it." She'd made it plain to him that she felt something for him. Yet he hadn't attempted to take the relationship any further. Take it? He'd all but pushed it back into her hands.

"Welcome to the world of romance. The path of which never runs smooth." She ought to know, June mused.

"Tell me about it," Kristina murmured. She perched on the arm of the sofa, hugging the pillow she had just finished plumping to her. She watched the unexpected rain obscure the world outside the window. "Just when I think everything's going well, Max pulls away from me." She turned imploring eyes on June. June knew him far better than she did. For that matter, June knew *her* far better than she did. Maybe the older woman had a clue. "What am I doing wrong?"

Moved, June rounded the front desk and crossed to her. She placed a comforting hand on Kristina's shoulder.

"Nothing. Just give him time to work this out. Max's been burned once before."

Kristina hadn't even thought that it might be something besides her. Her eyes grew wide. "He's divorced?"

June shook her head. "Never got the chance to get that

far." She saw she was confusing Kristina, and backed up. "He was going to be married."

The frown came of its own accord. June had never cared for Alexis. With the unerring eye of a woman who had experienced a great many things in six decades, she'd seen Alexis Wexler for what she was. A heartless social climber.

"Max was engaged to this prissy little thing." June lifted her nose disdainfully. "A knockout as far as looks went, but someone forgot to put in a heart. All she was interested in was someone to take care of her." Max was better off without her. "As soon as she found someone whose future was more promising than Max's, she dumped him. Royally." June could have cut her heart out for hurting Max. "Took him a long time to get over that." She sighed softly as she shook her head, remembering. "Sometimes I don't think he ever got over it entirely." Her expression softened as she looked at Kristina and hoped the hope of the optimistic. "So if he hesitates a little, maybe he's remembering Alexis."

"That was her name?" June nodded. "Alexis," Kristina repeated. She supposed she was grateful to Alexis, as well as angry at her. The latter because the woman had hurt Max and made it more difficult for her to break through his barriers, the former because if Alexis hadn't walked out on him, Max wouldn't be unattached now.

And she was very, very glad that he was.

Sinking onto the sofa, she continued hugging the pillow. Wishing it was Max. "So you're saying that I shouldn't give up?"

That, and other things. "I'm saying that you should keep an open mind," June said diplomatically. "And forgive him."

She didn't see what she had to forgive him for. It wasn't as if he had actually done something she needed to forgive. "For pulling back?"

"For anything that needs forgiving," June answered vaguely.

She'd said too much, and yet she did so want this to work out between them. They were meant for each other, she could feel it.

June peered into Kristina's face. She would see the truth, even if the girl lied. "Do you care about him?"

"Yes." There was no hesitation. "I can't remember, of course." And that was frustrating. She would have settled for just a scrap of a memory. "But I have a feeling that I've never met anyone quite like him."

"I'm sure you haven't." She had no doubts about that. Maybe she was a little prejudiced, but she felt that Max was one of a kind. And very special. "Remember that, when you remember."

Was it her imagination, or was that couched as a warning? "Do you think I ever will?"

June thought of the newspaper she had just barely managed to hide before Kristina came up behind her. The newspaper with the article about Jake Fortune in it. She might be overly optimistic about some things, but June knew they couldn't manage to hide things from her forever. "It's very likely."

Kristina rose from the sofa. He wasn't coming tonight. She might as well call it an evening. "June, have you seen the newspaper? I thought I'd take it up to my room. It doesn't look as if Max'll be coming tonight—"

To June's relief, the front door opened just then and Max walked in, bringing with him a sheet of rain.

His disposition was not the best. Rain meant another setback. The rainy season was supposed to be over by now. Why was the weather being so whimsically unpredictable?

He glanced in Kristina's direction. Why should the weather be any different?

"Speak of the devil!" June cried, nodding at the front door.

Kristina smiled broadly. There was no denying that she felt exactly the way she'd described to June. Like a crepe being flipped on Sam's spatula. It was a wonderful sensation that enveloped her, and she cherished it. Being around Max made her feel alive, conscious of everything and everyone around her. Maybe she had been asleep until now, and he was her awakening.

She rather liked that interpretation.

"Hi." Not waiting for an invitation, she crossed to him. She took his wet jacket as he shrugged out of it.

"Hi," he echoed. "I can do that," he muttered as she hung up his jacket.

"So can I," she countered. God, she was glad to see him. "I was afraid you were going to stay up in Newport, with this weather."

"I was." He had tried to hold out, and found he was a lot weaker than he was happy about. "Decided against it at the last minute."

The only guest they had was upstairs in his room. Jimmy was away on vacation. Sydney and Antonio had gone into town that afternoon and were probably spending the night there. Their romance had heated up considerably since Valentine's Day. Amazing what store-bought roses could start. Kristina felt a twinge of envy, thinking of them. Her eyes shifted to Max. Except for Sam, in the kitchen, and June, they were alone.

"Why?" She wanted to hear him tell her what had made him change his mind.

She saw through him, but he pretended not to notice. He pointed toward his office. "I forgot the plans on my desk. The ones I want to review before I go ahead and order the building materials."

Her mouth curved invitingly with a knowing smile. "Is that the only reason?"

He drew her into his arms. How could she fit there so comfortably after such a short time? And how would he feel once she wasn't there anymore? He tried not to think of that, only of now. And her.

"What other reason would there be?"

She shook her head innocently, slowly, her eyes never leaving his. "None that I can think of."

He had an uncontrollable urge to nibble on her lower lip. And then her upper one. And then all of her. "Try hard."

As if reading his mind, she turned her mouth up to his. "Give me a hint."

Suddenly aware of her, Max glanced toward June. She was watching them with rapt attention, as if she had a front-row seat at a much-loved movie.

June took the cue quickly.

"Sorry. There must be a manual I'm supposed to be reading." She grabbed one without looking at it, and left them alone with their feelings.

Kristina took his face in her hands and turned his head toward her. "Now then, about my hint?"

He could eat her up. "One hint, coming up."

Max lowered his mouth to hers, and no longer felt tired. His blood sang as he deepened the kiss. God, he was going to miss this when she left. There was no doubt in his mind that she would go. Quickly, and probably with stinging words in her wake.

But that was later. Now was all he had. Now and her. He made the most of it.

Her body pressed urgently to his as his mouth sampled, savored, and took more. How was it that he couldn't control this situation, the way he could others? What was it about this small woman that untangled him so?

Kristina twined her arms around his neck. When he began to draw away, she rose up on her toes, not letting him make the break just yet. With a skill that came naturally, she kissed him hard, long and passionately. And then *she* broke the kiss.

"Mmm..." She smiled up at him. "You should hint more often." Releasing him, she stepped back. "Hungry?"

"Yes."

And getting more so by the minute. Each time he held her, he came that much closer to making a fatal mistake, one he wouldn't forgive himself for. Not when she didn't know.

She laughed. "For dinner."

He loved the way she laughed. Damn it, Paul was right. He loved her. "That, too."

She took his hand, leading him to the dining room as if she belonged there and he were just a visitor.

Sam was just about to go to bed.

"Sam," Kristina called out, her voice echoing in the empty dining room. "Home is the hunter. Home from the hill." Abruptly Kristina stopped as the words replayed themselves in her head. They were familiar. And yet she'd never heard them before. "Where did that come from?"

Max shrugged, watching her eyes intently. *Home is the hunter* had been the first words she uttered when she saw him. "From something you once read? Looks like your memory's trying to come back."

She shrugged carelessly. "Maybe. I'm not in a hurry to get it back." They settled at a table. "I'm very happy where I'm at right now." Of late, the past actually held a threat for her, like a darkened room she was afraid to explore. "Maybe I'll remember things I won't want to remember. Won't want to know."

Kristina searched his eyes, to see if he understood. Or agreed. She saw something there she couldn't read.

"You know, baggage to clutter up my mind. Right now, I know all I need to know. Even about you." Rising, she quickly stuck her head into the kitchen and asked Sam for a roast beef sandwich. Max's meal of choice.

When she returned to the table, Max looked at her. He hadn't followed her line of thinking. "What's that supposed to mean?"

Maybe she wasn't supposed to say anything. But guile was beyond her. "June told me."

He cocked his head. A blind man would have seen the sympathy in her eyes. "About—?"

She sat down opposite him. "About why you're stand-offish."

"Oh?" He felt like a man trying to pick a safe path over a minefield.

"Yes, I understand."

Well, that didn't clear up anything. "And just exactly what did she tell you?" He was almost afraid to find out.

Kristina looked at her hands as she spoke. She didn't want to embarrass Max, or raise any painful memories. She just wanted him to know she understood.

"She told me all about Alexis." She raised her eyes to look at him. "You don't have to worry."

"I don't?"

"No," she said firmly. "I'm not here for the money, and I'm not about to run off if someone offers me a better future. A better deal. I like it here." As she said it, she knew she'd never meant anything so much in her life, no matter what the past held in it. "I like the people, the tranquillity. And I love the plans you've got for the inn." He'd gone over them with her, at her insistence, right from the beginning. "Funny, I've been studying them so much, they almost feel as if they're mine. You know how things seem familiar sometimes?"

It was time to tell her. Paul was right. It would be better coming from him than having her discover it by accident.

"Yes, I know." Here went nothing. "Kris?"

"Yes?"

There was no way this was going to be easy. "About your past…"

He looked as if this were painful for him. She stopped him before he got any further. "You don't have to say it. June mentioned that, too."

If this kept up, he was going to require a codebook to decipher what she was saying. "Mentioned it, how?"

"Well, I asked her." She was tripping over her tongue. "About us. You and me." This wasn't coming out the way she wanted it to. "If we got along."

All right, June had set the stage for him. He could work with that. "And she said—?"

"That we didn't. Exactly."

Bless June and her understatement.

"That's when I told her that I was grateful for the accident." She spoke quickly, while her courage still held up. She wanted him to know. "Because if it hadn't happened, then maybe I wouldn't have seen what a terrific guy you were."

He sincerely doubted that Kristina Fortune would ever think of him as a "terrific guy," especially in light of the present situation. "Quite possibly."

She read a great deal into his answer. And flushed. "Was I a very big pain in the neck?"

He couldn't help laughing. "That wasn't the part of the anatomy that came to mind when you got started," he confessed fondly.

"Oh." She wasn't offended. "Then I'm sorry. Sorry for everything I put you through."

He reached across the table, his hand covering hers. "Kris, before you apologize any more, there's something I have to straighten out—"

"Max?" June stuck her head in. Her sharp eyes homed in on their joined hands. "I *really* hate to interrupt this, but there's a call for you. It's Paul. Something about an emergency."

As if he weren't up to his neck in one right now. Max sighed and rose, tabling his confession for another time. He could feel his courage flagging already.

"Tell him I'll be right there."

Twelve

Max stood in the dim hallway, looking at Kristina's bedroom door. There was no sound echoing on the floor save his own breathing.

That, and perhaps the sound of his heart, being torn in half by indecision. By two diametrically opposed desires.

He'd spent the past three hours in his office, mostly on the telephone, trying to buy himself some time. The unexpected deluge would set them back more than a day and a half, even if it stopped within the next ten minutes. He already had two full crews on standby, ready to shift into action as soon as the land dried.

After that was arranged, Max had remained in the office, going over the cost projections for the inn's remodeling.

He supposed another word for what he was doing was *hiding*. He was hiding from Kristina, and from his feelings about her. Right now, he figured, he was in the running for saint of the century—if his deception was disregarded.

Temptation sizzled through him, nudging him forward. Whispering in his ear. It was late, but not that late. He could just knock on her door and...

No, he couldn't. Not when he knew where that knock would lead him.

He was in living hell. The first woman he'd ever been deeply in love with—far more than he'd ever loved Alexis—wasn't real. Oh, she breathed, all right. And walked and talked and melted selected parts of his body when she looked at him with that way of hers he'd come to look forward to.

But she wasn't real. Not in the sense that she would remain the way she was. Not once her memory had returned, destroying forever and irrevocably what there was between them. The best he could hope for was a mellowing on her part toward the inn. But not toward him.

Every day, they were one day closer to the inevitable. One day closer to her reverting back to a woman who would leave his life with great relish. There was no way she'd remain, not once she became aware of the way he'd kept the truth from her.

Paul was right. She had to be told, and by him, not anyone else. He owed her that much. But how did he go about telling a woman he'd fallen in love with that he'd thwarted every attempt to restore her memory? That he'd lied to her from the start, for selfish purposes, without caring how it might affect her?

No, that wasn't entirely true. He did care. Had cared. If he hadn't, guilt wouldn't have been his constant companion, wouldn't be riding shotgun beside him now. And he'd almost blurted the truth out to her tonight, just before Paul's telephone call rescued him in the nick of time.

Or prematurely cut off his courage, whichever way he wanted to look at it.

Damn it, he shouldn't be standing here, mooning at her door. He needed to be fresh tomorrow morning. They were on the last leg of construction, and their time was running out.

So was his, he thought ruefully.

He wanted to see her, now, before everything blew up in his face.

Look at yourself, Max thought with disgust. He was behaving like some weak-chinned adolescent, pining in front of her door, wanting her so bad he couldn't think straight. Kristina was all he could think about when his nose wasn't pressed to the grindstone.

And even then, she managed to sneak through, penetrating his thoughts like vapor. Like air. Sweet and clean and life-giving.

Damn, he had it bad.

He raised his hand to knock. One knock and he'd be in her room, and then the mental battle he was waging would be taken out of his hands, done in by the look on her face, the scent of her body. One knock and he'd be out of hell and in heaven.

Temporarily.

The word echoed in his head.

Max let his hand drop to his side. If he went in, it would only be asking for trouble. Why was he torturing himself like this? Why compound this tangled situation even further by taking that next step that he knew was waiting for him?

He couldn't make love with her. It wouldn't be fair. When her memory returned, she'd accuse him of taking advantage of the situation. And she'd be right. She didn't know who she was.

And once she did, it wouldn't be fair to him. He'd want her for the rest of his days. He knew it as surely as he knew his name.

More.

Better not to start anything than to spend the rest of his life wanting what he couldn't have.

He was making himself crazy. He should have sent her back to her family that first day, with a note pinned to her blouse—that was what he should have done. Not let her remain where she could make Swiss cheese out of his head. With the best of intentions, he'd succeeded in messing things up royally, and making himself miserable in the bargain.

With a sigh, Max turned and walked back downstairs, to his own room. With any luck, he'd get a few hours' sleep before he had to get back to the site.

He sincerely doubted that luck would be with him tonight.

* * *

Kristina jerked her head around, listening. She thought she'd heard something in the hall.

Someone.

Straining, all she heard was the sound of the rain as it tapped out an impatient tattoo on the roof. And the wind as it moaned low from time to time, mourning this late-in-the-season rainfall.

It wasn't him.

No longer alert, her shoulders sagged. She'd been "hearing" Max approach for hours now. She'd nursed the hope that he'd come upstairs to see her once his work was done.

Of course, she could go downstairs to his office, but Kristina knew better than to bother him there. He did have work, and she'd only interfere. Want to interfere, she thought ruefully. She'd want to take his mind off whatever had prompted the "emergency" call and onto her.

Was it too much to hope that he'd come to see her once everything was as resolved as it could be for the night?

Apparently, she thought, suppressing a pout.

Feeling listless, she moved toward the window, watching the rain come down. It obliterated the world beyond the glass, making her feel isolated. As isolated as the amnesia that haunted her had initially done.

Before she discovered her attraction to Max.

Attraction. What a paltry word to describe what she felt when she was close to him. There was something in his eyes that melted her, made her want to give herself up to him. Just thinking about him made her blood hum. Made her yearn.

A piece of a shingle danced away by her window, riding on the wind.

Max was beginning work on the inn none too soon, she mused. She wondered if that meant he was going to be around full-time.

The thought made her smile for the first time in hours.

C'mon, Max. Where are you? Why aren't you here? How

hard do I have to throw myself at you before you catch me?

Restless, Kristina roamed around the small room, looking for something to get her mind off Max for a little while. Despite the hour, and the drowsy sound of the rain, she felt too keyed up to sleep.

She looked at the wide bed that was the focal point of her room, thinking of the changes Max had told her he wanted to implement. If she concentrated, she could just envision them. He wanted to transform the rooms, with their homey, haphazard decor, into something far more romantic-looking. She'd suggested replacing the double beds with king-size, canopied ones. Canopied beds with soft, filmy white curtains that gently swayed in a breeze, inviting lovers to fulfill their dreams.

He'd liked her idea. He'd made a note of it and asked her to tell him if she had any others. That had pleased her. She wanted to help, wanted to make this a place that would create precious memories for people that they would always cherish.

She'd certainly cherish the memory of their making love in a bed like that.

If it ever happened.

It didn't have to be a bed, really, she thought, wanting him. It could be anything. A sofa, a tabletop, the floor. Anywhere. Anytime.

Though her mind still held her past hostage, Kristina instinctively knew that she'd spent her entire life waiting for someone like Max. Someone kind and gentle, someone who knew how to hold back and wait.

Maybe a little too long, she thought, frustrated, glancing at the door again.

She *had* to get her mind on something else.

Moving in front of the bureau, she began opening drawers, rummaging around. It had been a while since questions about her past rose up to plague her. Tonight, with nothing to occupy her mind and no one to talk to, they returned.

Had she been an avid reader before the accident? she wondered. Was there something here she could start reading and, hopefully, fall asleep over?

Kristina frowned as she looked at the small piles of clothing neatly arranged side by side. She certainly didn't have much in the way of possessions, she thought, sifting through one drawer and then another.

She'd been so busy trying to fit in, trying to get things right, trying to make a difference, that she hadn't spent much time in her own room. She certainly hadn't bothered consciously assessing it.

She did now.

Obviously, she had to like living like a Spartan. She couldn't find any trace of knickknacks, no photo albums, nothing. Just a few changes of clothing. All high-quality, she judged, from the feel of them. Kristina supposed that meant she didn't have much money and only bought the best. Quality, not quantity, seemed to be her motto.

She rolled the thought over in her mind as she closed the lingerie drawer.

It sounded right.

A cryptic smile lifted the corners of her mouth. Too bad she wasn't secretly an heiress on a madcap vacation, running away from an estranged lover.

In her case, she was running after the lover, not from him. A very reluctant lover.

With a sigh, she crossed to the nightstand and opened the top drawer. It was painfully empty. So was the one below it. Finding them so irritated her.

Didn't she have any hobbies? Any interests? No magazines that had been thumbed through, no novels, nothing?

How dull was she? She certainly didn't feel as if she were dull, but this was a room that belonged to an incredibly dull person. Maybe that was why Max was trying to keep her at arm's length. He couldn't believe the transformation.

Believe it, she thought.

In desperation, because she wasn't tired and she didn't have anything else to do, Kristina opened her closet. The same clothing she had seen for the past two months and more were hanging neatly above two cream-colored suitcases. Curious, she took out the larger one. Something thudded inside, sliding from one end to the other.

She placed the suitcase on the bed and flipped the locks. There was a hardback book inside, but nothing else. The suitcase looked as if it were brand-new. She obviously never used it, never went anywhere. But then, if that was the case, why was there a book inside it?

Curious to discover the sort of thing she'd read before the accident wiped her mind clean, Kristina took the book out and plopped down on the bed. When she opened it, something she'd apparently been using as a bookmark floated out from the middle of the book. She flipped it over.

It was a photograph. One of those large, panoramic group shots. But there was no one from the inn in it.

She scanned the photograph, going from face to face. Her heart skipped a beat when she found herself. She was standing off to the side, in the midst of a group of strangers. A lively-looking redheaded woman was casually resting one hand on her shoulder.

Kristina laid the photograph on her bed, abandoning the book. She looked at the photograph intently.

Strangers.

Familiar strangers.

Slowly, as if a cloud were moving away from the face of the sun, she became vaguely aware that these were people she had once known.

People she *did* know.

The thought pierced her suddenly, like the tip of an arrow. She *knew* that redheaded woman standing just behind her.

That was...was...

"Rebecca," Kristina whispered, almost afraid to say the name.

Tears rose to her eyes, shimmering, making everything swim. Blinding her. Kristina brushed at them impatiently. She blinked twice, attempting to clear her vision.

''That's Rebecca,'' she said louder, her voice trembling. She remembered.

Dear God, she remembered.

Excitement poured through her veins. She sat up on the bed, her body alert, as she looked at another face. ''And that's Grandmother.''

Kate. Kate, who had died in a plane crash. And Rebecca—she had called Rebecca from here. From the inn. From this room. Rebecca had told her that she wasn't satisfied that her mother was really dead.

Her hand flew to her mouth, holding back a noise that was half gasp, half moan.

When had that been? How much time had she lost?

One by one, she began naming the people in the photograph, her excitement growing with each recognition, with each face that was suddenly familiar to her.

She remembered.

Kristina jerked her head up, looking at her reflection across the room in the mirror over the bureau. Scrambling to her knees for a better view, she stared at herself as if she hadn't looked into the mirror each morning for weeks.

The woman looking back at her wasn't the maid.

With a shaky hand, she traced the tips of her fingers along her cheeks, her mouth, her brow as she continued to stare at her reflection in stunned disbelief.

''And I'm Kristina. Kristina Fortune.''

The woman in the mirror opened her mouth to form a perfect O.

The rest returned to her with such lightning speed that it almost overwhelmed her. Memories emerged, full-bodied and vivid, crowding their way into the space that had been so sparsely populated just moments ago.

Kristina sank down on the bed again, weak. Her eyes

blurred again. Through the tears, she looked at the photograph again.

She was Kristina Fortune, not Kris Valentine. And she owned this place, at least half of it. Kate had willed it to her. Willed her her share.

Slowly, still holding the photograph, Kristina swung her legs down and rose from the bed. She walked around the room as if she hadn't seen it before. As if she hadn't been prowling around it restlessly just a few minutes ago.

And she remembered.

Joy mingled with confusion. She really remembered. She knew who she was, what she was doing here. Everything.

She knew—

That she'd been duped.

Kristina dropped onto the bed again, as if the air had been completely let out of her, leaving her limp. The next moment, indignation and anger erupted, filling the empty space.

"That dirty, conniving bastard."

She caught her tongue between her teeth, trying to steady herself. All this time, she'd thought he was being kind, gentle, patient. Holding back his own desires to be fair to her because her memory hadn't returned. And the bastard was really just toying with her. Leading her on, making her jump through hoops for his own amusement.

Laughing at her.

She jerked up, and she was halfway to the door before she stopped herself. No, she had to think this through. This merited more than just telling him what she thought of him in loud, colorful terms. Letting out a long, shaky breath, she returned to the bed and sat down again.

Kristina clenched her fists in her lap as a fresh set of tears rose in her eyes.

Damn his sorry hide. She was going to make him pay for that. Really pay. Big-time.

* * *

Hurt, devastated, Kristina plotted all night. By morning, her desire for revenge had been honed to a sharp point.

The situation didn't look better to her in the morning, it looked worse. There was no excuse for what Max had done. None.

In the dark, staring at the ceiling, she'd tried, really tried, to come up with something, anything, that would absolve him. That was due to her weakness. No, she amended, her stupidity. She still cared about him. Why was a mystery she didn't attempt to explore.

But there was no excuse and no absolution. Kristina couldn't find any reason for his behavior except the sole purpose of humiliating her.

What other reason could there be?

But why? It made no sense to her. Despite the argument on the beach, and his stubborn behavior, he'd obviously liked her ideas well enough to want to set them in motion once he stamped *his* name on them. They both seemed to agree on that now. Their only bone of contention would have been the staff, and she'd changed her mind about terminating them.

They would have had to be in on it, she realized suddenly. June, Sam, Sydney—all of them—they had to be in on it.

Tears continued to sting her eyes. They had all pretended to like her, to be her friend, when all the time, they were just laughing at her behind her back.

That, she thought, hurt almost as much as knowing what Max had done. She had grown to really like these people, to enjoy their company. To discover that the friendships she thought surrounded her were only a sham really devastated her.

It was going to be payback time, she promised herself. And the one receiving the special delivery was going to be Mr. Max Cooper.

And she knew just how to do it.

Kristina showered and dressed quickly, then settled in with the telephone. There were people she had to call and wheels she had to set in motion.

And one big wheel in particular. That one she intended to drive right over Max's body.

Max knew he was in trouble the minute he walked in. He'd passed June in the front room. The woman had grinned from ear to ear and told him that Kristina was waiting for him in the dining room.

She certainly was.

Sitting at a table for two, Kristina was wearing a hotpeach dress that seemed to defy the laws of simple gravity as it adhered to her breasts. Her blond hair tumbled about her shoulders invitingly, showing them off to their best advantage. Sleek, perfect, they made his fingers itch.

She looked like sin, served up hot and tempting.

He felt his resolve dwindling even as he crossed to her. The dining room, empty now, was dim, except for the candlelight that added a warm golden sheen to the color of her skin. Soft, supple skin. Skin he wanted to touch, to press his lips to and caress.

He wanted to possess it, and her.

This was not shaping up well where his good intentions were concerned, he thought.

Max found his tongue, but it wasn't easy. Not when it felt too thick to manage. "Aren't you cold?"

It was not a warm March evening, but she had thoughts of righteous indignation and revenge to warm her.

"Not a bit," she murmured.

It hadn't been easy, pretending today. Talking to the others and acting as if she didn't know about the ruse they were perpetrating. It had taken effort for her to act as if she were still the woman she'd been the day before, when she wanted to take each of them aside and hotly demand to know why they had done this to her, when she had put her faith and trust in them. She had believed them when they told her things, believed them when they acted as if she were their friend. And she had become one, and trusted that they were hers.

Lies, all lies.

But she had continued the charade, biding her time. She had a bigger fish to catch. There was no sense in ruining that by sending shock waves through the water.

She'd borrowed the dress from Sydney. It had taken very little convincing. Sydney had almost seemed eager to have her take it. Sydney was taller, but less amply endowed. The fit was tight, enticing.

And it had taken equally little persuasion to get Sam to prepare a special dinner for two. June had been the one to put out the candles. Then all of them had conveniently decided to leave the premises. They were all eager for her to get together with Max.

They'd fooled her before, but not now. Not again. Undoubtedly they thought Max could get her to sign over her half of the inn if she was besotted with the man.

Well, surprise, folks. Little Kristina's back, and I'm nobody's fool.

She smiled up at him. It took an effort for her not to shout names at him. *Dirty, lying bastard.* Not to double up her fists and pound on him until she felt better. Avenged.

"You don't look so cool yourself, either."

That was for sure, he thought.

Max gripped the back of the chair, but didn't sit down. "No, I think my blood pressure's gone up about ten degrees in the last minute or so."

She leaned over, slowly, deliberately, as she curved her fingers around the neck of the bottle that stood chilling beside the table. Her eyes on his, she ran her thumb over the tip of the cork.

"Stay, have some wine."

Eve, offering Adam the apple. *Just take a bite, what harm will it do?*

If he knew what was good for him, he'd turn and run for the exit. For the hills. Somewhere, anywhere.

He didn't move a muscle.

Max dug his fingers into the chair. "Kris, I don't think that's a very good idea. I have to—"

Apparently the mountain is going to have to fall on Mohammed. Kristina rose, coming to stand beside him.

"You work too hard," she murmured. She covered his hand with hers. "Stay. Sam went to all this trouble. Have a little something." Her eyes made it clear to him just what that little something might wind up being.

The scent she wore was making a more forceful argument for her than the dress she almost wasn't wearing did. Against his better judgment, Max sat down.

Kristina moved something onto his plate, urging him to sample it. It could have been rusted nails, for all he noticed as he chewed. What he did notice was the way the light made love to her. Just the way he wanted to.

Reinforcements. He needed reinforcements. Max looked around. This was usually the time of day the others took their evening meal, but they were alone tonight.

Damn, he wished she wouldn't look at him like that. As if she were parched and he were the only glass of water in town.

Max cleared his throat. "Where are all the others?"

Why did you have to be like this, Max, why? I could have really cared about you.

"The inn's empty." She took a sip of her wine, fortifying herself. "June and Sam said they were on their way out to the movies. I'm not sure where Antonio and Sydney went, but I'm sure they're happy. Jimmy's still away," she reminded him. "That leaves only us." *So I can't kill you, because the finger'll point to me. Too bad.*

He watched, mesmerized, as her tongue slowly moistened her lips before she took another sip of wine. He felt his gut tighten like a fist about to deliver a punch. Except in this case, he was the recipient, not the deliverer.

"Kristina, are you trying to seduce me?"

A wicked smile curved her mouth. It was in direct contradiction to her innocent tone.

"Me?" She waited a beat. "Maybe." She raised her eyes to his. "How am I doing?"

How could his mouth be so dry when he'd drained an entire glass? "You're succeeding incredibly well, incredibly fast."

He looked down at his plate. There was no sense in eating when he couldn't taste anything. Max pushed the plate away, wishing he could somehow get himself to push her away as easily.

"Kris, I really don't think that this is such a good idea."

Kristina rose from the table. Very deliberately, she laced her fingers with his, drawing him to his feet. "Then don't think." Her voice was low, drifting like a warm caress along his skin.

He was looking at her as if she were something precious. If there was something within her that wished the look belonged to her exclusively, instead of being tangled in some plot, she was going to have to deal that with later, not now. Now was the time for revenge. She was going to make him sit up and beg.

And just when he did, she would pull away, telling him that she knew who she was. She'd walk out on him, leaving him wanting more, begging for more.

That was the plan.

Thirteen

Entranced, unable to resist, Max allowed himself to be led up the stairs. Their shadows played along the wall as they approached her room, mingling, a precursor of things to come.

Max could feel a trickle of perspiration beginning between his shoulder blades, zigzagging down along his spine. He wanted what he couldn't have. What he shouldn't have.

They had the inn to themselves. There was no one to suddenly turn up in the hall, to stop and exchange words with. To use as an excuse to leave.

And no excuses seemed to want to materialize on his tongue of their own accord. In fact, his tongue felt as if it had grown thick and unwieldy in his mouth.

That happened a lot around her.

Damn it, he was a thirty-two-year-old man, not some lovesick boy being led around by the nose by his first crush. Not that he knew much about being one. He hadn't had time to be a boy, not even when he was one, not since he was very, very young. He'd become a man very early on. And his fate had always been in his own hands. Always.

So why and how had he allowed it to dribble away into hers?

Allowed? Hell, he'd had no choice. It had been snatched away with that first kiss, with the first promising whisper of her body along his. Snatched away as if he hadn't had a firm fix on it at all. Kristina was taking a hostage, and he was it.

But he cared about her too much for this to happen between them. He didn't want to take her to bed. Not this way. It was all wrong. Nothing good could come of it. And he wanted it to be good. He wanted it to be good so desperately.

When she came to him, Max wanted her to know who he was, who *she* was. Something rooted in a lie didn't have a chance of growing, flourishing. It would be in the dark. Nothing grew in the dark.

Except desire.

And his was engulfing him.

With almost superhuman strength, Max gathered his resolve to him. He had to tell her. Now. Before it was too late. Before she wound up hating him forever.

It wasn't her hatred he wanted forever. It was her love.

"Kris. Kristina," he amended, using the name she preferred.

Her hand still laced in his, heart hammering a tad more than it should for a woman who felt she was in complete control, Kristina turned to look up at Max. Turned and felt a little of her steely resolve turn into mercury within her. Liquid mercury.

Kristina pointedly ignored it. Feeling weak-kneed wasn't part of her plan. Conquest and revenge were.

With a seductive toss of her head, she sent her hair flying over her shoulder as she leaned her body invitingly to his.

"Yes?"

Disengaging his hand from hers, Max took hold of her by the shoulders.

Big mistake.

It was a gesture meant to define space between them and keep it defined. But touching Kristina made him want her so terribly, so completely, that for a minute his mind went blank. Being noble was all well and good on paper, but it was playing hell with him now.

Desire, hot and ripe, was licking the sides of his body

with long, demanding tongues that seared him as they passed.

For two cents, he'd crush his mouth to hers and deal with the consequences later.

"Kristina…" he began again.

"You already said that." Kristina rose up, bringing her mouth tantalizingly close to his. And raising the flame on the torch of her own desire a notch. "And you've got my attention."

Lightly, ever so lightly, she passed her mouth along his, barely touching her lips to his. It was enough to set off a warehouse full of sparklers. She could see it in his eyes. If some of those sparklers found their way to her, well, she could handle that.

Kristina drew back just a fraction of an inch. She could feel her pulse accelerating in her wrist as she grasped the front of his shirt—not to steady herself, she insisted silently, but to hold his eyes on her face.

"All of my attention," she whispered.

Her body wasn't supposed to be throbbing in anticipation this way, she admonished herself. She was just going to bring him to the brink, tangle him up in a knot so tight he couldn't undo it himself, and then leave, triumphantly crowing that she'd known all along. Known who she was. And what he was. A rotten bastard.

She'd laugh in his face and tell him that she'd only been entertaining herself at his expense, to see just how far he thought he could carry this ruse.

She'd—

Releasing his shirt, Kristina tangled her fingers in his hair as she felt his arms tighten around her. Her body began to hum. No problem. If she had a good time bringing him to his knees, so much the better. There was no danger if she allowed herself to enjoy the man a little. She'd always had the upper hand in relationships, and there was no reason not to feel that she would go on having it.

If her body heated whenever it was near his, well, that

was just physical. Nothing she couldn't handle when the time came.

She just didn't want the time to come now, that was all. Nothing wrong in that. After all, he did have an incredible body. It was his personality she hated, not his body.

If he didn't get this out now, Max was going to lose his nerve. She had to let him talk before his mind clouded over completely. But even as he spoke, her mouth raced over his.

"Kristina, there's something you have to know."

Her head began to swim. Held tightly in arms that felt as hard as the desire she felt flaring within him, within her, Kristina groped behind her for the doorknob. It took a moment before she found it. Turning the knob, she managed to push the door open a crack.

Just as the first fissure opened up in the wall she was trying to maintain between them during this final act of the masquerade.

"Yes?"

Was that her voice? It sounded so strange, so thick. As if she were already halfway drunk on desire. But that was impossible. She was in control, complete control. He was the one in trouble, not her.

The single word glided along his skin, undermining his noble intentions, drawing them away, as if it were a magnet and the words that were to follow were just simple iron filings.

If he told her now, his conscience would finally be clear.

And his body would be bereft.

A second longer, just a second longer, so that he could kiss her again, hold her to him again. Then he'd tell her. What was a second in the scheme of things? In the sum total of a lifetime? Nothing.

With a firm, desperate grasp, he snatched up that nothing and held on to it.

Instead of answering her, he brought his mouth down to

hers. He kissed her as if his very soul depended upon it. Because maybe it did.

His mouth working over hers, deepening the kiss until it was a symphony that involved every fiber of his being, Max picked her up into his arms. He tried not to think of right and wrong, of deeds and payback. Now was no longer the time for debates.

Now was the time for loving.

Moving the door open with his elbow, he stepped over the threshold.

And into paradise.

Something small and urgent still whispered that he was only compounding the mistake, but he closed the door with his shoulder anyway. The click that echoed in the room and in his ears sealed his fate as finally as a firing squad raising their weapons at a condemned man sealed his.

We who are about to die salute you, Max thought with resignation. And rapture.

Slowly, with patience he hadn't known he possessed, Max moved his mouth over hers, fanning the fire he'd raised within her. Being consumed by the flames himself. It was a good day to die.

Good, he was hooked, Kristina thought shakily. Her plan was working very well.

Her plan?

Her plan. She had to hang on to her plan, she told herself fiercely, fighting to focus her mind, even as she was numbed by the power that underlined his kiss.

Max fought for breath. He couldn't seem to get enough as he found himself pulled into a vortex of passion. Couldn't get enough of her. Struggling to regain precious ground, Max set her down on the floor.

Her body slid fluidly along his, every inch of the way. It seemed as if an eternity passed before her feet reached the patterned scatter rug. During that eternity, she felt a thousand eruptions rumble through her body, like a thousand tiny earthquakes. She kept her arms wrapped around his neck, afraid to let go. Afraid to test the stability of her legs.

"You're trembling," he murmured.

Or was that him shaking? Where did she end and he begin? He wasn't certain anymore. Wasn't certain of anything, and he didn't want to think about it any further. All he wanted to do was to enjoy this sensation that was battering his body, demanding release, demanding tribute. Demanding her, with a voice so loud it almost echoed in his head.

He wrapped his arms around her more tightly. "Maybe you are cold." Her dress certainly wasn't covering enough to make her warm. Only him.

"Warm me, Max," she said as pulse points quivered within her body.

A part, she was just playing a part, Kristina told herself urgently. Maybe with more feeling than she'd ever played anything with before, but it was just a part. A part she was going to take great joy in terminating at the right moment. But it wasn't just yet. If she played it out a little longer, he'd be more humiliated, just as she had been when she realized what he was doing.

The urgency in her loins took her by surprise. It wasn't her body rebelling against her. It was…it was… She didn't know what it was.

"Warm me," she urged again, with more feeling.

"You're making this hard." Max breathed the protest against her skin, trailing kisses along her throat. He could feel her response to him, gloried in her response to him even as his own pulse rate went into triple time.

"I hope so," she whispered hoarsely.

Kristina gave herself up to the delicious feelings just a moment longer. A moment longer. Maybe two, tops. If her fingers seemed to act independently of her mind as she tugged his shirt out of the waistband of his jeans, it was just part of the plan. She was improvising, creating, as she went along, nothing more.

He felt her fingers, long and cool, trailing along his body and could feel that knot growing in his stomach, tightening so that he could barely catch his breath. Buttons rained on either side of him as her eagerness increased.

Her hands spreading out along his chest, sapping the last of his self-control, Max felt for the zipper in back of her dress.

And found none.

"How do you get out of this thing?"

"You tug." Catching his lower lip between her teeth, Kristina did just that, demonstrating the power of the word.

Damn, he was going to rip the dress off her in another minute. Did she have any idea what she was doing to him? How she was making him agonize?

He hadn't wanted to make love with her until he told her the truth. Now he was afraid that something would happen at the last moment to bring this all to a careening halt. A sense of urgency flooded him, warring with his desire to savor this, to memorize every nuance, every movement.

Hands that were so sure at their craft fumbled as they came in contact with her dress. He did as she'd instructed, and tugged. As if in slow motion, the dress moved erotically down her body until it freed her breasts to his gaze.

Max stopped, his breath caught in his throat. The moment was frozen in time as his eyes feasted on the banquet before him. And then he filled his hands with her flesh.

Kristina cried out then, not in protest, though the game had gone more than a step further than she had first anticipated, but in wonder at the sudden flash points that ignited throughout her body at the feel of his rough, callused palms against her breasts.

Dazed, her eyes filled with wonder, she arched into his touch. The ache she felt was both sweet and agonizing as Max bent his head, anointing first one breast, then the other, with his lips, with his tongue.

She wanted him to stop. She wanted him to go on forever. Her very stomach quivered as she felt his tongue flick so lightly, so tantalizingly, over just the tip of her hardened nipples.

Kristina bit her lip to keep from crying out.

Her fingers tangled again in his hair as she urgently pressed his head to her burning flesh, trying to absorb him, trying to absorb the wild, heady sensation he created with just his mouth.

Eager for the very sight and taste of her, Max tugged more urgently at her dress, pulling it away from her slick body until at last she was free. It floated like a peach cloud down her long legs.

She wasn't wearing anything beneath the dress. Kristina stood before him like a bronzed goddess, her body calling to his.

She'd meant for the silhouette of her body, moving beneath the silken fabric, to tantalize him, to drive him crazy. That part of the plan had backfired. Feeling the soft material gliding seductively along her body with every move she made had managed to heighten her mood, as well. It tantalized not only Max, but her, too, making her feel more sensual, more desirable. And leaving her vulnerable to that feeling.

Her anticipation increased, even as she insisted that she was in control.

Control? It was a word that no longer had any meaning to her. All she wanted, as she stood there with the peach fabric pooled around her sandaled feet, was him. Nothing but him.

The worshipful wonder in his eyes made her forget everything else that had come before. And everything that might come after. Right now, she wanted this drunken feeling to continue. To reach its peak and sweep her away with it.

There was such wonder in his eyes, it gave her pause. "What?"

His smile was soft, gentle, and so damn sexy she had to

grit her teeth to resist begging him to take her here and now.

Max passed his hand over her reverently, hardly touching her, and exciting her more than if he had plunged himself into her this moment.

His eyes made love to her. "I never got to unwrap gifts as a kid. I thought I'd enjoy this present for a second longer."

A line. It was just a line. A lie, like all the others must have been. Had to have been. So why did it tug at her heart so? Why did it fill her with a bittersweet sadness to think of the boy he'd been, lost and unloved?

She wanted to take him into her heart and love him, to make up for all the people who had ever neglected him. Kristina called herself a hopeless fool. But she remained rooted to the spot, unable to leave.

"You're overdressed for the occasion." She licked her lower lip, undoing him completely. "I have to do something about that."

Eyes on his, Kristina opened the snap of his low-slung jeans, her fingers fluttering along his taut, hard belly. She saw something flash within his eyes. Smiling, tempting, she began to ease the zipper down with the tip of her finger.

She felt him shudder as she coaxed it down, a fraction of an inch at a time. Felt him grow in anticipation of her, and almost cried out.

"You're making me crazy," he breathed.

"That's the general idea." His desire only quickened her own pulse.

He wanted to shrug out of his jeans, to take her here, now, but somehow, he managed to hold himself in check. Having her do it for him was sweet agony. He gloried in the feel of her long fingers along his hips as she inched his jeans and briefs from his body.

And then they were both free, free to enjoy each other, free to be imprisoned by emotions and feelings far greater than the sum of both of them.

Bodies pressed tightly against one another, they tumbled onto her bed and tumbled into a world neither of them had ever visited before. Neither of them had known of its existence.

They knew now.

He wanted to take her immediately, to end this throbbing in his loins. But he struggled against it. He wanted to savor this, to enjoy her. To bring her such pleasure that it tempered what he knew would come later.

A fragment of a thought occurred to him, and he pushed it away with both hands. He didn't want to think, to feel guilty, to risk abruptly ending this before it reached fruition.

He had to have her or die.

Tell her or explode.

Gathering her into his arms, Max looked down at her with such feeling that it took her breath away. It made her afraid of the words to come.

"I've never felt this way about a woman before, Kris. I just wanted you to know."

She didn't want to know, didn't want to hear anything that would make her even more confused than she already was. Because if she heard, she might believe. And she knew she couldn't. Couldn't believe a liar.

And yet she wanted to, so desperately, she wanted to.

This had gone so much further than she had imagined. And not far enough to satisfy her. Her body ached for release. Ached for him.

Cupping his face in her hands, Kristina brought his mouth back to hers and ended any words that he might have said, any confessions he might have uttered.

He gave himself up to the kiss, deepening it quickly as his tongue found hers. And all the while, his hands played along her body, bringing forth a melody that only they heard.

She turned, bucked, arched, greedy for the feel of him, greedy for the sudden star bursts that occurred as he played the melody to a crescendo.

His fingers found her soft inner core and worked their way in, teasing, toying, tantalizing them both. He felt her breath shorten until it was almost all short spurts, felt her body arch and shudder as the release came.

Peaking, she gasped his name as she curved into his hand.

Fascinated, excited beyond belief, Max experimented, bringing her to a fever pitch that had only begun to match his own. His mouth raced along her body, struggling to hold on to the final strand of control before it snapped irrevocably.

Kristina, limp and frenzied at the same time, grasped his shoulders tightly. Her eyes silently begged him for the joining. He slid his body, poised and hard, along hers. Lacing his fingers through hers, his eyes watching her intently, he sheathed himself in her.

Joined, one, they took the last journey together, slowly at first, quickly as their goal came into view. And together they experienced the final lightning storm.

Fourteen

Reluctantly, Kristina made the descent back to earth. Back to her room, and the rumpled double bed. Back to the man whose body blanketed her from head to foot. She hardly felt his weight skimming along her skin. And yet felt it enough to remind her of the journey they had just taken together.

Reality and remorse, with their cold, scratchy fingers, began to prod at her, bursting the thin soap bubble of euphoria that surrounded her.

The plan had gone too far, slipping from her fingers too quickly for her to grab hold of it. She tried to rally, making a quick assessment of the strategy that was still left to her. She could still get him where it hurt. His ego.

Satisfaction, soft and sensual, curled through his limbs, drugging him, even as the wave of pleasure receded from him.

Max felt Kristina stirring beneath him. Shafts of desire shot through him. Every movement erased his fatigue a little more, magically taking it down a notch until, somehow, it vanished altogether.

He wanted her again.

He'd enjoyed a fair share of women. None had remained in his life for too great a length of time. None had ever urged him on to another plateau. He'd taken his pleasure, offered the same in kind, and then, when it was over, it was over. He left. Case closed.

Nothing was closed here. If anything, it made him want to pry the door open even farther.

Max had never thought of himself as insatiable before. But he was. Insatiable for her. Ready to begin that wonderful climb up the mountain all over again, knowing that she was waiting for him at the summit and that together they would go skydiving over the edge once more.

Drawing his elbows in to his ribs, Max rose over her. He smiled into her eyes as he tried to still the erratic beating of his heart.

"Wow."

She tried not to let the word fill her with pleasure. And she wished he wouldn't look at her that way. That way that was guaranteed to melt her bones down to nothing.

It wasn't real, she insisted silently. Max was just having fun at her expense, nothing more. That should have made her angry. Instead, she felt mellow. Why did he have to turn her on this way?

Why did the feel of his breath along her skin make her shiver with anticipation? She was supposed to be finished with that part of it. Hadn't she just experienced everything a woman could? And more? Now it was time to pull back and gather the troops together for her own assault, not wander through the battlefield, picking up daisies and humming to herself.

What the hell was wrong with her? Why did she feel like laughing and crying at the same time?

She was vulnerable and exposed and needed to shore up her breached defenses, not give in to her emotions.

All she could think of was him.

Damn him, she wanted to be loved again. To make love with him until there was no breath left in her body. Until she couldn't think of this thing, this betrayal, that could hurt her so if she paid attention to it.

Trying to summon anger, all she could do was look at him. And want.

Lovingly Max framed her face with his hands. He ran her silken hair through his fingertips. Soft, like rainwater. Like her body. How could he be ready to make love with her so quickly? It was as if someone had lit a torch inside him.

"You're really something else, you know that?"

His words whispered along her skin as, ever so softly, Max pressed a kiss to each temple. Kristina could feel herself heating again. Her body felt like something that had been slipped into a microwave oven.

Her lids were so heavy, she could hardly keep them open. He was drugging her, even as he was raising her to greater heights.

"What else am I?" she asked hoarsely.

Now, he should tell her right now, he thought. She'd given him the perfect opening. But if he took it, something else would be closed to him. Telling a nude woman she'd been duped wasn't exactly something the faint of heart should attempt, and right about now, he wasn't feeling very brave about facing her reaction. He was feeling...other things.

"Perfect," he answered. "You're just perfect."

It was the coward's way out, but he would be a coward if it meant he could hold her in his arms just a little longer, love her just a little more.

Soft, sensual openmouthed kisses rained on her neck and face, trailing down her throat, her breasts, her belly, until Kristina writhed, twisting and mindless, wanting only to be allowed into paradise again. The hell with everything else.

Nipping the tender inside of her thigh, Max coaxed her to open for him. Then, with short, quick passes of his tongue that stoked the flame of her inner core, he reduced her to a mass of pulsating needs. Needs that could only be satisfied by him.

Kristina whimpered as she twisted away from the heat of his mouth and then into it, wanting him to stop, wanting him to continue. Ecstasy merged with agony until, clawing frantically at the quilted comforter, she was swept over one peak and passed to another. And another, until she was so exhausted she barely knew any name, least of all her own.

Max's face glistened with traces of her perspiration as he moved, snakelike, along her body, working his way up to her mouth again.

Once there, he could feel her heart pounding against her ribs, her heart pounding so hard that it seemed to pound against his own. The rhythms merged until the beat was one and the same.

Holding back the dawn and tomorrow, with all its consequences, he looked into her eyes and found himself hopelessly trapped by a woman who didn't even realize she had the power to imprison him.

"You're mine, Kris. Whatever else happens," he whispered against her ear, "you're mine."

She had never wanted to believe a lie so much in her life.

Lifting her hips, tempting him, Kristina offered her body to Max, and he took it, joining with her again.

The ride was just as exciting as the first had been. More, because she knew the destination, knew the mind-numbing power of the final moment. He did that for her. Made it more wondrous than anything she'd ever experienced before. More wondrous, she knew, than anything she would ever experience again.

With a muffled sob, holding on to him as if she were holding on to a piece of her soul that threatened to break away, Kristina took the plunge again.

They dozed and made love all through the night. It was an evening lost and a haven found. And neither of them allowed thoughts of tomorrow to rob the breathtaking wonder of now.

Dawn stealthily announced its presence with wisps of sunlight streamers preceding it into the room. It parted curtains and parted dreams as it entered.

Max roused slowly. He opened his eyes to find himself in Kristina's bed, his arm possessively wrapped around her waist. She was curled against him, nude and sleeping peacefully. Her blond hair lay across his shoulder like a flag flown at an enemy fort.

Somewhere during the night, they had both capitulated, he mused affectionately. For a moment, he was content just to look at her.

The moment didn't last. Desire came knocking insistently again, bringing with it the same familiar ache. But there was no way to put off the inevitable. Last night, the lovemaking, it had all happened out of order. He'd meant to tell her, then make love with her, not the other way around.

Now he had to tell her. Today. But he still hadn't a clue as to how.

Something tickled her cheek. Kristina stirred, unconsciously trying to hold on to sleep as it receded from her. But even as she reached for it, she could feel it fading away. She was awake, or nearly so. Awake, and not alone.

Her eyes fluttered open.

Oh, my God. She was hardly aware of suppressing her groan.

"Max."

It was a cry of surprise, horror, and a whole host of other things Max couldn't begin to readily identify. He decided to play the scene out lightly. His arm tightening about her waist, he smiled.

"Yes, it's me."

She felt his arm, felt the light hairs along it tickling her, and looked down. She yelped in surprise as she yanked the sheet up to cover herself.

Her embarrassment was almost endearingly touching. His mouth curved. "Isn't that a little like locking the barn door after the horse has run off?"

Right now, she felt like burning down the damn barn, not just locking the door.

Frustration and anger licked at her as she felt her cheeks heating. She might be just as much to blame as he for last night, but she didn't feel like being gracious and sharing the honors. Those belonged to him alone.

Fury raised in her eyes. "Get out," she ordered.

He hadn't expected this kind of reaction. "Kris—" He reached for her.

Her eyes narrowed. This wasn't the way she wanted to do it, but the words rushed to her lips, not heeding any plans that had gone awry until now. "It's Kristina, remember?"

Something cold and icy slid down his back. A premonition. He looked into her eyes. And knew. "You remember."

So, he wasn't going to try to snow her or act innocent. "Damn straight I remember. Everything." *The way you lied, the way you made me care, everything.* "Both before and after." Accusations blazed in her eyes.

Her response left him reeling. "You knew last night?"

She waited for the excuses, for the denials. Why wasn't he offering them? "Yes."

He didn't understand. "Then why—?"

Even as he asked, he reached for her. If she'd known last night and they'd still made love, then it was all right. Wasn't it? She did feel about him the way he did about her.

Why? There had to be a reason why she'd done what she had that wouldn't cause her to lose face. He'd like that, wouldn't he? To rub her face in it.

Quickly, Kristina improvised as she went along. "Because I wanted to make you suffer, that's why, make you see what you could have had, but won't."

He played her words over in his head. "I'm not sure I follow you here. We made love. I did have you." He was going to add, "And you had me," but he never got the opportunity.

"For one night." She shot back at him. And she'd been a fool to allow it, even though everything in her body had screamed for it. For him. She was supposed to have more willpower than that. "Just one night," she emphasized. Her eyes narrowed. "It could have been longer."

It could have been forever, a voice whispered. *It still could.* Stubbornly, Kristina shut down communications.

"It still can," he insisted, reaching for her again. Damn, this was complicated. But not impossible. Nothing was impossible. He could fix it. If she just let him. She *had* to let him.

This time Kristina didn't move back out of reach. This time, she held her ground and slapped his hand away, insulted.

"What do you take me for, an idiot?" she demanded hotly. "Why would I want to be with a man who lied to me? Who played me for a fool?" *A man whose sweet, tangy mouth secretly laughed at me.* She cursed herself for feeling tears building. She truly *was* an idiot.

Because he couldn't touch her, he dug his knuckles into the mattress on either side of him. "No one played you for a fool, Kris."

Wrapping the sheet around her like a cumbersome toga, Kristina rose to her knees, indignation flashing in her eyes.

"Oh, no? Oh, no?" she repeated incredulously. Even now, he was lying to her. How much gall could one man have? "Then what was making me into a maid supposed to be? It's a little early for Halloween."

His best weapon was the truth. Max vainly attempted to make a clean breast of it and hoped for the best. "I admit I did that out of spite—"

She'd known he had, but hearing him say it hurt. Hurt more than she would have thought possible. Just the butt of jokes, that was what she was.

Her eyes blazed. "Well, then—"

Max continued as if she hadn't tried to cut in. "But I did that for a good reason, too."

Was that how he'd justified it to himself? That he was doing it for a good reason?

"I'll just bet." Sarcasm vibrated in her words. "What

was it? You wanted to show the others how to humiliate me in one easy lesson?'' To think she'd tried so hard to blend in. What a fool she'd been. What an addle-minded, idiotic fool.

Max felt the sting of chagrin. She'd hit the nail on the head. But the head was bigger than that. She had to be made to see it.

"It was to show you the perspective from the staff's side. I wanted you to get to know them. For however long it lasted, I wanted you to see what they see, feel what they feel."

No, she wasn't going to let him charm her out of seeing this for what it was. Kristina raised her chin. "You wanted to ridicule me."

God help him, he was going to pay for that. *Was* paying for that already. "It started out like that, but you dealt me another hand."

Poker metaphors? He'd ripped her apart, and he was making poker metaphors?

"What?" she demanded.

"I wanted to put a royal bitch in her place." He waited until the barrage of words flowing from her lips was stilled. He had it coming, he thought. "But you weren't a royal bitch. You were sweet, eager to help, and so goddamn sexy you made me swallow my tongue."

"It's in working order now," she said coldly.

She didn't believe him, couldn't believe him. He'd lied to her, not once but continually. How could she believe anything he said ever again?

She'd been up against this kind of thing before, she reminded herself. Resentment because of who and what she was. She wasn't going to allow him to talk his way out of this just because her body still vibrated at the thought of his touch.

When he reached for her a third time, she doubled her fist, pulling it back. "Get out of my room."

Did she really think he was afraid she would hit him?

She might be athletically built and agile, but she couldn't hurt him. Not physically. But she had other weapons at her disposal. Weapons he had inadvertently handed her.

"I'm not leaving, Kris. Not until you calm down."

She gritted her teeth together. "I already told you, my name is Kristina. And I'm not going to calm down anytime soon." Like a queen issuing a proclamation, she raised her head. "I am, however, going to throw you out, get dressed, and leave this godforsaken place."

Her threat made his heart quicken. Leaving? She was leaving? "Where are you going?"

If that was shock and fear she heard in his voice, it had to do only with the inn, not with her. "As far away from here as I can, as quickly as I can."

He had to find a way to make her stay. He needed time to make her see reason. Max seized the only weapon he had. "What about the inn?"

The inn was the only thing he cared about. She struck him there. "I've already made plans to sell my half." She'd toyed with the idea last night, as she got dressed for dinner. Selling would be the best way to go, but she hadn't had time to find a buyer, so she'd lied to him. It seemed only fair. He'd done nothing but lie to her. "You'll have a whole new owner to plot against and seduce."

He couldn't believe she would do that so cavalierly. She cared about the inn. He could have sworn she cared. "You're selling?"

Good, it hurt. "It's already a done deal." She twisted the knife a little more, just as realizing that he had lied to her had twisted the knife in her. "I made arrangements yesterday afternoon. My lawyer is drawing up papers right now." She talked quickly, not giving him an opportunity to ask who the new owner was. "So get out of my room. We have nothing else to talk about."

Oh, no, she wasn't getting rid of him that easily. "Oh, we don't, do we? Then what the hell was last night about?" he demanded.

Her eyes narrowed to slits. Why wouldn't he leave her alone? Why did he want to continue to torment her? "About twelve hours too long," she spit out.

He refused to believe she meant that. Those were hurt feelings speaking, nothing else.

"You made love with me." He pointed out angrily, "Not Kris, but you."

Her cheeks flamed. He wasn't supposed to realize that. "I already told you—"

No, she wasn't going to talk her way around this. He knew what he knew. "Nobody's that good an actress," he told her. "You wanted me."

Yes, she had wanted him. Still wanted him. But that was something she had to deal with. Privately. She lifted a shoulder and let it drop disinterestedly.

"As far as bodies go, yours isn't bad. But not so terrific that it clouded my thinking. I was in control every second, understand?" She dared him to say otherwise. "Every second."

He'd been wrong. There was no reasoning with her. "Well, that makes one of us," he snapped.

Max got up off the bed, not bothering to take the sheet with him. He stood before her, a magnificent specimen of manhood, completely unselfconscious in his nakedness, wrapped only in his anger.

His eyes grew cold as he looked at her. "And to think that I wasted all that time feeling guilty about deceiving you. I should have spared myself the trouble." Talk about being a fool—he took the prize. "Go ahead, run. Sell your half of the inn. But before you go, I want you to know that for what it's worth, I thought your ideas were good." If nothing else, she couldn't accuse him of lying to her in the end.

His admission caught her off guard, but she recovered after a beat. "Thank you," she said stiffly. "I already figured that part out. And I intend to utilize them at the bed-and-breakfast inn I'm buying."

His mouth dropped open. "You're buying—"

"Another inn, yes."

It was hard carrying on a conversation when he was standing in front of her like that. He was doing it on purpose, she thought angrily, just to unnerve her, to undermine her resolve. Well, it wasn't working. She forced herself to look only into his face and nowhere else. Even though the temptation was tremendous.

She delivered the final coup de grace. "I still intend to go through with the national chain, Cooper. It was a damn good idea, and it was *my* idea." She'd be damned if she'd let him take the credit for it. Holding the sheet to her like a shield, she struggled off the bed and went toe-to-toe with him. "I've got more money, more resources, and I can beat you to the punch. So save your breath and your 'emergency' savings. Keep the inn just as it was." Incensed, she waved her hand in dismissal. "I make you a present of it."

She was contradicting herself. "I thought you said you were selling your half."

"I am," she snapped. Damn, why couldn't she keep her mind on her story? Because he was scrambling it, standing there like that, that was why. "Maybe I won't sell it to that other buyer after all. Maybe I'll just give it to you. A parting gift."

She liked the sound of that. She didn't want to have anything to do with the inn anymore, even if it had belonged to her grandmother. She never wanted to see this place again.

"You can stay here and not do a damn thing, just the way you were doing before I got here."

Exasperated, not wanting to continue talking to him, especially not when he wasn't dressed, Kristina snatched the book from her nightstand. The book she'd found in her suitcase, the one that had brought her back from the brink of oblivion.

"Now get out of here!" she shouted as tears stung her eyes, threatening to spill out.

The next moment, she hurled the book at him. It hit the door as he swung it closed behind himself.

"Well..." He blew out a breath. "She's back."

Muttering under his breath, Max made his way carefully down the back stairs to his room, grateful that the inn wasn't booked and that everyone who was there was still asleep.

That belief died abruptly when he passed Sam in the hall.

The latter looked him up and down slowly, raising his grayed brows in open amusement.

"Not a word, Sam," Max warned. "Not one damn single word."

"As you wish." Smiling to himself, Sam shook his head as he went off to the kitchen. Times had certainly changed since he did his share of wooing.

Fifteen

"How long have we known each other, Max?"

Max looked up from his desk. June was standing in the doorway. From the look on her face, she'd been standing there awhile, watching him.

Every available space in the crammed office was filled. There were brochures, samples of wallpaper, swatches of fabric, pictures of bathroom fixtures, order forms and bills, spilling out and melding together in a giant hodgepodge. Everything there was directly related to the inn's renovations. With Kristina's threat ringing in his ears, Max had thrown himself into refurbishing the inn at full throttle.

Paul had agreed to hold down the fort at their construction site until he was finished. And they'd just won a bid on a new development going up in San Clemente. There would be less than a week between the completion of the one and the start of the other. Max had never felt so damn swamped in all his life.

Or so damn alone.

He shrugged vaguely in response to June's question. There wasn't time for guessing games. He had to settle on a motif for the rooms. What the hell did he know about "motifs," anyway? That was *her* department, not his.

Except that there wasn't a *her* anymore.

"I don't know, June." He made no effort to curb the irritation in his voice. "Ten, fifteen years."

Entering, June crossed to the desk and unceremoniously dumped a stack of papers onto the floor. She sat down on the newly liberated chair.

"God, it's a good thing you never went into accounting. Nineteen years, Max. I've known you nineteen years." She frowned at him, but there was concern in her eyes. Ever since Kristina left, he'd been biting everyone's head off. She was the one who'd volunteered to finally come in and talk to him. "In all that time, I've never seen you like this."

Max dragged a hand through his unruly hair. The patterns for the wallpaper were beginning to blur and run together. Damn it, why did everything have to be so complicated? With a resigned, frustrated sigh, he made his choice. Then, in the next second, decided against it.

"It's a new phase," he grumbled.

She watched him agonize over the book of wallpaper patterns. Just as she'd watched him agonize over everything in the past two weeks. He was like a wounded bear who wouldn't let anyone pull the thorn out of his paw.

"The hell it is. Don't lie to an old woman, Max. I don't like it."

That got his attention. He raised his eyes to her face, and a hint of a smile curved his mouth, though it went no farther. "You're not old, remember?"

This was more serious than the gentle kidding they usually indulged in. She was really worried about him. "I'm older than you. And old enough to know when I've made a mistake."

He thought he detected a serious note in her voice. "Did you?"

She wasn't here to go into her own past. June blew out an impatient breath. "I'm talking about you, boy. Pay attention here."

Leaning back in his chair, Max thumbed through the thick book of fabrics on his lap. Despite Kristina's parting shot about beginning a chain of Honeymoon Hideaways of her own, he'd decided to go ahead with the renovations she had suggested. The ones, he reminded himself, he had resisted so stubbornly for his own sentimental reasons.

Now, just as stubbornly, he held on to them. It felt as if

he were engaged in a race against time, trying to get the inn finished and ready for guests before Kristina managed to do the same somewhere else. He felt he owed it to his foster parents to make a success of the inn. In theory, it was supposed to give him something to do and not allow him any time to think.

No time to think about how soft her skin was, or how she'd felt, curling up against him, as dawn threaded its way into her room. No time to remember what the taste of her mouth was like. Certainly no time to remember that it had reminded him of fresh strawberries. Ripe, and ready to be eaten.

He was going to be certifiable in less than a week if he didn't stop torturing himself this way.

Max looked at June, trying to focus on what she was saying to him.

"What? What mistake have I made?" Snatching up the latest drawings he had, he spread them out on his desk for June to look at. They conceptualized what he thought Kristina had meant when she talked about a romantic setting. Every last one of them reminded him of her. Of the bed they had warmed. "Are the bathrooms too small, or—"

June swept her hand over the drawings, dismissing them. "The bathrooms are fine, Max. It's your head that's too small. It hasn't let in a decent thought since she left."

He wasn't even going to ask her what she was referring to. His mouth hardened as he looked back at his work. "She walked out. Her choice."

June's voice was patient without being patronizing. She'd been there. "Agreed. And it can be yours to go after her."

His head jerked up. "And do what? Crawl? Beg? Not my style, June." He'd always had a fond spot in his heart for June, but right now, his heart was in no shape for visitors. "No disrespect meant, but back off."

She wasn't going to be budged that easily. "No disrespect taken, and I won't back off." She saw the surprise on his face and continued. "We're not talking about style, Max, we're talking about mistakes. Mistakes that can haunt you for a lifetime if you don't do something about them." There was a sad shadow mingling with the smile on her face. "Take it from someone who knows."

He was on to her. She meant well, but right now, he just wanted to be left alone to work this out for himself. He'd always worked everything out for himself. This was no different. Just because there was a hole in his gut the size of a cannonball, this was no different.

He couldn't help the sarcastic lilt to his voice. "And what story are you going to tell me, June, that's going to instantly clear the cobwebs from my eyes and make me see the light?"

If he'd meant to make her leave, he didn't succeed. June only shook her head sadly. "God, you are a bitter son of a gun, aren't you?"

Tired, he laced his hands behind his neck and leaned back, blowing out a breath. He had no right to talk to her like that. "I'm sorry, June. Really sorry. I shouldn't be taking this out on you."

June wasn't about to argue that. "No, you shouldn't." She took the largest oversize book of wallpaper from him and began to page through it as she spoke, one eye on the array. "What you should be doing is coming to your senses."

What was June talking about? Was she taking the side of the stuck-up snob who had run out, leaving her belongings and everything else in her wake, to be retrieved later by one of her lackeys?

"And you liked her?" he asked in disbelief.

"Yes, I did." She saw the surprise wash over his face. "Not the her who started out, but the her who was here most of the time."

Yeah, so did he. Until he learned better. "That was an aberration, June. She's not like that." More the idiot he, for thinking that she was.

June had lived longer and seen a hell of a lot more than he had. She knew better. And so should he. "Kris couldn't have behaved the way she did if she wasn't like that at bottom," she insisted. Didn't he understand? "Amnesia robbed her of that sharp tongue of hers, it didn't perform a lobotomy on her. Ask your friend the doctor, if you don't believe me."

June was certain that she was right and stuck to her guns. "Under all that big, brazen talk is a sweet girl, maybe even afraid to be sweet, because then no one'll take her seriously." Making a choice, she flipped the book over and showed the pattern to him, her finger stabbing it in the center. "Did you ever stop to think of that?"

June could make a better choice blindfolded than he could poring over the book for hours. He nodded, taking it from her. "No, I was too busy checking myself over for snakebites."

Maybe he was just being obtuse. June shook her head. "Time for that story, Max."

Max didn't want to hear stories, real or otherwise. He just wanted to be alone. He looked toward the door, the hint clear. If she didn't leave, then he would. He began to rise.

"I—"

June clamped her hand down around on his wrist, tethering him to his seat. "Shut your mouth and listen, boy. I'm only going to tell you this once."

Pausing, she gathered herself together. When she spoke again, it wasn't in the voice of the lusty woman Max had always known, it was in that of the young woman she'd once been. Max listened, fascinated by the change.

"When I was a lot younger than you, I fell in love with someone." She smiled, remembering. "He was the kindest, sweetest man God ever created."

Max laughed shortly. Those adjectives couldn't have been used to describe Kristina Fortune. "So far, I don't see any analogies.'' June looked at him warningly. "All right, I'll shut up.''

"The problem was, my parents didn't like him. Oh, they didn't know him,'' she said quickly. "They wouldn't take the time. They only knew what they had heard about 'people like him.''' Her eyes shifted to Max's face. "That was the way they said it in those days. Politely. 'People like that.''' It would have been funny if it wasn't so sad. "You see, Joshua was of a different, ah—'' June searched for the word her father would have used "—'background' than I was.'' She enumerated. "Different heritage, different religion. Things that in those days were guaranteed to make life difficult for a young couple just starting out. So my parents forbid me to marry him.'' There was no humor in her reminiscent smile. Only pain. "Joshua begged me to run off with him, but I was the good daughter. Afraid, I said no. And broke the heart of the kindest, sweetest man God ever created.''

Finished, June sighed again. "We would have been married forty years this spring, if I had said yes to Joshua.''

Moved, Max reached for her hand and covered it with his. Words weren't necessary. "Where is he now?''

June shook her head. "I lost track of him. Not a day goes by that I don't regret not saying yes.'' She paused, as if debating saying more. But Max was important to her, so she continued. "I tried to find him once, after my parents had died, but it was too late.'' Raising her head, June pinned him with a look. "Don't let it be too late for you, Max. Go after her. Make your peace.''

She rose, and then headed toward the doorway, careful not to upset any of the scattered piles on the floor. "You're absolutely no good to any of us, least of all yourself, until you do.''

He nodded slowly, held in the grip of the story June had shared with him. "Maybe you're right.''

Her bawdy grin was back. "Sure I am. Now get out of here.'' She gestured toward the phone. "Book yourself a flight to Minneapolis and show that girl what you're made of.''

Satisfied that she had lit the proper fire under Max, June retreated. She ran into Sam just outside Max's open door. He nodded approvingly at her.

June raised a questioning brow.

He shrugged. ''I couldn't help overhearing. Touching story.''

June's eyes glinted as her smile grew. ''Yes, wasn't it?''

Sam studied her face in surprise. She'd almost coaxed a tear out of him with that narrative. ''You mean it didn't happen?''

June raised her head as she walked out to the front room, a queen leaving her loyal subject. ''That, Sam, is for me to know, and for you never to find out.'' With that, she turned down the hallway and disappeared.

Sam laughed to himself. A hell of a woman, he thought with a shake of his head. A hell of a woman.

''Um, Ms. Fortune?''

Kristina massaged the area just above the bridge of her nose. Another headache was beginning. Or was it the same one as yesterday making a reappearance? Ever since she returned from that blockhead's inn, she'd had one damn headache after another.

At her mother's insistence, she'd gone in and had a CAT scan. It had turned out negative, just as the tests she had in La Jolla had. There was nothing wrong with her. Nothing that a long vacation and perhaps another bout of amnesia wouldn't cure. Amnesia, so that she could forget that lazy bastard with the killer smile and get on with her life.

The last thing she wanted right now was another interruption. Biting off her annoyance, she looked up as her secretary peered into her office.

''Yes, Jennifer?''

Jennifer looked over her shoulder uncertainly. It was one of the few times Kristina had ever seen the woman appear flustered. "There's a man outside who says he has to see you."

Kristina glanced at her calendar. There was no name written in for this hour. What there was was another meeting. She had forty minutes to approve a new presentation for the unveiling of their new formula before it went to Frank. She waved a dismissive hand at Jennifer.

"Tell him he'll just have to wait. I'm busy."

"Tell her I've been waiting for over two weeks and I don't want to wait any more," Max said to the secretary as he pushed his way past her.

Kristina's mouth fell open. For one single, unguarded moment, joy leaped in her veins. Then she squelched it. She fervently hoped what she'd felt hadn't registered on her face.

Jennifer looked up at Max as if he were King Kong, newly freed from his chains and about to take Kristina and scale the Empire State Building. The wariness on her face intensified. "Do you want me to call security, Ms. Fortune?"

Rising, keeping the desk between them, Kristina shook her head. "No need, I'm quite capable of handling this myself."

God, but she looked good to him. The way she was standing there, cool as a freezer filled with thirty-one flavors of ice cream, it was all he could do to keep from sweeping her into his arms.

"Can you, Kris?" He moved into the room slowly, like a panther stalking his prey. "I'd say running away isn't handling anything."

Kristina clenched her hands into fists, telling herself that her palms hadn't gone damp.

"You can go, Jennifer." She didn't need to have her personal life played out in front of the rest of the office. The woman quickly withdrew. Kristina waited until she heard the door close. And then she turned on him, her eyes riveted to his. "What do you mean by coming in here and causing a scene?"

He'd thought of calling her, but that would only have given her fair warning. He didn't want to play fair anymore.

"I thought it would be the quickest way to get your attention." He leaned a hip against her desk, making himself as comfortable as possible for a man with his life on the line. "I brought you these." He dropped the credit cards he'd taken from her wallet on her desk.

She didn't bother picking them up. "I've already replaced them." Did he think he could just saunter into her life like this? After what he'd done? Her eyes narrowed. "Get out of here, Cooper."

His smile was slow and lazy, winding along his lips like the morning rays of the sun, reaching across the darkened land. "I'm only leaving with you."

The man was the poster boy for gall. "No, you're not."

He spoke slowly, evenly, but there was no mistaking the fact that he wasn't a man to be messed with. Max raised a brow.

"Want to bet? I've just spent three hours stuck in a little silver canister a hell of a lot higher than I'm comfortable about to get here. There's no way I'm making that kind of trip back unless I've got something to occupy my mind with." Max hooked his thumbs on the loops of his jeans to keep from touching her the way he ached to. "I figured that would be your job."

She couldn't believe she was hearing this. For a minute, she thought of buzzing Jennifer and telling her that she did need security. But that would mean she couldn't handle her own affairs. And she could. Very capably.

"I have a job," she said pointedly. "A career. I'm an advertising executive."

Unable to help himself, he leaned forward and toyed with a wisp of her hair that had come lose. "I liked you better at the inn."

She jerked her head away. "Yes, mindless, a puppet you could order around."

His eyes narrowed. He hadn't thought she would lie to herself.

"Did I do that, Kris? Did I order you around?" His voice was soft, seductive. "Did I make you do anything you didn't want to do?"

She came very close to physically shaking off the effects of his voice. "You made me a maid."

He wasn't going to lose his temper. This was going to be played out with patience. He figured he had a few blows coming to him. He let her take her best shot.

"We've been through that. I didn't have you sweeping out the ashes in the chimney. I thought a little physical labor for a person like you would be good." Max saw the fire in her eyes and continued without missing a beat. "You surprised me by turning out to be better than I expected." Again his mouth curved as his eyes swept over her. "In every department."

Damn it, she could feel herself heating in response to the look in his eyes. What was wrong with her? "Am I supposed to be flattered?"

No, it wasn't going to be easy getting her to come around. But he hadn't expected it to be.

"You're supposed to be forgiving." He dragged a hand through his hair, wishing he knew how to proceed. He'd gone over this again and again in his mind during the flight, and come up with no pat answers, no solutions. "You want me to beg?"

No, she wanted him to go away. She thought if she egged him on, maybe he would leave. "That would be nice."

Max took her hand in his. "All right, please come back."

She had expected him to turn on his heel and leave, not comply. For a moment, Kristina could only stare at him, dumbfounded. Then she pulled away her hand.

"There's no reason to come back. I'm not part owner anymore, remember?" She turned her back on him, pulling her portfolio together. She couldn't stay here arguing with him, she had to get ready for the presentation.

He wasn't about to talk to her back. Max moved around to face her. "You can still be half owner."

What the hell was he talking about? Over her father's protests, she'd had the title of the deed transferred to Max. "How? I—"

"Husbands and wives own everything straight down the middle in California."

She looked at him. "What does that have to do with us?"

He took her hands in his again, partly to hold her in place, partly to prevent her throwing something at him. "Everything. Marry me, Kris. The inn's going to be a Honeymoon Hideaway, just as you originally planned. It needs honeymooners in it."

Oh, no, he wasn't going to do that to her again. She'd been duped once, and once was too much. Pulling free, she turned her back on him again and continued to gather her materials together.

"Then get some."

Obviously, the calm approach wasn't going to work. He grabbed her arm and forced her around to look at him. "I would if I could think straight, but I can't. You're in every part of my brain, messing things up, making me want you." This wasn't going well, but he wasn't much good at apologizing. He'd had no practice at it. "I'm sorry I lied to you. It was a desperate action, but once I was in the lie, I couldn't get out. It just kept snowballing on me." She had to understand. She had to forgive him. "I wanted to tell you, tried to tell you."

Despite everything, she could feel herself wanting to believe him. Desperately. But that was due to the part of her brain that couldn't seem to learn from her mistakes.

"When?" she demanded coldly.

"A dozen times." It took all he could do to keep from shouting at her. "But every time I tried, I kept thinking of the consequences. These consequences.'' He gestured around the office. He'd been afraid that he would make her leave and return here, to this sleek office, with its ebony furnishings and its wide abstract paintings. And he'd done just that anyway. ''And I didn't want to risk them.'' His hand tightened on her arm. ''I didn't want you leaving me.''

Damn it, she wasn't going to give in. She wasn't. She was going to face him down and make him leave. ''You expect me to believe that?''

His eyes never left hers. He searched them for absolution and understanding. ''Yes.''

She lifted her chin defiantly. ''Why?'' *Convince me, Max. Convince me. Make me believe you.*

Frustration licked at him with a coarse, skin-stripping tongue. ''Because it's the truth, damn it.''

''Prove it.''

How the hell did she expect him to do that? ''How? I can't get an affidavit stating that— Oh, hell.''

Max yanked her into his arms and kissed her, allowing all the passion that had gone begging these past two weeks to envelop them. Kissed her until the room spun for both of them and the heat that was generated between them melted away the rest of it.

Her knees were watery when he released her. She could barely focus on his face. Instead, she focused on the way she'd felt when she had discovered that he had humiliated her. It almost worked.

''And that's supposed to convince me?'' she asked weakly.

''Sure as hell convinced me,'' he breathed, resting his forehead against hers. She might be saying no, but he'd tasted a different answer on her lips. ''Give me another chance? Everyone misses you.''

If she believed that one, he'd be selling her a bridge next. ''Right.''

"They do," he insisted. Why did she find that so difficult to believe? "Hasn't anyone ever missed you before?"

"I don't know," she answered truthfully. "But they've lied to me before."

If they were going to make it on any level, she had to put that in perspective. "Get past that, Kris."

"I can't." It cost her, but she told him the truth. Maybe if she did, *then* he would leave her in peace. "I cared about all of you." This wasn't working out the way it was supposed to. He was grinning at her with the look of a man who had just won the lottery. "All right, I said it, don't look so bright-eyed and bushy-tailed. I didn't know any better. I didn't know that you were all getting your kicks out of watching me make a fool of myself."

Her accusation angered him. She was too intelligent to misinterpret the signs so badly. "When? When did you make a fool out of yourself?"

"When I— That is, I, um... Oh, you know." Did she have to spell it out for him? Wouldn't he save her this final embarrassment?

"No, I don't."

"When I threw myself at you," she hissed between clenched teeth.

Was that what was at the root of all this? "And I didn't catch you."

He kept moving toward her. Carefully, she shifted, maintaining the distance between them. "Right."

She was his, he thought. She just hadn't admitted it to herself. "Did you stop to think why I didn't 'catch' you?"

Boy, he really wanted to draw blood, didn't he? "Because you didn't want to bother."

"Oh, is that why I'm here now, why I left everything in a mess, because I don't want to bother?" Couldn't she give him a scrap of credit where it was due? "I didn't catch what you were throwing because I didn't want to take advantage of you."

He really had to think she was simpleminded, if he be-lieved she'd buy that argument. "Then why did you?"

"Because I was going to die if I didn't have you," he told her quietly. Fiercely. "There, satisfied? I wanted you more than I wanted to breathe. I still do. Now, are you going to make this easy on me, or not?"

He was confusing her. She didn't like being confused. Kristina began to pace. "I—"

Giving up, he caught hold of her. "I'm through reason-ing with you." The next instant, he picked her up in his arms. "You are coming with me. Get used to it."

God help her, she already was. Without realizing it, she threaded her arms around his neck. "And I have no say in it?"

His gaze warmed her. "You can say yes."

Yes. "I can have you up on kidnapping charges, you know."

"They'd have to catch us first." He pressed a kiss to her temple. "I figure it's worth the risk."

"Why?" She wanted to hear why, needed to hear why.

"Because I love you."

She hadn't expected him to say that. Overcome, Kristina snuggled closer in his arms. "You love me?"

He laughed. "Hello? Haven't you been paying attention here? I just left an inn hip-deep in renovations, not to men-tion my construction company, to come here and grovel. To most people, that would mean that I'm a little more than just infatuated with you."

She only heard part of his explanation. "You love me?" she repeated.

He grinned. "I love you."

She felt dazed, as if this were all a dream. A wonderful dream. He'd said something about community property. Her eyes widened as the rest of it sank in. "And you want to marry me?"

He nuzzled her neck. "You *are* catching on."

Kristina settled back in his arms, content to remain there

forever. ''Are you planning to carry me all the way to La Jolla?''

''If I have to.''

She smiled seductively. ''Put me down, Max.''

''Why?''

She lightly skimmed his lips with her fingertip. Max could feel his mouth going dry. ''Because I want to feel the length of your body against mine when I kiss you.''

''Finally, something we can agree on.'' Releasing her, he let her glide along his body.

''We can agree on other things,'' she offered.

''I'm counting on it.''

The buzzer went off on her desk. Reaching over, still entwined with Max, Kristina pressed the intercom down. ''Yes?''

Jennifer's voice filled the room. ''Are you all right, Ms. Fortune?''

''Never better. Hold all my calls, Jennifer.'' Her eyes held his. ''For a long, long time.''

Jennifer was saying something in protest about the meeting when Kristina released the intercom.

''Where were we?'' Kristina asked.

He drew her closer to him, his mouth inches from hers. ''Right about here.''

Her warm, contented sigh whispered along his face. ''Oh, yes, I remember.''

He grinned just before he kissed her. ''Don't worry. If you forget, I'm here to remind you. I'll always be here to remind you.''

It was a promise he intended to keep.

Epilogue

It was a room that was seldom used, conceived more for show than for hosting functions. But since it was large, it provided the space that was necessary to accommodate a gathering of this size. He could, Sterling knew, have asked the members of the far-reaching Fortune family to come to the Lake Travis mansion, but there was something within him that wanted neutral ground for this bombshell that he was going to lob within their midst.

Besides, it was here, in his own place, he had come to feel in the last few months that had passed, where Kate really belonged. It was here that she was not just a larger-than-life woman who helmed a huge family business, the tentacles of which were far reaching, but a woman who was vulnerable. A woman who needed protecting.

And, a woman who needed him.

So, he had called them, all of them, reaching out by wire, by telephone, by postman, by any means necessary, and asked, no, actually told, them to come and meet with him here.

Sterling smiled to himself. He supposed that the instruction smacked a little of a 1930s mystery, but for once, he thought he'd indulge himself. It was harmless enough. And the effect, he was certain, would be interesting to watch.

Besides, it was the swiftest way possible to accomplish what Kate wanted. Now that Jake knew, the others had to be told. It was only fair and Kate Fortune had always been fair.

Sterling Foster paused for a moment longer before entering his living room, savoring the aura of charged excitement and mystery that abounded, consciously and un, just a few feet away.

Though she was as much in the dark as to why she had been summoned here as everyone else, confusion took a back seat to joy for Kristina. It made her heart glad just to be here. To look around at each of their faces and silently press their images between the pages of her mind. After having lived, however briefly, with a soul-consuming void, the very sight of her family had become indescribably dear to her.

Every single last one of them.

She wasn't so besotted with the idea of remembering them, with the myriad of memories that spun through her mind, that she forgot that some of them had feet of clay. She didn't forget, but she just didn't care. It was precisely those very feet, those very foibles that made them more dear to her, more human.

It felt wonderful just to be alive.

She was grinning like a loon, Kristina thought, and she didn't care.

Max leaned his head in toward hers. Since he'd been ushered in by a near-silent, nondescript man who might or might not have been a butler, he had been feeling increasingly more awkward with each pass of the pendulum of the imposing grandfather clock that stood guard over them in the corner.

He slanted a glance at the unsmiling man by the fireplace. The man who would soon be his father-in-law if all went well. Max didn't exactly feel heartened by the man's expression.

"There're more people here than at a rehearsal for the Mormon Tabernacle choir," Max whispered in her ear. "Are they *all* related to you?"

Since they'd only entered a few minutes ago, at the

height of a discussion, introductions had yet to be made. Max couldn't picture having a family that he couldn't count on the fingers of one hand, with a few digits left over.

Kristina nodded, turning her head so that she could whisper her reply into Max's ear. "In one way or another."

Almost all of her cousins had arrived with someone in tow. Someone, she had a strong feeling, who would come to matter a great deal in the general scheme of things for them. Just as Max had come to mean so much to her.

Rebecca smiled as she looked at Kristina and Max. They looked adorable, she thought, their heads together like two schoolkids lost in a world of their own. It made her long for someone like that in her own life.

But if she wanted a significant other, she mused, she would have to create him herself, giving him life and wit on the pages of one of her books. A hero worthy of her heart. A hero, if she sketched him quickly, who might even resemble...

Rebecca banished the thought from her mind—though she made herself a promise to start thinking about having an adorable child like Caroline's Katie *very* soon—and crossed to Kristina.

She tucked an arm around one of her favorite nieces as she smiled at Max. "What are you two whispering about?"

Nate snorted, eyeing the doorway impatiently. Where was their damn "host" anyway?

"Maybe she knows why His Majesty summoned us here." Nate's frown emphasized the lines around his mouth. "First he makes it sound like it's a matter of life or death, then he pulls a vanishing act on us. Who does he think he is, Houdini?" He looked around at the others for support. "It's not as if I were cooling my heels with nothing to do."

"Yes, dear." Barbara winked at her daughter as she placed a soothing hand on her husband's shoulder. "We all know what a very busy man you are."

''And a happy one,'' Rebecca put in, pinning her brother with a look.

Rather than shrug off Barbara's hand, Nate slipped his over it and linked his fingers with hers. The lines about his mouth relaxed. The smile was genuine. Barbara was his anchor, his port. His haven, and he was lucky to have her. He, more than anyone, understood that. ''No argument there.''

It was Lindsay who rolled her eyes. ''Ah, a first time for everything.''

Zach Bolton looked from one senior Fortune to another, his confusion mounting rather than abating. It was an easier matter for him to try to learn all the changes the world went through in the past hundred years than Jane's family. Everyone blurred into someone else.

Jane had coached him, patiently showing him photographs and repeating minibiographies for his benefit, but Zach still found himself stumbling as he attempted to affix the right name to the right face. It would have taxed Einstein's mind.

The advent of yet another pair coming into the room had sent him reeling back to square one, especially since introductions hadn't been declared. The pair had just been swallowed in a show of affection while he had lingered on the outskirts, looking on. He turned now to Jane, hoping for clarification.

''And these two are?''

Jane threaded her hands around Zach's arm, ushering him forward with the pride of a woman in love.

''This is Kristina Fortune, my half sister, and this is—'' she paused, confused herself. She raised a brow to Kristina, waiting for assistance.

Well, if he was going to be part of them, he might as well jump right in, Max thought. He extended his hand toward the other man, an instant kinship forming at the sight of the latter's discomfort. *You're not alone, Mister.*

"I'm Max Cooper." The other man's grip was firm, strong. The bond between them grew.

The name was familiar. Jane raised her eyes to Kristina's face for a clue, trying to remember what it was her father had told her about the man.

"Kristina's partner?" she guessed.

Max and Kristina exchanged amused looks that were not wasted on anyone close to them.

"For life, I hope," Max put in before Kristina could say anything.

For eternity, Kristina added silently, taking immense comfort from the thought. "There you go," she teased him, her eyes laughing, "stealing my thunder."

The next moment, there was a whoosh of bodies moving in toward them, arms reaching to embrace, hands extended to grasp and well wishes and surprise ringing through the room.

"A wedding?"

"Congratulations."

"Hey, welcome to the family."

"Why didn't you tell me?"

Acceptance felt good, Max thought. Damn good. He hadn't realized until this moment that he had been holding his breath, waiting. Having Kristina agree to marry him was the most important step, but it was incomplete without her family's blessings. Because he knew it mattered to her, it mattered to him.

He felt a hand clap him on the back and found himself looking into a rugged, tanned face split open with a broad grin.

"Finally! Never thought anyone would be fool enough to take my little half sister off our hands." Grant McClure laughed, catching Kristina in his arms and hugging her. He looked at Max over her head. "Welcome to the madhouse, brother."

Brother. It had a nice ring to it.

"Is this why Sterling asked us here?" Michael wanted

to know, taking his turn at hugging his half sister. "To announce your wedding?" It didn't sound like the man, Michael thought, but he'd learned not to make assumptions. They didn't always pan out.

"Hardly." Kristina brushed his cheek with her lips and then hugged Kyle. "For one thing, he doesn't know." She looked at her mother, a silent apology in her eyes. She'd meant to get a moment alone with her to break the news first, but it just hadn't worked out that way. "Nobody did, until now."

"Speak of the devil," Kyle murmured under his breath, loud enough for everyone to hear. He nodded toward the entrance to the room.

In a disjointed motion that resembled a wave breaking on the shore, the others turned their heads to look.

Sterling Foster remained in the doorway, his mouth pulled in a somber, straight line. He had the ability to make each individual in the room feel as if his eye were fixed exclusively on them.

His expression was unreadable. It was what made him an excellent poker player as well as a lawyer to be reckoned with.

On opposite ends of the room, Allie and Rocky took a step forward, unconsciously mimicking one another. The worry in the twins' eyes was mirrored more than a dozen times over.

The good wishes and joy faded from the air as if it had never visited the spacious room.

Allie voiced the question that was on all their minds. "Is it about Dad?"

She felt Rafe's reassuring grip as his hand closed over hers in silent support.

Luke placed his hand on Rocky's shoulder, as if to anchor her in place. She looked ready to leap out of her skin when the lawyer didn't answer immediately.

He'd had enough of this, Nate thought. "Damn it, out with it, man." Moving toward him, Nate shrugged off Barbara's hand. "We don't have time for theatrics. Did you issue your royal summons to tell us something about Jake?"

"No, this isn't about Jake," Sterling replied. "Not directly."

"But indirectly?" Adam pressed. He'd only just recently found himself on the path to reconciliation with his father. He didn't want to be detoured or turned away from that road now.

Like the others, he found comfort in the silent joining of hands with the woman he loved. Laura said nothing, but he felt her support. It helped. Some.

"In a way," Sterling agreed. It wasn't his idea to call them together in the first place, but then, very little of this had been his idea, or even had his blessings. Still, he never could deny Kate anything and she had wanted to make the announcement to all of them at once.

He was struggling, Natalie realized, watching the tall, thin lawyer. It wasn't his expression, but the way he held himself that gave her an inkling of a clue.

But why? Why was he struggling? And with what? It had to mean that he had something devastating to tell them, something that would affect them all. She felt a knot forming in the pit of her stomach as she thought of her father and the possible fate that waited for him unless something miraculous happened.

"Please." She placed a hand on Sterling's arm, reinforcing her entreaty. "In what way?"

There was no way to say this, but to say it. He took a breath. "Kate—"

Eyes wide, Rebecca elbowed her way forward. "You've found Mother's killer?"

Kate was tired of waiting in the wings, a place, in her opinion, she'd occupied far too long. She stepped forward, coming out of the library where Sterling had instructed her to wait until he prepared the others for her appearance.

Though her expression remained regal, exhilaration tingled through her body at the moment of entry. "No," Kate said quietly, "he found Mother."

"Omigod."

No one knew who said it. It was as if Death had walked into the room, moving silently among them, rendering them mute.

No one spoke, no one breathed.

To a person, they became a still life, a depiction of shock that had been forever frozen into place, taking on depth and breadth.

Rebecca was the first to recover, if being completely numb could be called recovering. She stared at the tall, redheaded woman.

"Mother?"

In her head, Rebecca screamed the name, but it came out barely a whisper on her lips. She was afraid to move, afraid that if she did, her mother, her beloved mother, would fade away like smoke, like an illusion that mass hysteria had somehow tricked them all into seeing.

Kate Fortune looked around at these people she had held suspect, these people she loved more dearly than life itself. Without them, she knew, there was no life. She had come to understand and firmly believe that during her endless months in exile.

"Yes." Kate's voice was no louder, no stronger than her daughter's. "It's me."

"How...?" Lindsay couldn't find the words to complete her question, not even in her own mind. Not yet. Her mind was paralyzed, as was the rest of her.

As if in a trance, Kristina, closest to the apparition who was her grandmother, stretched her hand out and touched her grandmother's hand. The long, aristocratic fingers were warm.

Kristina's eyes widened in awe and wonder as she looked at Kate, and then tears filled them. She flung her arms around her grandmother.

"Oh my God, you're alive," she sobbed against Kate's thin shoulder.

Kate had to swallow before she could speak. Funny thing, emotion, you went so long without displaying it and then it undid you, as if to pay you back for the audacity of ignoring it. Her arms tightened around her granddaughter.

"Very much so," she whispered against Kristina's hair.

And then, the silence broke and a torrent of words, of questions, came pouring in from all sides as more than two dozen people made themselves known, vying for the attention of a woman they had all believed had been ruthlessly taken from them.

Sterling stepped back, allowing Kate to have her moment.

Kate had always had her moment, he thought with just the slightest hint of a smile gracing his lips as he looked on the scene. And it was a scene. Straight out of a heart-tugging movie. Kate Fortune, the matriarch, had returned to reclaim her rightful place in the scheme of things, he mused.

No matter what the circumstances, Kate had always made him think of a queen. Even at her most bedraggled, she'd had that quality. He'd felt it from the first moment he'd laid eyes on her.

Sterling supposed that could only mean one thing.

He was in love with her. He always had been. He'd overheard Kristina and her young man with their announcement. There would be another in the offing soon, but for now, it could wait. He could wait. Kate needed her time with her family right now. And he was a patient man.

Kate hadn't fully realized, until this very moment, until she looked upon their faces, just how much she had missed them all.

Just how much she loved them all.

It was as if she'd been fasting all these long, lonely months, hanging around the fringes of their lives to steal a glimpse of them, for the sound of her family's laughter.

And now she felt she couldn't get enough. Quite possibly would never get enough.

"Nothing is so dear," she murmured aloud, running her hand through Rebecca's hair, "as finding something you thought was forever lost."

Nate pressed his lips together, afraid that for once, his softer emotions might get the better of him.

"We could say the same about you, Mother." He felt like a small boy again, wanting to hold on to his mother's hem to keep from getting lost. From losing her.

That was how he'd felt all these months she'd been gone. Lost. Rudderless. The woman cast a hell of a long shadow, even over a man his age. But then, she always had.

He cleared his throat. He wanted answers that made sense to him. "Where have you been? Why this elaborate charade?"

Nate looked at Sterling as he asked. He didn't blame his mother. She was a hard woman, a tough woman because life had made her that way, but she wasn't cruel. This little drama had to be Sterling's fault. But why? Why put them through all this?

Recognizing the challenge, Sterling began to answer, but Kate shook her head, silently telling him that she would explain, even though it was hard for her.

"The plane crash wasn't an accident. Someone wanted me dead." Her eyes swept over them. *Someone,* she thought. *But not you. Never you. I realize that now.* "I felt if they knew they had failed the first attempt, they would try again. Or they would try to hurt you. I didn't want to keep looking over my shoulder, constantly wondering, constantly worrying, so I let them think they had succeeded."

"And let us think they had succeeded." It was harsh, but at the moment, emerging out of hell, Nate didn't feel all that magnanimous. How could she have done this to them, her own flesh and blood?

Barbara tried to temper her husband's tone. "But why—"

Lindsay elbowed her brother out of the way, hugging her mother—something she had despaired of ever doing again. "I don't care why, I'm just happy that it isn't true."

"Jake," Erica suddenly cried, looking around at the others. "Someone has to tell Jake."

"Jake knows," Kate replied quietly. "I told him first."

"First?" Nate repeated incredulously.

A murmur rippled through the crowd. Rebecca saw Nate's brow furrow and knew what he was thinking. But this wasn't a time for hurt feelings, or a show of competitive instincts Nate was so capable of displaying.

"Then I say this calls for a celebration," Rebecca declared. She looked at Sterling expectantly.

This one, Sterling thought, was most like her mother. He was glad of the diversion. "My sentiments exactly. There's champagne chilling in the dining room." He looked around the room, fascinated at observing the way shock was giving way to joy and relief. "Let's adjourn there now, shall we?"

Stepping forward, he presented his arm to Kate. With a laugh that vividly brought back the young girl she had once been so very long ago, Kate threaded her hand around his arm and inclined her head in assent. "You think of everything, Sterling."

"I have to," he replied. "To stay one step ahead of you."

Kate pressed her lips together to keep the smile in check. "You mean one step behind, don't you?"

"It's a draw," Kristina declared, coming behind them. "You're abreast of each other."

Both nodded, accepting the compromise. "Abreast," Kate echoed. That was just fine with her.

And that was the way they walked out of the room. Side by side.

*   *   *   *   *

FORTUNE'S CHILDREN

continues with
THE BABY CHASE
by Jennifer Greene
Available in June

Here's an exciting preview....

The Baby Chase

The entire view offended Rebecca Fortune. It was a dark and stormy night—how trite was that? Lightning speared the midnight sky, haloing a big, gaudy, ostentatious mansion that looked like a fake set in a grade B Hollywood movie. Worse yet, she was about to break into that mansion.

Rebecca wrote mysteries. She'd thrown her heroines into every dangerous situation her devious mind could come up with—and her imagination was considerable. But she'd throw her word processor in the trash before forcing a heroine into a stupid, cliché plot setting like this.

The shiver of fear that suddenly ran through her was motivated solely by love. She wanted so badly to come through for her brother, and she was scared of failing. Somewhere in that house there *had* to be clues, information, evidence—*something* that would clear Jake of Monica Malone's murder. Dozens of people, including quite a few of her own family, had reasons for killing the old bat. Monica had been an evil, greedy, selfish woman who'd done her damnedest to destroy the Fortune family for more than a generation. A two-year-old could find suspects with motivation.

Rebecca circled the house again, crouching low, battling the bushes in the flower beds to shine a flashlight over one basement window at a time until she found a window that seemed only painted shut. On the third try she finally managed to edge the crowbar under the window's ledge. It squeaked and creaked open.

Hesitantly, she aimed the flashlight through the opening. She was probably going to kill herself if she tried this.

On the other hand, this appeared to be her only way in— and giving up the search certainly wasn't an option.

She poked her feet in first, then her legs, then wriggled her fanny through the window. Then came trouble. Her hips wedged in the opening, and suddenly she couldn't move. At all. In or out.

Cripes, there were times she'd groaned about not having enough hips to fill out a pair of jeans. Now she wished she'd had three less cherry doughnuts this week. Her fanny was stuck. No kidding, no joke, seriously stuck.

She sucked in a breath, braced her arms, found some purchase of the ground and pushed hard.

The push worked. Sort of. She was still alive when she crash-landed on the concrete floor, but that measure of success was hardly worth applause. On the route down, she'd cracked her forehead on the window frame, and both her breasts had been squished and scraped. She landed on a hip and a wrist. She wasn't positive it was possible to break a fanny—she'd certainly never seen one in a cast or traction—but she was damned scared she'd done it.

To add insult to injury, a light suddenly flashed in her eyes.

The obnoxious glaring light came from a bald lightbulb in the middle of the basement room.

And to top off the worst debacle she'd ever gotten herself into, the man standing by the light switch, shaking his head, was familiar. Painfully familiar. So was his unmistakable gravelly tenor. She had to look like something a dog would bury, but there wasn't a rip, a tear or a smudge of dirt on him. His square jaw was freshly shaved and his shoulders stretched the seams of a long-sleeved navy T-shirt. His boots didn't even look muddy.

"I thought at least ten kids were breaking into the place. You made enough noise to wake the dead. I should have known it was you. Dammit, Rebecca, what the *hell* are you doing here?''

Rebecca squeezed her eyes closed and spoke softly. "At the moment, I'm sitting here with forty-seven broken bones, feeling sorry for myself. Please God, make this a nightmare, and when I wake up, try and fix it so he's someone else. Make him a Russian spy. Make him a serial killer. Make him anyone but Gabe Devereax.''

But when she opened her eyes, Gabe was still there. This was *not* a good night!

AMERICAN ❖ ROMANCE®

LOOK FOR OUR FOUR FABULOUS MEN!

Each month some of today's bestselling authors bring
four new fabulous men to Harlequin American Romance.
Whether they're rebel ranchers, millionaire power brokers
or sexy single dads, they're all gallant princes—and
they're all ready to sweep you into lighthearted fantasies
and contemporary fairy tales where anything is possible
and where all your dreams come true!

You don't even have to make a wish...Harlequin American
Romance will grant your every desire!

Look for Harlequin American Romance wherever Harlequin
books are sold!

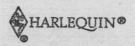
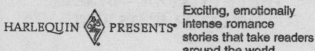

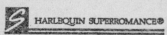

Harlequin® Historical

If you're a serious fan of historical romance,
then you're in luck!

Harlequin Historicals brings you
stories by bestselling authors, rising new stars
and talented first-timers.

Ruth Langan & Theresa Michaels
Mary McBride & Cheryl St.John
Margaret Moore & Merline Lovelace
Julie Tetel & Nina Beaumont
Susan Amarillas & Ana Seymour
Deborah Simmons & Linda Castle
Cassandra Austin & Emily French
Miranda Jarrett & Suzanne Barclay
DeLoras Scott & Laurie Grant...

You'll never run out of favorites.

Harlequin Historicals...they're too good to miss!

HARLEQUIN PRESENTS

HARLEQUIN PRESENTS
men you won't be able to resist falling in love with...

HARLEQUIN PRESENTS
women who have feelings just like your own...

HARLEQUIN PRESENTS
powerful passion in exotic international settings...

HARLEQUIN PRESENTS
intense, dramatic stories that will keep you turning
to the very last page...

HARLEQUIN PRESENTS
The world's bestselling romance series!

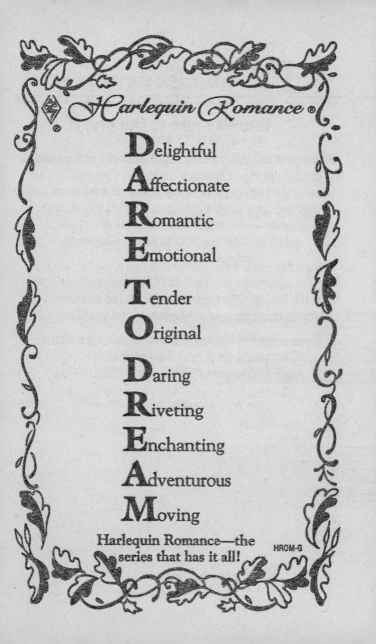

Harlequin Romance ®

Delightful

Affectionate

Romantic

Emotional

Tender

Original

Daring

Riveting

Enchanting

Adventurous

Moving

Harlequin Romance—the
series that has it all!

HROM-G

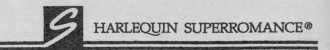

HARLEQUIN SUPERROMANCE®

...there's more to the story!

Superromance. A *big* satisfying read about unforgettable
characters. Each month we offer *four* very different
stories that range from family drama to adventure and
mystery, from highly emotional stories to romantic
comedies—and much more! Stories about people
you'll believe in and care about. Stories too
compelling to put down....

Our authors are among today's *best* romance writers.
You'll find familiar names and talented newcomers.
Many of them are award winners—and you'll see why!

If you want the biggest and best in romance fiction,
you'll get it from Superromance!
Available wherever Harlequin books are sold.

Look us up on-line at: http://www.romance.net

HS-GEN